THE WAY BACK

A Soldier's Journey

S.K. Carnes

skcarnes.com

I dedicate this book to my heroic sister Mary Lou,

*the perfect blend of our mother's grace under fire
and our father's pluck.*

Our Mother:
Beautiful and Brave

*Able to leap the insurmountable
in a single bound!*

Our Father:
Veteran Of World War I

*When the sky falls,
we will catch larks.*

And The other daughter Lori offers as her excuse
for running amuck, the words of Antoine de Saint-Exupéry:

"One runs the risk of weeping a little, if one lets oneself be tamed."

CONTENTS

My Barn Burned Down and Now I See the Moon

April 12, 2013

SIPPING EARLY MORNING COFFEE, I WELCOMED THE E-MAIL from my son, Dan. "Hi Mom," it said. I smiled, picturing him in his home by the river in far away Wisconsin, land of snowdrifts and lakes. I imagined him typing while enjoying first light sparkle on the river Flambeau, watching the shy deer drink, then, like phantoms, disappear into the forest. I depended on Dan to be my watchdog over the memories of early times, while I fled to a new gentler life 2700 miles away on a pacific island. He was my oldest son, like me, born into a wilderness both savage and unbearably sweet. I read on:

> They are tearing down the dairy barn on your old farm and selling it off in pieces. I thought you might like me to try to get one of the cupolas for you. I know it had been a show barn—really the last of its kind in Douglas County. Since Grandpa built it, I thought you would like something to remember it by. Let me know.
>
> Love, Dan

Mechanically, I hit "reply" and began to write my acceptance.

Of course I wanted a piece of that barn—a substantial part of my father's dream.

What—they are tearing down the barn? I stopped typing as realization set in. Anger flooded over me. Tears drenched my disbelief. How could Dan let this happen? Hadn't I left him in charge—in charge of nothing changing?

Did those people back there think this was just an ordinary old building? All those children of farm families, moved to the city, making suburbs of the dairy land. Traitors! In a flash of insight, I saw the barn as it must now be, surrounded by houses and fenced little yards. But it was a show barn—yes— the pride of a time and a way of life, and they were tearing it down.

I spent the morning sending e-mails, making phone calls, pleading for life for the big dairy barn, now abandoned, dishonored, a prisoner on death row, guilty only of losing purpose. Over and over came the same message back, blasting against the steel of my will. "Let it go," said my friends. "Let it go," said my family. Finally, I came to ponder the signature I had used on my e-mails for several years. I had adapted it from a haiku and thought it said everything. Ironically, I had enlightened my companions and friends with the very under-standing I needed now.

"My barn burned down and now I see the moon."

There was no moon to be seen in my mind, only the fading shadows of a living structure being sold off in pieces. What stories could these walls tell? Who remembered the glowing eyes of the animals sheltered there, felt their raw uncondi-tional love, remembered their birth and their death? Who still lived to tell the stories? What about the builders? Who would tell the story of how they fashioned the barn and how it fashioned them? Who would tumble words together, until like agates disguised as stones, they reflected polished layers of magic? Who would write the obituary of the barn so that others would know and care? I must do it, I thought, and once honored, the stories told, I would be able to let it go—this symbol enshrined in my heart of who I was—a dairyman's daughter from Wisconsin.

No one to call, no one left to question. My mother and father were 30 years gone and so many of the stories died with them. My memories were murky, but the need to write nagged at me. A cousin remembered that the barn was raised in 1930 with the skill of Danish carpenters following plans sent out from Madison. It was the state of the art dairy barn of its day: 100 feet of burly and brash, classic red with white trim. It was efficient, audacious, splendid, and built hell for stout. John saw to that. My father, the Dan I had named my son after, had hired a man to help build the barn, and handle the herd. His name was John Chapman, and he came from Portage, a town 60 miles south of Superior. Like my father, John was a World War I veteran. Perhaps he was the reason I have always favored warriors, for he showed me tenderness and selfless courage I figured he learned on the bloody battlefields of the "war to end all wars." I grew up under his watchful eye. He saved my life the first time when I was two, and many times after that. When I was nine or ten, he stopped working for us and I lost track of him. Years later, when I was a grown, married woman, I realized how important he had been to me. I called Portage looking for him. So often, we neglect to thank people until it is too late. Sure enough, Phone Information gave me the number of John Chapman, but it was his son's number. I spoke with his daughter-in-law who seemed like an old friend as soon as I gave her my name.

"Well of course I know who you are, Lori," she said. "John

spoke about you often. You were his little girl. I wish I could put him on the phone to you, but he died last year, he was 81."

"I'm so sorry," I stammered out, "I missed my chance to tell him—to tell him how dear he was to me."

40 years had passed and I still remembered that conversation with regret. I reminded myself how often I had failed to express gratitude, or to say the words "I love you." Ashamed and remorseful, I sat at my computer and typed John's name and hometown into a search engine to see if cyber space held news of my old friend, my first love, my champion. I selected the first of two news articles. At once a surprise filled the screen.

From Portage Advocate, Portage, WI

September 11, 1925

A posse of about 100 men, led by Sheriff Waggoner, scoured the countryside near the home of John G. Chapman on Sunday, looking for some trace that might lead to the whereabouts of Mr. Chapman, a farmer residing near the Evergreen schoolhouse who has been missing since last Saturday afternoon. The search proved in vain.

John came to work for us in 1930, and stayed 10 years. This article was five years earlier. They must have found him, or he found himself. I selected the second article:

September 18, 1925

John Chapman of the town of Evergreen, who was reported to have been missing from his home for several days last week, was found in the hay loft of his barn late Tuesday. Though the barn had previously been searched, it is thought that the man, in a dazed condition as a result of severe headaches with which he was afflicted at the time of his disappearance, wandered back to the barn during the search. His reappearance is a great relief to relatives and friends.

"Found in his hay loft." I repeated that phrase over and over in my mind. I thought about the old dairy barn back home, and about John who had fashioned its loft. Old memories of my childhood settled in, like autumn leaves, lazily drifting, shifting. I began to remember the light in the loft of our barn, twinkling like a star through the branches of the apple tree outside my window, shining night after night. I pictured John working in the high loft. Or was he hiding again—perhaps from the pain in his head, or from the horrors of war? What comfort did he find in the loft of the barn? How does a warrior, homeward bound, find his way back to everyday? If only the walls could tell the tale, but soon, they would be gone, and John's story with them. Before its too late, I should write his story, "from my memories," I thought. But leaves move with the wind and clouds dim the stars. I needed more.

The following week, I got another e-mail from Dan:

Hi Mom:

I was too late to buy a complete cupola tower for you. They split the roof all along the top beam and removed the three ventilators and the motor for the hay lift and anything else they could get of value from the roof itself. They already had removed all the metal stanchions, the granary machinery, timber and pen boards. I wonder what holds the barn up. With the roof opened, it won't last long. What you are getting is a part of one of the ventilators. The owner had already sold all three dairy cow weather vanes that were on the top. I didn't get much, huh. But there was one thing.

When they were stripping boards from the loft, someone found a little compartment built into the wall. It had a book in it—a journal from a guy by the name of John Chapman. I got that for you because I think he was once one of the hired men on your farm. No one here knew him—only you. I'll send it to you.

Love, Dan

Found in the loft, I said to myself. And now another chance to hear John's voice—the sound of it, a cherished memory locked safe within my mind, his caring crafted in the walls he built, his meaning floating to me on the words he wrote—alive again with the reading of his journal, revealing as it must, how he changed as he built and tended the barn. Perhaps I could write words that expressed what it meant to me—and at last—between us, the story would be told—one of love.

The package finally came, and I eagerly tore away the outer wrapping to reveal a doeskin sleeve smelling faintly of sweet grass clover, tobacco and Old Spice, its velvety cover protecting the journal hidden inside, where handwriting un-apologetically strong, yet a touch elegant, ran with purpose edge to edge across yellowed pages, and then again, with a flash of surprise, waltzed with poetry, or hovered like a solitary bird in a vanilla sky.

I remembered John as very physical, loving the outdoors, an introspective and solitary man, and was surprised to read his thoughts so masterfully written. What could have caused this literate and well-read man, to leave his home to work at hard labor on our dairy farm? Puzzled, I researched the happenings of the times, beginning with the Great War. Ten million soldiers were killed in World War I, many never found, unidentified pieces shoveled into mass graves grown over into vast fields of poppies between the crosses. In the unearthly silence when the guns ceased firing, allied soldiers found themselves tortured by loss and foreboding, returning home torn, bleeding and unable to extract the barbed wire grip of no man's land from their hearts. In 1918 influenza broke out killing 20 million more around the world. The wounded numbered another 20 million, many terribly mutilated. Human masks were given to hide wounds—new faces, new legs, new arms were fitted. New minds were more difficult.

Europe had changed drastically. There were new nations with new names building upon the ruins of four great empires. Beginning again. Germany had ceased to fight, but since She had not been invaded, and was not convinced She had lost the terrible struggle, war was brewing again. Like a tsunami flooding in, eleven years after the 11th hour of the 11th day of the eleventh month of 1918 (the date marking the end of World War I) the longest and most severe depression ever experienced by the industrialized West drowned prosperity. Along with many survivors of combat, John felt diminished, unsure of himself and unable to cope with the crumbling world around him. Hoping to shore up his memory, and clear up his mind, John began his journal, "A Necklace of Words." Perhaps it was by chance or destiny but I preferred to believe the journal, the Necklace, was John's gift to me, his little girl.

That night, I imagined the looming bulk of the barn silhou-etted before a star spangled sky. I thought I saw John's light in the loft where he was writing to me from another time, but I was mistaken. It was the rising moon through the broken roof.

Waiting to Begin Again

My Johnny Comes Marching Home

The old church bell will peal with joy
Hurrah Hurrah
To welcome home our darling boy
Hurrah Hurrah.

From the gas in the trenches, the hungry mud
the bursting shells, the rivers of blood
And, victorious music we happily sing
When Johnny comes marching home.

Back to us in disarray
Hurrah Hurrah
For the ghosts of war fight night and day
Hurrah Hurrah

The bells they toll, the pipes they play
For the dead 'neath the poppy fields far away
And those lost on the way back to everyday
And for Johnny come marching home.

Afternoon sunbeams played over the dusty Mohawk bus as it lumbered off the main street and came to a stop by the station door. The banner above the driver's window said "Superior." The door swooshed open, and out spilled a motley bunch of folks. They were the curious, downtrodden and hopeful, most looking for work in Wisconsin's city at the head of the lakes. With the unemployment rate topping 25 %, there were still jobs here for fishermen, loggers, farm laborers, railroaders and dock workers. Shrouded in gasoline fumes, the bus puffed and coughed, while the driver set out suitcases and trunks from its belly. Breaking past the welcoming hugs and chatter, two drunks linked arms, singing a song of hard times. They tottered off down the alley toward some unmarked speakeasy, words drifting back along with the smell of their illegal booze.

Once I built a railroad,
I made it run, made it race against time.
Once I built a railroad now it's done.
Brother can you spare a dime.

A tall solitary man, lean and dapper in his fedora hat, picked his small tan suitcase out of the mêlée and followed them. While the revelers lurched along, sloshing thru puddles of sooty water, the gentleman stepped with care, touched his hat in a "so long" gesture, and cut out of the alley and on to Tower Avenue toward the business district. The drunks slogged past the bowery Mission, waterfront bound, their melancholy song drowned in street sounds, but the words played on in the mind of the loner. His long strides kept the rhythm while the lyrics marched in his head.

Once in khaki suits, gee we looked swell,
Full of that Yankee Doodly Dum,
Half a million boots went slogging through Hell,
And I was the kid with the drum!

He checked the numbers of the buildings and the names of the streets, looking, seeking 1004 Broadway. There it was, the Unemployment Service window on the second floor of the office building across the street, and it was lit from inside. *Still open!* He sped up the stairs, taking them two at a time, and found the door, its window glass etched with the title across; blurred movement inside. He took a breath to bolster determination and opened the door. A buxom lady, her pink flowered dress stretched tight over her beyond ample form, glanced at him sideways as she filed papers into an oak cabinet. Beaming at him from behind stacked forms and a typewriter on a massive desk, she looked welcoming. Beyond her, he saw a waiting room he presumed to be full—there would be competition for jobs if indeed there was one he could do. He introduced himself, hat in hand, smiling his best. "Good afternoon madam, my name is John Chapman. I am looking for employment and I thought I would begin my search here."

"Mr. Chapman, it is a pleasure to meet you," she said, extending her hand with a flourish. "My name is Myrtle and you can call me that. I will get some forms into my typewriter and we can fill in your information—get you started—could be your lucky day!"

Myrtle liked the look of Chapman. He was handsome, she thought, a ladies man. His voice was soft and his manner charming. His hand felt work hardened, his grip firm but gentled for a lady, and she loved that. But the dark circles under his eyes betrayed the gladness of his smile. "Muckelty-dun eyes rimmed in blue" she thought, remembering her mother's warning that eyes of that color could steal your heart away. *The color of camouflage*, she thought, as she set up for an interview. *You never know what thoughts lay behind such eyes.* She liked his mustache too, full and dark just touched with silver, like the hair at the temples. She noted his suitcase, pictured it parked in her bedroom, and mentally rebuked herself as an addle-brained old fool.

"Now, lets find you a job," she said, hoping her voice sounded professional. As he gave answers to her questions, Myrtle typed first his name, John G. Chapman, then his age, 36, and his address on Chapman Road in Portage. His skills were: a carpenter/mechanic, a builder, a horseman and a dairyman. He had served in the Army during the First World War. He had a wife and three children to support, and wanted long term employment. She stopped typing, flashing a look of encouragement at John.

"Mr. Chapman, a farmer came in earlier today seeking a man with your skills— a mature responsible man— he said he wanted." *Just the man I am looking for also*, she thought, blushing a little, averting her eyes lest her obvious approval seemed to him as unprofessional. "It is late now, but I will try to ring him up and set up an appointment for you tomorrow. Please take a seat in the waiting room while I give it a try."

John sat alone by the window, held his head, and thought about the day, his mouth grim and tight as he recalled the early morning argument with his wife. Lingering bouts of depression, loss of memory that accompanied mind-bending headaches, crippling disorientation and the lack of work due to the Depression, were the white noise excuses behind what had been happening in his marriage. The war had ended 12 years before, but not for him—he fought its battles nightly.

When he didn't get ready for work that morning, he had to admit to Ida that he had been fired from his delivery job. He wished he could forget what she had said, but words that hurt his heart from the inside continued to scream at him like a stuck record.

"What good are you," she shrieked, her voice rising to a crescendo. "You can't keep a job—who would have you? And how can we pay our bills and feed our children? I can't stand it. I can't stand you!"

Blood boiling with rage beyond reason, he had thrown a chair, breaking it against the wall. The children were crying. He tore through the house swearing, driven by anger and fear of the man he might be, jammed some clothes into his suitcase, seized up his favorite book, and stuffing it in too, left without a word or a backward look. "Slam" went the door behind him, muffling the wails of his new baby. He ran from them, ran from himself, stumbling off his porch, down the drive, catching a ride and then the bus north. John rocked back and forth in his chair, head in his hands, feeling shame as he remembered the baby's cries.

Myrtle opened the door breaking his reverie with a call back. John rose shakily, then stood tall ready to shoulder disappointment, and marched after Myrtle wagging her hips at him as she received him into her domain.

"Good news Mr. Chapman." She beamed into those beguiling eyes (surely the ones her mother had warned her about!) and continued in a confidential manner. "Our farmer—oh he has a name—Mr. Daniel Moyer, will be in to visit with you here in this office tomorrow morning at 10:00. You should be prepared to go with him, God willing, on a trial basis. He has a homestead in the county and is building a barn for the dairy he calls Green Meadows."

Profoundly grateful, John felt like hugging Myrtle—she looked so huggably soft and presented herself in such a manner that it was his first thought; but he was a proper gentleman and gave her instead, his best smile wrapped in relief. "How can I ever thank you enough," he said, and then he left abruptly, not waiting for her answer, lest she see the tears in his eyes.

John sought out a drugstore to stock up on headache medicines. While there, he bought a book to write in. He had decided to keep a journal. That way, if the headaches came again, he could remember who he was, where he was, and what he was doing. He resolved that if only he could find work, he would not run again. He walked back to the bus station looking for a place to eat and a cheap bed for the night. The nearby café owner kept such a room to let upstairs, two flights above the street. After sipping some soup that tasted like chili made with dishwater, John climbed the rickety back stairs and sat alone on his bed. *"Tomorrow I will start a new life"*, he told himself. In his mind there was a dangerous black hole of doubt. He circled his thoughts around it, careful that they would not slip in. *"Will someone want me?"* he wondered. Out of the depths of his fears he heard Ida's voice again, as if in answer. Words that would haunt his days and nights echoed off the bare wooden walls, bouncing back at him from all sides. *"Who would have you? You are crazy, good for nothing but war, and now you are old."* He stood up soldier-straight and walked to the window where the last light of the day shone like hope. He saw cold grey Lake Superior battering the piers of old Duluth. Black granite hills rose up behind the red brick warehouses and stone Port buildings—all old—all beaten, but surviving—like him. He commanded his mind to focus: *"I can't go back."*

The next morning, John was up early. He went down to the café and washed up in its restroom before a breakfast of oatmeal, and strong coffee. He wanted to walk the waterfront alongside the shipyard, grain elevators and roundhouse. The ground shook under the pulsing weight of engines bossing around miles of cars filled with Mesabe Range Iron Ore. He caught the odor of creosote, fishy nets, gasoline, and burned oil. Harbor lights glimmered through lake mist, laden with sounds near and far, as the twin Ports of Duluth and Superior awakened to the hiss and thunder of the steam locomotives, the chug of a tug headed out the harbor entrance, squealing brakes on Duluth's Thompson Hill, and the eerie scream of whistles. When he found a store open, he bought a newspaper, pencil and pen and then went back for his suitcase.

9:30 found him sitting in the waiting room of the Unemployment Office, reading the newspaper about Herbert Hoover's latest attempt to avoid financial meltdown. "Blessed are the young, for they shall inherit the national debt," Hoover said. More news from the depression came from Chicago as John read that Al Capone had sent out a wage cut order for his employees, saying income from gambling, beer and liquor was down a third from the days of prosperity ($100,000,000 income for his gang). Indeed Al Capone was now Chicago's Public Enemy Number One, but there was also a photo of the Free Lunch restaurant Capone operated during these hard times. He had been the first in the country to open soup kitchens and he ordered that clothes should be distributed at his expense. John saw an ad for the Packard Auto that posed the dilemma: "*A DOLLAR FOR DOLE - OR AN HOUR OF WORK? Which do you prefer to give?*" Under International News, he perused an article about the rise of the Nazis in Germany. He noted that Japan, driven by its growing hunger for raw materials, was expanding into Manchuria. Nervously, John skipped to the comic strips to read that Dick Tracy was coming soon.

The farmer who might hire him was late for their 10:00 appointment, and that made John edgy. He found himself pacing around the waiting room. His hands were shaking a little, and he forced himself to sit and settle down. He took a deep breath that sounded a little ragged, glad that he had bought the journal so that he could fill in time writing until the farmer arrived. A smile crept cautiously onto his face. Soon he would know if someone wanted him. He must write something clear for his journal that set his bearing. He used his new pen to write in a firm hand:

April 10, 1930 Waiting to begin again.

THIS PLACE OF
WATCHFUL WAITERS

VOICES IN THE ADJOINING ROOM, LOW CONFIDENTIAL MUM-blings, spiked with giggles from Myrtle. *She is flirting with someone. I'm betting its Moyer*, John mused, as he held his breath to distinguish the words.

The window of the waiting room door filled with the wide silhouette of a woman's backside. Laughter again, the knob turning, and there she was, beaming, wearing honeysuckle perfume and an orange flowered dress. She crooned, "Mr. Chapman, come in please." A scene flashed in his mind. For the briefest moment, he saw himself in a canoe pushing off into the rapids—the river of fate perhaps?

A man in bib overalls and a green woolen shirt looked up from the forms he was reading; John judged him to be younger than himself. "Dan Moyer here," he said extending his hand. "Chapman is a good British name, eh?"

John felt energized by the man's firm grip.

" Myrtle here tells me you are the man I am looking for," Dan continued, "and she is giving us a room to chew over our deal." He directed a charming smile toward her and said, "Thank you Myrtle, don't bother yourself further my dear." Turning, he instructed John, "Bring your things and yourself along then John, follow me, I know the way." He stepped lightly down the hall to an interview room. Moyer had hired many men out of this office, and he had confidence in Myrtle's judgment. He loved to play to her sultry side, and for not noticing her matronly appearance, she rewarded him with her pick of top prospects.

"I suppose Myrtle told you I am a town chairman and hiring all sorts to build roads and bridges." While John shook his head puzzled, Dan continued. "This time, I am looking for someone to live and work on my farm. Mr. Chapman—"

"Call me John," Chapman interjected.

"yes—John, I need a herdsman for what I want to be the finest dairy in Douglas County, and I'll be frank with you John, I love farming, but have to be gone a lot with county and town business. I need a man who will work from early to late, can drive or break a team to pull, can build a herd to produce milk, and deal with the breeding of 48 cows. We milk at 6:00 and 5:00 everyday-but you know how it is. I'm looking for a man who can handle an ax and a saw, can build fences, and follow a blueprint. Did Myrtle tell you we are finishing the barn?"

John nodded.

"The plans I have call for a working barn, but I want to be proud of the look of her. We are going to have to peddle milk in the city to pay the mortgage—especially now in this dratted depression. But my wife Lena and I will handle that part. Of course, we are still picking rocks and blowing stumps in our fields. I have another hired man, Dave, who plows an acre a day. Dave's not social—lives over the horse barn—and I only see him to pay him, and not always then. Which reminds me—I see you are a veteran of the War."

"Yes," John replied, looking away, and said nothing more. The two men stood drowning in a silence that said too much. Attempting to quell the uneasiness, Dan gestured to a chair.

"You have heard me out, let's sit here and talk about what

you want and expect."

John sat and composed himself. When he was ready, he looked Dan in the eye and made his case. "Dan, I can do all you ask and I can give you my best. The truth is, I left my family in Portage, and I need money to send to them. I doubt they will ever want me back for I am a failure at being a family man. But I am good with horses and can build and manage a herd. Animals like me. I guess I am best at building, and I have done barns before. There is something about the loft of a barn that makes me feel—well—I'm not a religious man, but it makes me feel like I'm, in God's pocket."

"God's pocket is it John? Well, that's a way of thinking I like. My Lena-now she is religious and looks to her Catholic Church for God to speak to her there, maybe from statues made of plaster lit by stained glass. Me—I love the wild places. Rivers— now that's where God would be—maybe washing his feet or fishing like the Bible says. That's why I'm here. My Dad was a lawyer and his dad before him. We had money once. Now, have lost it all. Me—I didn't care about money and stuffy buildings—just being outside breathing fresh air. The war taught me that. I was there too. You and me, we don't have words for the smell of that war. That's why I put up with that crazy Dave who works for me, and throws things against the walls all the night keeping the horses awake. He was in the war too and it messed with his mind. And you—I think that there is something of Dave in you, too. Brother, be as you are, but can you do the job I need done?"

"I think so Dan," John said. If I can be alone and quiet, but I do get spells when I am not myself." Having said that up front and honest, John glanced down, waiting to be dismissed.

"Well now John," chided Dan, "Truth shames the devil. It's a troubled world we live in and will be buried in soon enough, so Lord willing and the creek don't rise, we should just give this a try. Can an English gentleman work for an Irish rogue?"

Hearing understanding wrapped in dark humor startled John into a level look at Dan. He saw the face of a man full of mischief, malarkey, and the fatal vision of the Irish. Dan's black hair stood in a tall crew cut, above cerulean blue eyes. *"Black Irish"* thought John, *an unruly mix of Iberian warriors and fair skinned Celts.* He saw a man fun loving and a little untamed. *The presence of this man would clear a cloudy day.* A smile of agreement bridged between the two men as John answered, "Yes," confidently extending his hand.

"Lets give it a go then John my man," Dan said, grasping John's extended hand in a firm shake of agreement. John got his suitcase in hand, thanked Myrtle on the way out, and together they walked down the stairs into the sunlight of a new day.

They rumbled along the length of Superior in Dan's stake bed Model A truck, as Dan gave a travelogue: "Imagine if you can John, this place of watchful waiters," Dan said, pausing to see if John was interested in a good story.

John picked it up "Watchful waiters?"

"Yes-tis the way of it here before the railroad came. Superior was built as three towns between two rivers, the St. Lewis and the Nemadji. It was called the town of "magnificent distances", for its safe harbor was 20 miles long."

"Magnificent distances—very good," said John, turning the phrase in his mind, for he loved poetic sayings.

Encouraged by John's approval, Dan continued with zest. "Upper Town was called Superior City and had a brewery on the slough. Its people were Scandinavian or from eastern states, and the place developed by right of occupancy. Middle Town was settled by half-breeds and French Canadians in the same way, and Lower Town, which had attracted the eastern and southern wealthy, was platted and sold by development companies. They were joined by two wooden planks over the red mud so thick it swallowed your boots right off your feet and it took your two hands and a good back to pull them out if you could. All these people, John, were watchful waiters knowing that they had a piece of ground that would be worth millions when the railroad came."

John smiled, intrigued by the history and enjoying Dan's telling of it so much he forgot for a little time about his world in dire straights.

"There on Conner's Point", gestured Dan, "stood a mill the likes of which no one had ever seen. It turned out 4000 board feet a day to build homes for the great city that was to come with the railroad. And the Indians, why they were everywhere—gliding in and out of the slough in their birch bark canoes, come down out of the forests each spring to put their nets out for fish, and to visit their dead. Beyond Conner's Point, Wisconsin and Minnesota Point almost meet, giving Superior a harbor everyone here thought to be the best in the world. On these shores were the burial grounds of the Chippewa. Conner's point was a strip of stars at night from their fires, and their drums rolled like distant thunder."

"Oh, to have lived then," John murmured.

Dan liked that, smiling and nodding. "Soon enough John, you will meet mule skinner Whinneboujou—call him Whinn for short—a blacksmith, friend to me like no other, son of Steven Bungo who claimed to be the first white man ever born at the head of the lakes; though his skin was the color of the black spirit rock. Stephen was the son of an African servant to an officer stationed at Mackinaw, and a full blooded Chippewa. If you're lucky, Whinn will take you along the south shore, maybe even share a secret or two, for like his famous father, he speaks royal English."

"Look there, the sign for the old stockade site, built to protect the people from the rampaging tribes—the vengeful Sioux and their enemy the Chippewa, certain sure to be warring at each other, and newcomers twixt between. It was never used—torn down and made into canes as souvenirs—for the Chippewa remained loyal friends to the white settlers, and the Sioux never came."

The truck jounced along through Allouez, and across the Nemadji, out into the countryside past the gristmill on the Fond du Lac River, and then south. Dan shifted the little truck down as they began to gradually climb up out of the Lake Superior basin. On both sides of Highway 13, standing like gravestones, were natural groves of huge white pine stumps, the cutover great north woods. Black ash, maple and birch made little patches of leafiness amidst the devastation. John saw fences of stone and in the distance, a plowed field. Ahead a lone mountain of the Douglas Range faced the lake, its black basalt rampart dominating the horizon. He commented on it, "now where did that peak come from I wonder? It doesn't look to be part of anything around here."

Dan proudly answered, "That rock-hill is on my farm. We are almost home. Look right and you will see our new barn coming along to be tall as the cliff behind it."

John shivered. Was his excitement over the challenge ahead, the luck in the chance, or the look of this structure, undressed and showing its bones of timber—at once both massive and delicate. There were other main buildings—a log house, another barn, and a long low machine shed, all fronting onto a circle at the end of the driveway.

"We have a cabin for you, John, behind the woodshed over

there. You won't have to bunk with Dave (Lord help him) above the horse-barn. Why don't you put your things away and come out when you're ready."

With a "thanks" to the boss, John lifted his suitcase out of the cubbyhole. As he walked along the path to his bunkhouse, he tumbled Dan's words in his mind: "this was a place of watchful waiters" stuck in the mud but sure to be worth millions, they remained watchful, for luck was on its way—just around the corner—like the railroads, coming soon. Optimism. Hope. John recognized in Dan's words, a way of thinking he (John) had forgotten or maybe never knew.

Dan had said, "We should just give this a try."

It's easy to peg Dan-he's the picture of Irish optimism, John thought, adding, it would take just such a man to take a chance on me. What did he see in me I wonder?

Remembering the first entry in his journal—his own words—"waiting to begin again", John answered his own question. *Why, he thinks I'd fit in here—that I am a watchful waiter worth millions in the offing. Ha, he doesn't see that I am bankrupt.* And along with that thought, came the faintest whisper of what else Dan had said "Brother, be as you are." Wincing, John asked himself who that might be, and then realized what he was waiting for to "begin again". He was waiting for himself to come around the corner—whoever, whatever, whenever. *Waiting.*

Silver Threads
Lead Me Home

John washed up in a blue enamel washbasin set into a stand outside his cabin. *If there is room, I can move this inside in the winter,* he thought. He opened the door and entered, seeing first the window with its yellow flower-sack curtains and a view of the barn. A matching print fabric draped shelves. Three walls were rough sawn, smelling of the piney woods, and a cot sat in front of the 4th wall, papered in a blue color overlaid with wildflowers. The traditional wide stripes of a Hudson Bay blanket on his bed looked so inviting that he wanted to lie down on the soft red, green and yellow wool. Someone had carefully painted a table yellow and placed a lantern and Black Eyed Susans in a blue bottle upon it. Books fit underneath on a shelf. The pot bellied stove with its heating shelf, sat against a bricked chimney. Too nervous to enjoy his new surroundings, John hastily unpacked his suitcase, changed into work clothes, and was about to head off to find Dan when he heard the dog bark, then whimper-cry greetings to a lady walking down the drive. She was struggling to carry a huge bundle. *This must be Dan's wife, Lena,* John thought.

John ran to help Lena, introducing himself as he assumed her burden. She profusely thanked him.

"Ah, so Dan did hire you! I am so glad. We have high hopes for you, John. I bet you can guess I am Lena," she said. "I teach at Lakeside school and these are books and homework I'll be looking at tonight." She walked fast, with authority, glancing over her shoulder to be sure he followed, her dark flared skirt swaying with every stride. He took her in—thick blond hair done into a braid around her head, milk white skin, a fashionable polka dot blouse and jabot, and the scent of her like hyacinths in the spring. She seemed out of place on this wilderness farm.

"Excuse my haste, John, I am helping the men with chores first, and I must get the stove going to heat the stew I've made of venison, and—well you will just have to come join us for supper. We can talk around our table then."

They entered into a mudroom fronting the main house. Hooks along one wall held work clothes, jackets and boots, smelling of the outdoors and farm animals. The green printed linoleum looked freshly scrubbed. John promised to return for dinner, gave over the bundle to Lena and stepped with care over a threshold freshly painted in white enamel. "This is its one day to be bright white as Dan pays it no notice," Lena complained, adding "A spotless threshold shows an immaculate mind."

Dan was easy to find. He stood in front of his new barn with papers in his hand looking up and down checking the progress. Several men were on scaffolding, setting front double doors onto the mow.

"John, those are the Ritzen boys. They are barn-building brothers who travel around constructing them all over Wisconsin. They have the plan in mind, but here is the official one from Madison that some committee of educated blokes put together to please the government. Lena wants this barn pretty, I want it to work, and the Ritzens want to it to be done so they can get on to the next job with money for their wives and another feather for the Ritzen cap. When Myrtle told me you were a carpenter, and I asked if you could follow a plan, I meant it. I'd like to give over these plans to you—can't make heads or tails of them anyway, but since they were done by those who are supposed to know best (according to my Lena) someone should pay them mind. Also, I'd like you to work with the boys and be sure they do things proper. You milked cows for a living—should know things I don't."

Dan talked as they walked. "For now, we'll muck along in the old barn in the lean-to behind the horses. Out yonder, you can maybe see Dave and Nell plowing. I check on occasion to see they're still moving. Lena bakes him a loaf of bread now and then, and Dave cooks in the woods—whatever it is he shoots—comes back here at night so Nell can eat oats and hay, and he can get juiced up on moonshine from the still in that woods over there (Dan gestured to trees in the shadow of the rock) I hope you never find it. You'd be hard pressed to meet Dave, he's my man (and my heartache) and I'd best deal with him myself, as I have (or haven't)."

"Now there goes Lena to get the cows in, and she feeds the calves too." John glimpsed her and the collie headed along the road toward waiting Holsteins at the gate near the base of the hill. "She's a worker-that one. She can lift and carry with any man, and bake a pie tasty as Betty Crocker herself. And when we go dancing, well, she's fancy on my arm. She's even teaching me to write reports I give at County Board, and speeches to calm the rabble at Town meetings (I'm not everyone's cup of tea it seems). She gets rides to school and home now, but when the rains come, the mud is too deep for man or beast to get over, and she sets up at school."

The two men entered the horse barn to ready the stalls out back for milking. Each cow must have mixed grains to munch while being milked, then be turned into the night pasture. Soon John was immersed in a world he knew well. The cows looked him over, jostling each other to see the new man who would tend them, smelling him while licking molasses off their muzzles, raising a foot at him to let him know to be gentle while he captured their tails and set belts and milkers, his hands telephoning some sort of babble they liked. They waggled their ears at him when he turned them out. Still curious but clearly won over, full and happy, they finally paraded out between the stumps to lie and chew cuds near the safety of the barn. Lena had done her chores and disappeared into the house. With the milk cooling in cans in the milk-house tank, the men washed faces and hands in a barrel, pumping water up from a dug well, then work weary and relaxed, they strolled to the house for another wash over. While they waited for dinner to be set on the table, Dan spoke with enthusiasm about the park he wanted to develop in the Lakeland Township.

"The black Douglas fault that makes up our rock hill runs under this county. Alongside it is brownstone so pure big cities like Ashland come buy the stone to face buildings with. The Fond du Lac River spills off the basalt onto soft sandstone carving waterfalls. Where the river splits to form an island near here, there are three waterfalls, each different from the other. The land was long ago given to this town to be a park. Can you imagine it, John, whole families coming to picnic on the island by day, and by night people dancing to piano and fiddle music on a covered bridge. Children will wade in a kiddy pool where they will learn to swim, and the older ones will dive from the cliffs into the deep water. We are building a race track around a ball field on this land; such a gift it is."

John noticed Lena listening and saw a frown pass over

her face, like a cloud briefly covering the sun. She had set the table with white plates on a red-checkered cloth and made an arrangement of wild columbine, honeysuckle and trillium. She brought in biscuits still hot, bowls of butter, and blackberry jam. Then she set a wooden lazy-susan on the sideboard to receive a steaming casserole of venison stew. John breathed in the smell of deer meat simmered with onions and flavored with garlic, rosemary and thyme. Lena joined the men briefly, reminding Dan to lead the saying of grace. Coffee and creamy custard pudding topped with brown sugar hard caramel, shone tawny gold in the lantern light. As she served them, Dan joked that it was only after Lena knew that he could only cook milk soup, only after she realized that the cat did the dishes after every meal, only when she heard he was a bachelor living alone who loved to dance and brawl, only then did she agree to marry him to save him from disease, starvation and a trip to hell. She sat down at last with the men and traded stories, slapping her thigh, tears running down her cheeks laughing about the creatures and characters sharing the byways and back waters of these wild Wisconsin woods.

Tired to the point of exhaustion, John excused himself and borrowed a lantern to make his way along the path past the woodshed, the outhouse, then to his cabin, the table, his journal. Without pausing long, he began writing.

Tonight, I will begin writing of this new life and those who are in it. This journal will be like a playbook, or a book of poetry, or maybe it will be like a painting filled with the shapes and colors of my impressions. I write my journal so I can remember. For now, it is not for sharing but for me, groping my way along, lest I forget the path. The characters in this picture are showing up. Dan is the dreamer—color him sky blue. His dream is bigger than a farm—it is about opening this North Country to the world so that others might love it as he does. He has one foot in the mud, the other in the stars.

Lena is the worker. Blond and beautiful she is, a wild rose in bloom, but like the oak tree that is so proud and unyielding that it breaks in a storm, she uses her body like a hammer driven by her will. All must be perfect to please her unmerciful God. She has two people in her—the one is dutiful, a beast of burden, carrying wood too heavy for her, but the other dusts drudgery with loveliness and refinement, shining it with class. She would put bouquets on each fence post. Color her crimson and shell pink.

And of myself, I cannot yet write. I have no shape, no color.

We are gathered together to build this barn, the rhyme, reason and stage for this production. Help me find the words to make sense of it. On this, my first night here, I see the lake shining in moonlight and framed by the barn, her timbers like silhouettes of lace.

Silver threads-lead me home.

A Love Letter
Short of Words

John sat at his table trying to write. He wanted to send his first paycheck home to his family, and include a letter, but he didn't know what to say to his wife, and he found countless ways to divert his mind. He sat looking at what he had at hand. Paper was hard to come by during the depression, but Lena kept him supplied with scrap paper from school, and occasionally she brought by a new book of poetry. He had his own poem book by Walt Whitman to read and he wanted to lose himself in Whitman's rich images of war, nature, love, sweetness and power, and never get to writing a letter to his wife. He had met a new character for his journal. Tonight instead of letter writing, he found himself wanting to scribble his impressions of Whinn, Dan's friend who came by on occasion to needle Dan or to help. Whinn was short for Whinneboujou Dan had said, and now John knew that Whinneboujou was Chippewa for "the spirit who used the anvil of a blacksmith." Fascinating. *More fascinating than letter writing*, he thought. There also was a sheet of paper John had set aside to write about him, and it was blank except for his name. John decided to write some things down on that sheet and then put together something meaningful to send to his wife along with the paycheck.

He drew a maze on the "John" page. He thought it represented the way he was thinking—round and round, back and forth, lost and going nowhere.

Getting out another scrap of paper, John entitled it "Ida" for his wife. As he looked at her name, he remembered that he had first seen her when she was about 6 years old. Several years later, when he apprenticed to carve and paint carousel horses for the fair in Portage, his favorite of all the horses he helped restore, was a dappled grey charger with a red saddle and bridle. This was the very horse she chose to ride when the carousel opened. He watched her walk among all the horses touching their noses, caressing each one with wonder, until she saw the dappled grey. She squealed with delight and threw her arms around his curving neck. John fell in love on the spot.

He made a heart on her page and wrote the word "horses" in it.

Soon after that, John made friends with Ida's family. He encouraged her in every way, giving her a nickel—the first money she had ever earned, to play the piano for him. She played "Claire De Lune", still a favorite song for both of them. John worked as a teamster for a farm owner, and gradually developed a reputation as an expert horseman. Thus it was only natural that Ida would bring her unruly calico filly to John for training. John worked with the horse to make her responsive and taught Ida to ride and train her. When Ida and Calico became performers at the fair, John watched like a proud father as Ida carried the flag for the local horse club and Calico pranced proudly in parades.

Thinking about his wife brought a flurry of words to John and he wrote some of them down. Ida—chestnut hair streaked with sun—hazel eyes like the first leaves of spring— lilting laugh, refreshing as artesian water—Ida—: adventurous, energetic, spirited, loving.

John wrote "Ida" into the center of the circle on his own page.

When she was 16 and John was 21, they were married in a simple ceremony. They had two sons in two years. With the help of the bank, they bought an old farm and some cows. In love with life, hard work and each other, they were a handsome, happy couple. But bad things were brewing. In 1914, the Great War began over an assassination, complicated by treaties that brought the major powers into what might have been a local conflict. John was from a family that had migrated to the US from England and felt allegiance to Great Britain. For that reason, he joined the Royal British forces in 1915. The war ended in November of 1918 with the United States having been fully engaged for over a year—but by that time John had been fighting for 3 years.

Though the world was no longer at war, the war never ended for many who could not forget the trench warfare, hand to hand combat, the gassing, shelling and deadly toll. It was like an earthquake had opened a chasm between Ida and John. He could see her on the other side and made attempts to cross over to her, but something pulled him back, and the chasm widened. To make matters worse, the depression, and John's recurring debilitating headaches, which rendered him unable to work the farm, resulted in a bank foreclosure. John and Ida had tried to make the best of things, and for a time, without the terrible stress of paying a mortgage, it seemed things were getting better. John was working a job delivering milk in Spooner when they conceived another child, hoping this would rejuvenate their marriage.

John drove an old horse named Molly on his milk route, rising each day at 4 AM to curry and harness Molly, ending the route before noon each day. This was a demanding job for he had tickets to write for merchandise and empty bottles to collect, along with maintaining a friendly business-like manner with the customers and anticipating their every need with different products like cottage cheese and chocolate milk. Molly was so well trained that she walked ahead stopping to wait on the corner. One day a car lost its brakes and slammed into Molly as she stood, faithfully waiting for John. She had to be destroyed. John's headaches and nightmares returned and he lost his position.

Thinking about the war, John rose from his table and walked outside to sit on his stoop and breathe the fresh air. He remembered what Dan had said about it:

"We don't have words for the smell of that war."

It was a soft misty evening, and the moon gave little light, but a lantern was flickering in the loft above the horse barn. Dave- the man Dan called *"his heartache"*, had stopped off at the still for some shine on his way home. John could see Dave as a shadow image moving fast across the light, and then he heard crashes and thumps. Dave must be *"throwing things, keeping the horses awake"*, Dan's explanation of how the war continued nightly for this man who had been there.

"I was there too, and that's why I put up with Crazy Dave" he had said.

Another pulsating thump and John recognized the ferocity of feeling—this huge violent explosion of rage. Dave was launching missiles made of wood at walls of wood, hurting no one, but aimed at the demons that plagued him. John understood. For the first time, he saw something akin to what he felt: hopeless rage, directed at the universe and what God there was (or wasn't). A God that let the meek be defiled, the righteous be humiliated and the gentle be disposed of; a God that took the best and the sweetest, leaving only desolation, disappointment, destruction and this kind of damnation. With each thud, John shuddered at the futility of Dave's wrath, the pain of it, and the permanence of it. And how had Dan tied John in with Dave? Ah yes, John remembered the words: "*Brother, I see some of Dave in you too.*" John felt the kinship—he was not alone.

John went back in and sat down to write to his wife. If only he could get back to being who he used to be with her—a teacher, a mentor, her lover, capable and competent, making all her dreams come true. He wanted to apologize for himself, for becoming a liability who could not be depended on, who disappeared into another world of debilitating headaches, again and again bringing shame to his family with his crazy actions.

He wrote:

Dear Ida:

This is my first paycheck and I hope to send many more. I want to come home as the man I used to be. I have been like a stranger even to myself. Until then, I can at least provide money to help with school for the boys. Give little Joe a hug for me and you take care and buy something nice for yourself.

John wanted to end his letter with a poem of love. He scanned the poem books for something to say, and then read Ida's page, visualizing her with the words he had written there. His own so separate page was sadly empty, but he focused on the circle with Ida's name inside it and wrote his message of love, painfully short of words.

Love,
John

And the Woods Would Not Be Silent

THE WOODEN SIGN WAS BORDERED ROUND BY MULE SHOES and read "Blacksmith." It hung high from an arrow of wrought iron driven into a bare-trunk Norway pine. Turning off Moonshine Road, John followed the path as it twisted down through a dank smelling cedar grove, fragrant filigree boughs covering soggy silt, soaked by a brook that tumbled unseen over mossy stones. Now the path was edged by a rock fence climbing onto the shiny black ridge of the hill warmed by the sun. Near the top, he passed through another grove, this time of balsam fir, and smelled the mules before he saw them, craning their necks to watch him. Tarpaper buildings, a log barn, house and machinery shed, obscured in a wood smoke haze, lay snug in the trees. Trails end was a stone building with open double doors. Inside stood an immense anvil, flanked by a table of clamps, and behind it, the chimney of old bricks and its surround containing burning coals. A coonhound yowled to announce a visitor to Whinn's Forge, but Whinn already knew he was there. Water was simmering on a black box stove, for the steeping of a brew. Two fine china cups, clearly misplaced in this rugged landscape, stood the ready for entertaining.

"Welcome John. I've made you rose hip tea fit for an English gentleman like yourself. My grandfather taught me to make it, as he learned to do from his English master; and my grandmother, who was full blooded Chippewa, sweetened his recipe with sugar she boiled down from maples. She said that sweet maple syrup won over his heart." He grinned, dark wind hardened skin contrasting with pearly whites. John was tall, but he looked up at Whinn, taking in the rugged elegance of his dress. He wore the laced boots of a woodsman, a wool shirt and canvas pants, both from St. Vincent De Paul's treasure store, and around his neck hung a heavy gold chain with an elaborate golden cross. Donning his open crown felt hat generously adorned with feathers, he poured tea, and motioned for John to follow him around the building to his garden, as he called it. He had an artesian well surrounded by wildflowers growing in pockets in the black rock. They sat at a hand crafted table of bent willow and twig, upon chairs of white pine boards big and sturdy, the better to lean back and enjoy water music made by the spring spilling out of the rocks into the brook. White birch with birdhouses in every tree, stood ready with shade. "What more could a man want?" He asked John, watching for his answer.

John smiled, looked all around, marveling the best he knew how to do, with all the fitting "oohs and awes", and unwrapped the pastries Lena had sent with him for Whinn. "Dan said I should accept your invite, Whinn, for then (I am quoting him now) I'd get to see how a "boondoggler lives the life of Riley," but that description didn't set me up for such splendor as you have here.

Whinn laughed a rolling thunder, deep throated belly laugh. "That Dan loves to insult me with political terms knowing full well I'll have none of what he does—him building this swamp up fancy so city folk can survive out here—and so we jab each other in true neighborly fashion just to beat back boredom." Satisfied with the words he had chosen, he punctuated his insults with three fist-to-palm-o-the-hand blows, "bam, bam, bam."

"John, it looks to me that you are a stayer down there on Dan's leap of faith he calls a farm. I think it's my duty to set you straight. Like they say, "One beetle recognizes another," and I've bought into his folly too. He's the damnedest man, your boss Dan! Such a friend he is, but seeing him farm is like watching a goose sent as a messenger to the fox's den. Let me tell you a little story of early on with us here, and then you'll know the man you are working for and be ready." Whinn, clearly enjoying the opportunity to spin his yarn, stretched out his long legs, and leaned back in his Muskoka plank chair. He was the picture of the back woods storyteller.

John sipped his tea, munched his pastry and settled in like he was at the motion pictures, in a mood to be entertained.

"Dan came here as a surveyor. He was the oldest son of a lawyer from Saint Paul, loved to dance, sing and hunt; never did much in school, a lovable playboy was he; but he had the charm of the Irish, and some luck being wise, like a fox or a politician. Like he says, "It's not what you know, it's who you know." He got a room from the Christensen brothers on their farm. His great aunt had a homestead bordering the Christiansen's that included most of this rock hill and the land below it toward the lake. Dan loved to hunt on that land full of white tailed deer, bear, wolves and the like and he spear fished the rivers, keeping the Danes provided for, while whirling the girls around the dance floor and setting lines for the farms. Now those Christiansen's—they come by farming naturally. Soon, Dan set his mind to be like them, and they tried to teach him." Whinn shook his head and set down his cup like a judge pronouncing a sentence. "You can't build a barrel around a bunghole," my Daddy used to say, and that's just what us lumberjack dirt grubbers, born and bred in these woods, have been trying to do—make a farmer out of a dreamer, but there's no forcing the sea."

Whinn poured out more tea for them both—fuel for the next chapter of his tale.

"And to his own demise, Dan could talk a coon out of its tree; so he convinced the family that he was the one to turn a homestead of cut over pines and a world of rocks into green meadows for high class dairy cows, the kind determined to die if not properly pampered. Those of us that know these woods—me and the mules—we've been saddled with the boy ever since. There's a hundred stumps to the acre here, some five feet across and all needing dynamite to blow loose of the heavy red clay. Then, a team of good horses can pull out the roots one by one. Burning stumps could take a lifetime, but there's no dying before picking up rocks. Did you see my stone fence on the way up? Dan has 500 acres of rocks just like I stacked here, to build fences and lanes to keep the cattle in and the varmints out," Whinn gestured a 360 degree circle to show the full extent of the danger, "and this fate—for a boy whose mind is in the clouds dreaming of picnics and concerts by the river in St. Paul! I hope you will be the kind of man Dan needs to get his dream up and running; and if you'll stay, I'll keep you jollied up with tales of Dan, the would-be farmer.

But I confess I had something special in mind with inviting you, John. Today, I wanted you to come here to see the gift I've made as a surprise. I thought a long time about what I could make for this new barn that only God knows how Dan will ever pay for. He brags on your skills as a carpenter you know, and I'm hoping you'll help me set my gift in place while he's off one day working on the bridge at his park."

Now John, his curiosity aroused and his ego flattered,

set his cup carefully down next to Whinn's and pledged his help the best he could give. The idea of a barn-warming gift, a christening of back country sorts, appealed to his generous side. He liked the idea.

Whinn led the way to a workbench inside his shop where the gift was propped. In the soft light of the dying coal embers, John saw a large piece of white pine covered with hammered copper in the shape of Lake Superior. Along the bottom, a deerskin laced with Copenhagen snuff lids, formed a wind chime jingle dress that moved a little and sounded like rain on a metal roof in the slightest breeze. Where the deerskin was attached, a valance of feathers covered the nails. Most notable were the implements crossing each other in the center of Whinn's design. One looked like a primitive digging tool and the other looked like a formidable implement of war. Both were adorned with feathers.

"Like I said John," Whinn explained, "my Grandfather was an African slave—perhaps Dan told you—and had an English master. Anyhow, his master was an officer stationed at Sault St. Marie, and he had a collection of throwing axes. The Europeans traded weapons like this one I have made, to the Algonquins, who named them tomahawks." Whinn ran his hand down across the hand-forged head of the fighting tomahawk.

"Algonquins descended from the Anishinaabe, as did the Ojibwa, or Chippewa, as they are called here, and traded all the way across the North Atlantic and down the St. Lawrence River into the Great Lakes. The Chippewa already had something like this weapon, a primitive digging and chopping tool they made of stone or antler fastened to the wooden shaft with leather like this one that I found on the rock hill, broken of course. I fixed it, and have made several myself, to study how it was done and see how it worked. The black stone found here can be chipped to make a very good tomahawk as you can see on this head. I made these for the new barn, as a good luck omen for Dan and Lena and their new enterprise. I thought it showed the combination of hard work, and warrior guts that's needed to live and thrive in this wilderness; tools for work and for protection—and Dan needs both—especially the protection from his foolish self. Could you help me hang this charm above the rear door of the barn? I think it should face the lake—and I'd like it professionally hung so it makes its jingle sound. I want it to be a surprise gift."

John was sure he could do that job. He nodded as he examined the workmanship, while Whinn explained the symbolism in his design.

"The copper stands for the minerals found here. There was a copper mine just across the road from the still on our rock hill. The jingle dress came to me, like a lot of things in my house, from the Indians that used to call that rock hill 'sacred'. The barn is made of wood from timber cut on the crest of the hill and sits on stone blasted from its heart. And now I am asking you a special favor; for beyond the hanging of this gift, I would like you to create something to explain it. I understand from Lena that you have a gift for writing—or at least like poetry. John, could you write something —maybe a poem I can give Dan and Lena so they know what I mean by this gift? Dan and I have battled together against old Mother Nature to get his house in place and stay alive in this wilderness. The Chippewa knew about that. I have the heart and the hands to make things, but I don't have the words. What do you think John?"

John felt Whinn's eyes on him and wondered at what Whinn saw as he tried to conceal his shock at the request. He remembered he had tried to write a poem to his wife, and the dismal effort he had managed. Still, he could not say no. He promised he would do his best and with the help of Walt Whitman, Henry Thoreau and Mark Twain, maybe he could come up with something. He thanked Whinn, shook his hand and made his way down the path past the mules, through the sweet-smelling cedars, out onto the road, and back to the farm. All during chores, he mulled over his assignment and that night, sitting by his stove aglow with fire, he searched the poetry in his books for what to say. John found encouragement in the words of Henry Van Dyke,

"Use what talents you possess: the woods would be very silent if no birds sang there except those that sang best."

He decided to begin with Dan's vision, noting the setting and the idea that this barn would span lifetimes. All around the edges of his thinking, there was a memory from the war, but he could not entertain it. Instead, he wrote the words "safe fortress" and "the strife" as his acknowledgement of battle. Soon he had filled a page with words that he thought described a barn. He remembered how as a boy, he would climb into the loft of a barn and look out at the heavens from that height, and talk with God there. He wrote the word "inspiration." Then, he thought about Whinn's creation, and wrote of the music the breezes would play in the jingle dress. He considered the tools themselves, one fashioned to till the earth, the other to defend it. He wrote "wood, stone, and hide." And then he wrote something out of Whinn's meaning and being to suggest that this was a charm to call forth the help of the ancestors, chuckling at what Whinn had said, "Dan needs protection from his own foolish self." The words of love that ended the poem were at once prophetic and puzzling to John, but he wrote them anyhow.

He thought to rhyme some of the words; working well into

the night, until he had what he thought was right and fitting. He wrote the poem out carefully on a clean sheet of paper, kicking back the small mountain of crumpled scraps he had rejected. His last thought that evening, as sleep tumbled impressions together in his mind, was of the jingle dress music of his poem, and that the woods would not be silent for he had found his voice.

A Barn Christening Gift
From Whinneboujou and the Rock Hill

Here stands the dream on sacred ground.
This barn built to shelter life
Space to be born, to grow and to die
A fortress safe from the strife.

Magnificent storehouse, dairy-land home
These walls shut the blizzards out
Smell the earth, capture the sun, moon and stars
Inspiration vanquishes doubt.

These tools made of wood, hide, and stone
jingle music from copper and tin
Can be used to break ground for new plants to come
Or to keep evil from entering in.

Chippewa blessings set on magical walls
Expect that the ancestors know
And will worship, protect and send swiftly to us
Spirit arrows propelled by love's bow.

THE SONG OF THE JINGLE DRESS

THE DAY FOR SURPRISES FINALLY CAME. WITH LENA TEACHING
school and Dan off to do town business, John was left alone
to put finishing touches on the barn. Instead, he hitched the
team and drove over to pick up Whinn and his gift. To the
be-jangle of the harness, he sang to the horses, humming the
words he didn't remember:

> *"In the winter and in the summer,*
> *The times are bum and getting bummer,*
> *But in the meantime, in between time,*
> *Ain't we got fun!"*

Nip and Tuck responded with high spirits, tossing their heads
and blowing at the mules watching from Whinn's woods.
Whinn welcomed John again with tea and a story. John sat
back deep into the wooden chair, warmed by the tea and
Whinn's tale.

"Like I said John, I'll keep you entertained with stories
about your city boy boss, and I'll start right from the day I met
him. Dan had been surveying all around the county and got
into his mind how he wanted his farm to go. The backside of
the hill faced south with the log homestead house built right
next door to the Christensens—handy for them to build it
there all right, but not scenic enough for Dan. He had to find

a way to move the house across a half-mile of stumps and then down off the face of that rock hill and across Moonshine Road so he could have a farm yard facing north looking out at Lake Superior with a mile to the lake woods. That was his dream.

The boy is clever at finding people to put foundations under his dreams—he is that! And he has the luck of the Irish. Well, some say the Irish are lucky; but they ate mostly potatoes for generations, and then starved when the potato blight struck. The truth is, they knew how to make the best of things. That's the luck they have. Dan sums it up when he tells the 'Legend of Clover.' It's about the good old Irish boy that drank too much whiskey and fell off a cliff but landed in a field of clover."

John listened intently, for his father had told him of the great potato famine during the time Ireland was under British rule. In Gaelic, the famine was called "An Gorta Mor"—the great hunger. Many people died and many more emigrated, leaving Ireland's population diminished by 25%. John remembered the question Dan had asked him before he was hired, and now he understood it: "Can an English gentleman like your self work for an Irish rogue?" The Irish never forget, he was saying, but can they forgive?" Dan said his family came here during that time," John volunteered.

"Yes," continued Whinn. "And the boy came honestly by the magic of his heritage." You know, in olden Europe, red headed people were considered witches and were burned. Well the Irish, God love them, just to be safe they settled an island so cold no one would go there, but they didn't plan that their neighbors were the Vikings. Irish luck. Still, somehow when the Vikings conquered the island, mating with the Irish, there sprung up a people with angels as friends and many of them were red headed. Witches they are, and Dan is too. I've walked with him and can tell you this John. While he is talking as he loves to do—that being natural for a politician, he will just reach down and pluck him a clover—a four-leaf clover. He never looks for them at all—just reaches down and gets them! And, when it comes to water, he is a witch for sure. He has uncovered a spring on the hill with water enough for his dream dairy farm, and with the moving of the farmstead down off the hill, the water will gravity flow to cool the milk from the cows he wants to have.

To get back to my story John, the Christensens sent him to me to move the log house, for he hadn't a clue how to go forward. People like me and you, we have the know-how while fanciers have the notions. So, I raised up the house and put skids under it, and when the snow was deep over and around the stumps, we glided that house behind my mules. It took all winter to get it to the brow of the hill and 20 minutes to make the descent, my mules running for their lives." Whinn paused to refill his teacup, smiling at the remembrance of the near catastrophe. "And John, ask Dan if you don't believe me, but not one brick in the chimney was lost so smooth was the landing. The snow was banked high that year. Dan and I dug and packed in boards under that chimney and the plan was to lower the house down with the melt. But Dan was busy looking after his park and his people (for he early on got into politics) and one day when the sun came out of hibernation unexpectedly, the house crashed down in the mud breaking the chimney to smithereens. The luck of the Irish is no luck at all—just a smile that sends trouble to trembling. That's Dan. He can make a mob of angry men at a town meeting bent on tar and feathering him turn sweet as molasses, all with his humor and charm. But, lets load up and get our business done on your farm and see how long before they notice the new barn has a tribal blessing on it from the Chippewa to make good the luck of the Irish."

The two men stood in the double door entrance, looking over 100 feet of limed white passageway that shimmered in sunshine, out at the lake scene beyond. Straight before them above the double rear doors was white space for strong medicine. Whinn had hand-forged hangers, and relied on John's carpenter skills to set them. Together they hung Whinn's masterpiece as if they were setting stained glass into a rustic cathedral. They gathered up their tools and John delivered Whinn back to his home on the hill.

There was time before chores for John to have another cup of tea with his new friend and he relished the chance to hear more about the early days. Whinn obliged him, telling how Dan had managed to kill all 6 of the first cows he had purchased for his new dairy farm. The last cow had bloated on new grass and Dan realized it was too late for half measures. The extreme emergency called for him to bravely puncture her side to open her stomach. "Not taking time to read the instructions that came with the trocar and cannula, Dan missed the insertion point and killed the animal. It was then that he decided to join the war effort and put the farm on hold. He had married Lena by this time, but they lived apart for she had to teach to pay the bills."

John realized the time slipping away, and made mention that he must be getting home to do chores, but Whinn poured him the last of the tea and continued. "John my friend," he said softly, punctuating the words with a dark look, "Dan and Lena have had to struggle, and he is enjoying the fray. Like he says, "When the sky falls, we'll catch larks." But she is not like that—not like that at all. She has in mind to clean and polish the stars in the sky. She lives to work and is serious about it. She is a proud lady and strong beyond her size, but strength doesn't endure, and they have no children. Dan collects clovers hoping for an Irish blessing, but my medicine is better—the song of a jingle dress. Tradition has it that it was given by the creator of the Ojibwa people to heal. The jingles ward off bad spirits and welcome in the good. The sound is like waves crashing on the great lake where the tradition began. Here in this place, Dan and Lena will listen to the music made by the lake breeze rustling the metal pieces together, and I hope they will learn what the old ones knew—that the jingles dancing over the hips of their pretty young women sing God's promise of eternal life—children to fill their lives with laughter."

"Ah, said John, now I understand." He gave Whinn his copy of the poem he had made.

Whinn read it aloud. When he got to the last verse, he stopped for a moment considering the words:

Chippewa blessings set on magical walls
Expect that the ancestors know
And will worship, protect and send swiftly to us
Spirit arrows propelled by love's bow.

"Yes John, I think this is good! I will bring the poem to Dan and Lena tomorrow, and thank you for helping me do this thing to celebrate what we have all worked so hard to make happen — this barn and the magic within it."

Out of the Shadows

When Lena looked through the mail, she found a letter for John. Curious, she noted the lovely script, the address, and put it to her nose to sniff for perfume; for it looked to be from John's wife, Ida. Remembering the letters to Ida that John had asked to be mailed, and knowing that John never had money to spend on himself, Lena guessed that Ida got John's paychecks. This was the first letter John had received—how strange. *He will be excited to open it*, Lena thought, as she brought it to John's cabin, setting it on his table with a tinge of foreboding. John was constructing a lane on the far side of the night pasture, and Dan was in the Lake woods burning stumps.

It was Saturday, and Lena wanted berries for pie and bread. She had in mind treats for Dan and John and thought she would put berries into a loaf of bread for Dave. She hadn't seen Dave for weeks except in the distance plowing his acre a day. But she saw the light above the horse barn and sometimes heard him at night. She thought she might catch him bringing Nell home for her grain and hay, before going off to drink, spending his wages on hooch.

Lena didn't approve of drinking. Her rough and tumble lumberjack brothers who danced logs on the Mississippi, wanted to visit her, the darling youngest child of their old German family, but Lena's mother had taught her to "shun those who disagree with your principles until they comply," and since they remained drinkers, they were never invited to visit. Lena believed in punishment, Purgatory and Hell. The exception to her rule was Dave. Lena forgave Dave his drinking, and favored him with the sweetness she could bake in her oven, maybe because Dave was suffering his own purgatory already, or maybe because he brought wildflowers to her, treating her like she was his lady to be worshipped from afar; or maybe out of guilt just because he had golden curls, a handsome wide face and a roughish smile that reminded her of her banished brothers.

Lena tied her straw hat tight to keep the sun off her white skin. She covered her housedress with one of her Dutch aprons full of pockets. It was early fall. Above, thunderheads tumbled against each other threatening to crash, tall white sculptures in rounded shapes with dramatic grey undersides filling the sky. Below, stumps like sentinels were surrounded by fields of sienna, ochre and all shades of gold. What forest there was, showed as patches of shamrock and yellow with an occasional red. Lena climbed the path up the rock hill carrying a light bucket; her dog Shep was with her, ever watchful, sniffing for foraging black bears.

Finding berry thickets growing on rocky plateaus, Lena scrambled about getting scratched, wishing she had a ladder, while she plucked fat thimbleberries, black berries and tiny wild raspberries. Her fingers turned dark red as the berries plunked, then nestled together in the bucket, her mind set now on making blackberry buckle and berry tarts. Shep lay flat in a patch of sunlight on a mossy rock, all golden brown with a white collie mane, listening to Lena, and dreaming about his younger days. She talked to the dog, saying things to him she didn't tell anyone else, knowing his love was true, for he listened carefully and had done so for 11 years.

"A little girl Shep—think how you'd love to watch over a little girl—pretty as a doll in long white stockings and black patent leather shoes. What shall we call her Shep—this one?" There had been others. Last year's little girl had lived an hour before spina bifida claimed her life. She had thick auburn hair and blue eyes, but Lena never spoke of her and allowed no one else to mention her. She was buried in the graveyard with no stone. Lena had read that spina bifida was more common in Ireland than anywhere else and she blamed Dan for this thing that had plagued them, this thing you could not scrub away or hide from. She was afraid of it, afraid it was inside of her like an alien seed. Black as sin, it maimed and disfigured innocence, then it tore at your heart and drowned your dreams in tears. Disgrace came to call but "look away, shun it!"

Her hand trembled and she dropped some berries, so she reached hard into the bushes, the thorns drew blood as punishment for her weakness, and she swallowed the pain and spoke cheerily to Shep. "I was thinking of 'Lorelei', Shep. It's a German name. Poets write of her, Shep. Listen to the name— like music echoing. Lorelei was a mermaid who was splendid to behold, and sang so lovely a song that men challenged the rocks of the Rhine trying to capture her. But they perished in the trying for she was pure and could not be possessed. Yes, if I am pregnant again, then Lorelei will be her name." Lena decided the bucket was full enough, and wound her way around boulders to find the trail down.

Alert and protective, Shep followed at her heels, then stopped, looking into the woods. His old eyes were not as sharp as they had been and he didn't hear well—but there was something—something there. His nose told him so.

Hidden by stumps and rocks, the man watched her hungrily. His heart beat faster as he thought how he could bring her down, the chase, a violent fight, domination, her inevitable surrender, and the satisfaction of pounding warm flesh, her body against his. The liquor from the still had provided fuel for the fire now burning inside him. *Fate is sending her to me*, he thought, a change of luck not to be missed—this beauty —alone for his taking. He could see a cloud of smoke in the woods nearest the lake and guessed her husband was busy burning stumps, far away and out of sight. Riding his horse, tied nearby, he knew she could not escape him no matter how hard she tried, and afterwards, he would simply ride away and no one would ever know what happened to the Misses out picking berries alone. She wouldn't tell.

A fast moving shape in the woods, and Shep barked. His voice rose, a volley, half surprise, half warning not to approach. Lena paused like a startled deer, looking into the woods, seeing a man not a bear, and he was coming at her. She ran. Dropping her bucket, she ran, while her dog bought her time, his bark now vicious as he stood his ground between them. Lena snatched up her skirt, dashed on down the hill, sprinted across the road, out onto the flat meadow and faster she ran, not looking back, just knowing, and hearing the dog fighting the man behind her. She heard Shep yelp, then nothing. She ran to the sound of her wildly beating heart. And there, across the circle drive near the far gate was the team hitched and ready—the team she didn't drive—but the horses to take her to Dan in the far woods. Now she looked back and saw the man leading a horse out onto the road, mounting up, coming after her. Trotting out onto the field, he stopped his horse, closer now, watching. He didn't dare come into the yard after her. No Shep. She yelled for John—no answer. She was alone. Soon he would know she was alone. Breathless, frightened beyond all reason, Lena untied the lead horse, Tuck. Up onto the wagon she jumped, un-dallied the reins and lashed them against the horses backs. They responded, slowly at first, through the gate and toward the woods a mile away. She whipped them into a trot, shrieking at them to run.

John had been building a fence to enclose a lane out of the night pasture. He had hitched the team to deliver a load of sharpened posts to his project and gone back for another load. He soon realized that he had forgotten his ax out at the job site and left the horses tied to walk back for it. Such a beautiful day, he enjoyed the greys and tans of fall. The young stock were all around him and he looked at the heifers and thought what good cows they would be. Then he heard something— his name? He stopped among the stumps to listen and turned to look back. He saw a man on horseback on the meadow. What was he doing on Dan's farm land? Then, he saw the team starting out for the lake woods—and Lena was driving, fast and furious. Spurring his horse along the road, the man skirted the farm buildings but entered the field and rode to intercept Lena and the team. John knew he would catch her.

Lena saw him coming. She screamed. The sound of terror resonated over the fields, out into the woods. Behind her, the young cattle stopped grazing, came to attention, and crowded over to the fence to watch. John heard it, and scrambled in competition with the cattle to see. Out of sight in a clearing in the lake woods, Dan stopped shoveling dirt around his stump fire, stopped to listen for something disturbing, but it did not come again.

The fear in her voice and the sound of horse and rider galloping at them made the team crazy. They ran uncontrolled. The wagon often airborne over uneven ground, lurched just as Lena whipped the lines, her hands tight on the heavy leather.

It happened so fast. She lurched and tumbled forward and over the edge. The heavy wheel of the runaway wagon tore into the tender flesh of her leg. Lena lay helpless as the team raced on, circling around, free of a driver and unsure of where to go.

The man stopped his horse to watch Lena try to crawl away from him. He rode around her one time laughing, before he dismounted and ground tied the reins. She kept moving, face down, desperate to escape. He stepped down in front of her, his boot barring the way, playing a game like a cat does with a mouse. He slipped first one suspender off his shoulder, then the other, and spoke to her tauntingly. "My pretty! Do you think you can get away? Look at me! See who it is that will have you."

And then she rolled up and faced him, her eyes blazing. "Did you kill my dog—you bastard? You bastard! Did you kill my dog? You coward! I will bite out your tongue and I will scratch out your eyes—you Satan! I will not grovel before you." She rose up on one elbow, gathering her good leg under her to spring at him.

Now he laughed, dancing, excited by the hate in her eyes, her blood all around, and her challenge. He unbuttoned his fly, exposing himself to her. He dodged away from her a little, taunting in wait for her attack, knowing she would have to drag herself to pounce. Running his tongue over his teeth, stallion fierce he would rake her neck with his fangs—taste her blood—hot. It was then that the first bullet tore thru his abdomen. He looked confused by this, seeing his own blood spurting out, pulsing away. Then the second and third shot hit him and he fell, surprised by death, onto the ground, a lifeless form in the dirt. Shying from him with a snort, his horse trotted off, turning his head to the side to keep from stepping on reins, seeking safety with his own kind; for he smelled another horse in the woods ahead. Soon he was grazing alongside old Nell.

John had managed to get through the cattle herd and the barbed wire fence, and sprinted across the field to Lena. She was curled on her side, crying a little, trembling and pulling her skirt around one leg, trying to stop it from bleeding. John knelt by her, slipped out of his shirt and ripped it into strips while he talked to Lena, soothing her. He did not have to examine the man to know he was dead.

"Now Lena, he said teasingly, are you making race horses out of that old team? I've never seen Nip and Tuck get out of a trot before. I believe they were running their best for you sweet Lena. Here, let's see that leg. It's been awhile, but I think I can do a battle dressing still. Let's first stop this bleeding." He folded a piece of his shirt and pressed it to the gash in her leg. She was embarrassed and covered herself the best she could, then lay back and let him help her. He put his knee under her ankle, elevating it, keeping pressure on the leg, while watching the woods for the shooter. He could see the roan saddle horse and old Nell and now a man emerged from the woods. He caught up the dead man's horse, mounted up and approached leading Nell, still in harness. John guessed he was about to meet Dave.

Dave had a smile for John, stepping down, tying the roan onto Nell's collar hames. Nell stood like an anchor, where Dave parked her, twitching her ears, watching. Dave had shoulder length blond curly hair, a lean body and a wide handsome face. Glancing at the dead man, he loosened a bag slung over the saddle horn, and came to help John with Lena. He opened the leather bag exposing medical instruments and bandaging material. The outside of it said US Army.

"You're John, aren't you man," he said. "Hi Lena," looks like you're in good hands. Let me help John here make sure your fine. Guess I never mentioned what I did in the army, but I've kept some things, to doctor up women driving run away teams."

Lena smiled a weak smile and murmured—"No Dave, you never did mention much of anything."

As Dave worked to disinfect and bandage Lena's leg, he spoke softly to John. "See how I am doing this John. I can't stitch this gash-it's too wide. Dan will have medicines at home, or he might want to take Lena to a real doctor, but this will do 'til then. That man over there," gestured Dave, "He's been hanging around the still for several days now, drinking and disrupting, up to no good. No one will care that he's gone. I am going to ride over and catch up the team, then get Dan to drive them on home. I brought Nell along for Lena to ride."

Now, he spoke brightly to Lena. "Lena, Nell here would love to give you a lift home if you are willing and able to ride a plow horse. You really should stay off that leg for a while. One nice thing about Nell, she isn't likely to run away." Lena nodded. The men helped her up. She leaned on John while Dave brought Nell close, and then the two men lifted her easily up onto Nell, carefully setting her leg across, padding it from the horse's side with Lena's skirt.

"How is it Lena? You make that horse look good. Are you as fine as you look up there?" Dave joked with Lena, kissed her hand and placed it onto the horn. For a moment, he kept his hand over hers. "Good bye then Lena, you've been my angel, my only angel." He turned and leveled his eyes at John, "Slow and steady does the job, man." He gave Nell a slap of fondness on her muscled rump then mounted the dead man's steed and rode off to catch up Nip and Tuck.

Wary and wild, the horses were hiding out to graze, far from the action, and Dave had to circle them several times before they gave up and let themselves be caught. Tuck was still crazy from running away. He snorted loud as a buck in rut at Dave and his eyes showed white all around. Dave drove the team and wagon, the roan tied behind, to the Lake Woods. It was not a place to drive into yet, so filled with stumps to be dynamited and pulled. He tied the horses between two trees on the path Dan always took into the woods, talking to the horses all the time, settling them down with his voice and his touch. Dave mounted the roan and followed the trail, crossing several creeks to emerge in the clearing where Dan was working. Dan looked up from shoveling, startled by Dave on horseback.

"So Dan, do you like my new horse come to me and Nell out of the blue?" Dave grinned, Dan did not answer, and Dave continued. "The man who had him last doesn't need him anymore—probably stole him anyhow I am thinking. I always wanted a strawberry roan and I'm keeping him. I'm calling him Red. Come Dan and jump up behind me. I'm here to bring you out to your team so you have a ride home. Drive slow— the horses had a run and are remembering the taste of it. Your wife wants you home—no worries—she's fine enough, and has John with her. You'll need to bring your shovel."

"The devil you say Dave." Dan replied as he climbed onto a stump, Dave rode alongside and Dan transferred himself, shovel and all, onto the horse behind Dave. "What have you gone and done now Dave? Oh what troubles have you made for us, my man?" They rode on in silence, both men knowing this would be goodbye. By the time they reached the team, Dan had figured some of what happened. He jumped down and caught hold of the reins so Dave would not leave. "Dave—

those shots I heard—what did you shoot? For God's sake man, did you kill someone? Sure as hell you're gonna leave me with a dead man on my hands!"

"On your hands, yes, but his blood won't trouble your soul. He joins the legion or so waiting for me in Hell." Dave chose his words with care, speaking slowly, hoping Dan would catch his meaning. "You decide what to do next; and I hope you will figure it so no one comes looking for me after tonight. Remember Dan, this here horse found me and Nell."

"Wait Dave, wait! You'll need money. I owe you." Dan let loose of the reins, leaned his shovel on a stump and fumbled for his money clip. He gave all the money he had to Dave.

"You owe me nothing more Dan. We are square and good. You'll remember me with the crops you grow on the field I've been plowing. Just add in some fertilizer and you can grow wheat! And tell Lena I'll never forget the taste of her bread— or the way she drives a team! Ha!" Dave grabbed up the shovel and rode away with it, loping his horse out across the field. He stopped to plant the shovel in the good earth marking a spot, then waved and rode away toward his day camp.

Meanwhile, Lena was trying to get her mind around what had just happened. She was accustomed to being in control and helping others and had no tolerance for being fussed over. John was kidding her along as he would have done with Ida or any other woman, but Lena was having none of it. She got right down to it. "John, I think he killed my dog. Oh—I think he killed my Shep!" she said, and the tears streamed down her face wetting Nell's mane.

"We'll get you home and I'll go to find him Lena," John soothed. He's probably waiting for us even now. He'll be surprised to see you up on a plow horse, Lena."

"No, he's dead John! I know it!" She wailed, then caught

herself, and forced herself to speak in an even, low voice. "Please John, find him and bring him home. I want him buried by the back steps so I can have him near looking after me as he's been doing all these years. Please, John! Don't worry about me; but go and find my dog."

"Ah, Lena. Dan would have my head if I didn't deliver you home, don't you know? Have pity on me then, and stay sitting pretty and let me lead this horse so Dan can have his wife safe. He will be coming with the team soon and we can all talk about what to do. But for now, you just stay up on Nell and don't worry yourself further."

But Lena did worry. "John, Dave killed that man. The law will come for him and he can't be in jail. He'd rather die than be kept caged up like that. Oh—this is my fault! I should never have gone picking berries alone. Oh, I'm to blame!" she lamented, tears flooding down her face, wetting Nell's shoulder.

"No Lena, him who's to blame is lying cold in that field behind us." John's words held a current of anger tinged with bitterness. "You did nothing wrong, and he got what was coming to him. Think now my sweet Lena—think how many others are saved from him this day. He will do evil no more. And if Shep is dead as you say, then he died a hero Lena, and not of old age being feeble and useless. How are you feeling? Is the pain bad?"

"How can I worry about my own pain when Dave is in trouble and my Shep has died because of me?" She dissolved in tears. John stopped Nell who stood statue still, hoping only to please, drenched in the grief of her rider. "He's not here now John—Shep—who always was by me. I am alone."

"Lena, you are never alone," John comforted her. "We all love you and are around you like a castle wall. I am like Shep—

my wife always said so. She said I was sort of like an old dog. Don't I strike you that way?"

Lena tried to stop her tears, wiping her smudged cheeks with the back of her hand. "Yes, John. You old dog you."

John saw the team coming out onto the field, trotting home, moving briskly he thought, but under tight rein. "Ah—here comes your Dan now," he said.

Lena whimpered a remark about it being just like him to miss all the action, but John wouldn't hear what she said and proclaimed "everything is going to be fine now that Dan has come. He will know what to do."

Dan drove the team around John and Lena making their slow way onto the circle drive. He tied Tuck who had been looking for an excuse to bolt for the barn all the way home, and ran over to the house steps where John had stationed Nell, waiting for his assistance. John explained what had happened while Lena composed herself getting ready to be helped down. She smiled at Dan and tried to make light of her own condition—"just a little bruise from the wheel of the wagon," she said, "this man was going to...but Dave *shot* him before he...what has become of Dave?"

"I think Dave's probably half way to Brule by now," Dan answered. "Says he's keeping that horse and will make good time in case we plan on calling the police." He said something strange about hoping I'd add fertilizer into my field, plow a furrow and grow wheat. It all makes sense if he killed the man."

"He's lying dead in your field Dan. Dave didn't spare him any, nor would I have" said John. Dan nodded in agreement, cursing the dead man under his breath.

Lena, for all her trauma, wanted to be heard. "Dan, you can't call the police! We are the only ones that know. I don't want people talking about that trash chasing after me; or the

Town Chairman's man shooting someone on his farm. Besides, they'd catch Dave and put him in jail and that would be the end of him. Please, Dan, let's bury the bloody devil deep..."

"...and plow over him Lena, like Dave hinted at?" Dan finished her sentence. "We've got to keep that secret then, or we'll be in for it. Can we all do that?" He cast a keen eye on John and Lena followed his gaze.

John nodded, and spoke mostly to Dan. "Yes, I think that will work as long as no one else saw any of this. I've been looking around while we walked home. I don't see anyone watching. It's hard to see anything from the road, for the cattle are all along the fence. But, we've got to do it tonight. We can't have him laying out overnight. Also, Dan, Lena thinks he could have hurt Shep. I'm going to look for him after we help Lena into the house."

Thinking of Shep being hurt, Dan swore, invoking all the revenge an Irishman is privy to. He raised his arms up for Lena to slide into while John eased her bandaged leg over Nell's broad back, helping her down. Lena was not crying now. She had her head down dealing with the steps and the walk to the couch inside. "Cover the davenport with the blanket Dan," she directed, "blood is hard to get out."

John decided to get a wheelbarrow and some gunnysacks for Shep. It would look like he was working on the fence if anyone came by. He thought Lena had cut across the field where he had first seen the man, so he went that way, crossed the road and began his search among the boulders near the spring. The ground was gravely and showed some scuffle, a bloody stain, but no dog. He wished he had asked Dan for his rifle. He was afraid of what he would find. Then, under the trees where he guessed that the man had tied his horse, he spied Shep's white mane, now mangled and dirty, crumpled beneath his golden body. He had been stabbed and flung into the brush. John laid out the sacks and gently wrapped Shep into them, lifting him with care into the barrow, bringing him home from the hill for the last time. He thought of Lena without her dog and felt a painful tightening in his chest and the sting of tears blurred his vision. Dan came out of the horse barn to meet him when he arrived with his burden. All the horses were gobbling grain and Nell still wore her harness.

"Thanks, John. I'll bring Shep to the house yard. Lena already knows he's dead, and wants him buried by the lilac bush. I called the doctor and he will be by in the morning. Lena refuses to go into town, and I don't blame her. She won't admit to pain. I can't baby her— oh no—not her! She's praying—not for the bum lying dead in the field—never for him—may he burn in hell! She's praying for her angel Dave— he's a blooming archangel now—like Michael—you know the one. 'Prince', she calls him."

John didn't know about the archangel—his eyes still misty, as he looked one last time at the lump in the wheelbarrow that had been Shep, and stepped back to let Dan assume the burden.

"I'll be surprised if Lena is on the couch long. She's giving me orders about her part of the chores to be sure I do them proper, and is worrying about dinner for you and me. She said to tell you she put a letter into your cabin—wanted you to know—bossy as hell—won't speak of what happened ever again—just cover it over. Now. You and me, we can do that.

I've fed and watered Nell; can you grab up the shovel and take her to the lake field and start digging? I'll join you soon as I can. Dave planted my shovel in the field; I'm guessing that must be where it happened. But you should go dig where he was plowing."

ENDINGS

John coiled a lariat, tied it to Nell's harness, and then drove her across the field. His heart ached as he thought about how he had found Shep and wrapped him for burial. The young stock watched from the night pasture as the cows filed to the old barn for milking. Soon, they would find their places in the big new dairy barn. The heifers would freshen and join them and fill the newly made stalls. The loft above would be warmed by the animals below. It already held the new crop of hay. People and animals came and went away like circles turning, the new barn would stand and the old barn would be taken down. He realized that he would not see Dave's light any more above the horse barn, and again he felt sad. From the volumes of poetry he read almost nightly, Yeats' new poem came to mind. John had found it terribly disturbing, for it described change spinning out of control. Now the words of the poem nagged at him to be released, so he spoke them to Nell who turned her ears to catch every word.

> *Turning and turning in the widening gyre*
> *The falcon cannot hear the falconer;*
> *Things fall apart; the center cannot hold;*

Ida was his center—his sun, moon and stars. He thought of the letter waiting for him, and he felt a pang of fear. But they were nearing the shovel marking where the man fell dead, and he dared not think of her now. It was bad luck to revere the living while burying the dead.

John avoided looking at the stranger's face, but searched his pockets and took the holstered knife to give to Dan. Anger rose in his mouth as he saw the blood on the knife. He wanted nothing of this man except to put him into the earth, and tried not to touch his skin, already cold, as he tied onto him and dragged him north to where the furrows wrinkled the land, acre after acre of red clay shining in the low rays of the setting sun. Nell waited patiently while John began to dig, watching him, listening for his voice.

The lake sent its chilly breath sighing over the field. John tried to fight the gloom, feeling its fingers inside of him as the light slipped away. The clay was heavy as was his mood. Again he spoke to Nell.

"Nell my lady, we need a song—a song to dig by—a grave-diggers song is what we need. The melody will set our pace. At once, he remembered "Tramp, Tramp, Tramp, the Boys Are Marching". Soon he created a chorus out of war songs and anger and he sang it to Nell to fuel his power, changing the words 'til it was a bitter brew on his tongue.

Dig, dig, dig
The grave grows deeper
Unholy hole—a custom fit
The rain will never touch his face
Let him rot in his disgrace
Alone, unloved and colder by the lake

Suddenly, Dan was there, singing with him. "It looks to me like you have dug his damn grave all the way down to the door of Hell, so lets do the funeral. May the devil come out, greet him by name, and welcome him home," said Dan.

With that as the eulogy, they rolled the man into the grave face down and pelted him with dirt. While Dan finished the covering over, John hitched Nell to the plow and they put furrows up top like it had never happened. They tied the shovels to Nell's harness, unhitched her, and the two men with the horse between headed back. A wolf in the Lake woods bayed forlornly, and like shards slicing the moon thin, an unearthly chorus gave voice. "They are singing the devil's own to his doorstep," Dan said with a shiver.

They walked along in silence. John felt small in the vastness of the wilderness and appreciated the big horse's bulk, so near, so protective. "Dan, I'd like to tend to Nell if you don't mind," he said. "I'm thinking she will be missing Dave, and after such a day as this, a few minutes spent with a good horse helps it all settle down for me." Dan agreed of course, saying he'd rather spend his evenings with a good woman. "I'll bring you a sandwich to enjoy with your new horse then John."

And so it was John who took off Nell's collar and pulled the heavy harness away to hang it on its peg. He ran his hands over the wet places the collar had made, checking for sore spots, seeing and touching her satiny power, unsnarling the coarse mane, hearing an occasional stomp of big hoofs onto the wooden floor and affectionate nickers meant for him. He had missed this world of horses—their smell, their greetings to him and the way they leaned into him pleasured with his attention when he curried and brushed them. He had not let himself be attached to any horse since the milk horse Molly had died. "Nell," he said at last, "I'll be taking care of you now and I'm so glad to do it." He ate his sandwich slowly, giving himself as much time as he needed to gather his courage and regain his strength. When he was ready, he stepped out into the cold evening and made his way to his cabin and the letter that awaited him. He thought he would read it, and then go help Dan finish chores.

John lit his lantern and found the letter on his table. He had already imagined several versions of it. Now, here it was. He opened the letter without hesitation, glanced at its length and the way it was signed, and then began. He read first about gratefulness for the money he sent. Yes, they needed and wanted the things his money could buy. He had entertained the hope that sending home his paycheck would be enough. She was *"hoping he could keep his job on the dairy farm,"* she wrote.

He read next about support of another kind, and between the lines, he read that they were not getting that from him. She wrote, " I miss the intimacy we used to have. There was a time when you read poetry to me, we laughed a lot and loved each other. I could depend on you. But, in the twelve years since the war, you have become a stranger to me." He understood how lonely and disappointed she was. He read, " I think that it is best that we are separated from each other. That last day, the children saw a madman instead of their father..." Now the memory of her voice and her words, born of frustration, played again in his mind, "What good are you? You can't keep a job—who would have you? And how can we pay our bills and feed our children? I can't stand it—I can't stand you." He heard again the crash of the chair he threw against the wall— the shattering pieces, fragments blown from the volcano inside him. Rage had come over him. How to describe it? Was it fire or ice? Shells bursting in air, the roar of fire and then the whistle as flames erupt, higher and higher into a roaring column burning the rational, burning the "why", annihilating

humanity, leaving what? Leaving the animal—the wild man—
to pummel the wall. His rage was like a pulsing white light and
he did not know how to use its power; like electricity through
the broken transformer of his mind.

John stopped reading and looked out his window at the old
barn. No more Dave smashing, crashing wood against wood.
Dave was a wild man too. He had lived in a cave of wood,
slept on a bed of hay, and used his physical power to batter
against walls in his mind, perhaps to silence the bloody voice
of war—to break through to peace on the other side using the
force of his body driven by the fury in his mind.

Another paragraph, this one about how Ida had taken to
cleaning houses for money and that had led to her meeting a
man. Yes, there it was—his fears come real. "John, I've met a
man I want to be with."

John set the letter down. He couldn't read another word.
The world was all white now, like ice in a blizzard, and he
could see and puzzle about things, but order had slipped
away. He saw the bed. His head was aching. His world was
going round and round like an ever widening gyre and he was
the falconer and his bird had flown. The center would not
hold. He lay down on his bed and curled into a ball trying to
keep conscious. Circles of sadness slipping away from him.
Endings. Like a strobe, images flashed—Shep's white mane
showing in the brush, the knife with blood on it, the sound
of the dragging corpse, thuds of clay covering over the stiff
body. He saw another circle spinning and there was the merry
go round in the county park where he had fallen in love with
Ida. She was seated on the dappled grey charger, the carousel
horse he had painted. Round they went to the music. Then the
horse grew wings and spun off into the night sky. Ida soared
away, her eyes on the stars. The music kept playing—it was his

gravedigger song. And then he saw for the first time the dead man's face, and it was his face, "alone, unloved and colder by the lake."

Hands on the Plow

What was that noise? John heard the pounding, must be on his door, and someone was calling his name. The man was saying "Daylight in the Swamp." This was not a morning in the trenches, this was not his bed in Portage; this was Dan knocking to wake him up for chores. John rolled up to sit on the side of his bunk and try to remember, but it was all a blur and his head hurt. The sun was blasting through his window. Dan didn't go away, was asking if he was all right, and John didn't know. Finally, to stop the noise, John went to the door and opened it, to stand face to face with Dan, exuberant as ever, enthusiastically describing the day. John saw the lively good natured expression on Dan's face change to one of concern. "Come on man," he said, "Lena has coffee ready. Chores are done. Wash up and join us at the house." John wanted to go back to bed. If Dan had gone away, he would have shut the door and pulled the curtains and...but no, Dan didn't leave.

John could hear, like through a long tunnel, only catching a few words while there was an echo in his head and the world looked unbearably white. Dan got cold water on a rag and he handed it to John. "Here, wash your face, get shed of yesterday's grime. Wash your hands in this basin. Come on, let's go to the outhouse. I'm not leaving you man; just do what I say." It was easier to follow orders—he didn't have to think. Sort of like the army. He had been a good soldier, he thought. He fell in, doing what he could do automatically. Getting ready for muster? No, he would never pass inspection. He thought he might like to make a break for it; but he was a good soldier, hadn't he just told himself? And besides, Dan had him by the arm. Dan presented John to Lena in the house and they got him sitting at the table. Lena was limping badly and had a cane to lean on, but was serving a full breakfast. She fussed over John and through the fog, John felt some shame and tried to break out and be civil for her sake.

Strong coffee. The aroma and heat rose up, he breathed it in because it was there, and realized he was hungry because Dan was telling him so. "Here, you need to eat," Dan was saying. Lena lavished orange marmalade onto a warm muffin and handed it to him. Automatically, he ate. Next: the bacon and eggs. The radio was on, playing music, "Happy Days are Here Again", and Lena turned it up. It was all coming back to him now.

Dan's voice was telling him his new assignment: "You are good with a plow, John, and now that Dave is gone, and we still have weeks, I think, before the snows comes, that you had best plow in the Lake field breaking new ground. Nell has been doing it all summer, and is fit and ready. She is standing in her stall, fed, watered and waiting, looking for her driver to get to work. You can't disappoint her now can you John? John couldn't smile, but he thought what a crafty politician Dan was. "I thought I'd cut wood for the winter in the Lake woods and can bring you a lunch every day when I go out for a load of wood. I'll have the team to help you move some of the bigger rocks to piles. If I need help, you will be handy, and otherwise you'll be alone, just you and Nell. You can do this John," Dan finished with more enthusiasm than John could grasp.

John couldn't shake his head no—it hurt too much.

"Good. Lena isn't going to teach any more this year, so she can help me with chores when she's ready and until then, Mrs. Swenson will come to help her, and bring one of her big boys to help me with chores. We are going to begin to move the herd into the new barn. We will need you when we move the young stock. I see you've made pets of some of the girls—Bell follows along the fence as far as she can get, just hoping you'll notice her."

John thought there might be truth in that. There was something about his wife he couldn't remember—no—not now. At least the heifers liked him, Dan had just said so, and Nell. He found himself relieved about the assignment. He wanted to be alone, and he was glad it was fall. Soon the colorful leaves would become brittle and dull brown, curled and dead under a dramatic grey sky. He fit perfectly into that landscape. The idea of tearing into the dirt, smashing roots, shoving rocks, hard as it would be, suited him too. He mumbled a "thank you" to Lena, and managed to look at Dan and say "I'll harness Nell." Then he was out the door leaving Dan and Lena on the porch watching him make his dreary way to the horse barn.

Plowing was an art. The plow man must concentrate, keep the shear in the ground, and work in concert with a slow steady horse. John did not have to think about how to pay the bills or how to please anyone. He didn't have to think about his wife—only how to keep the plow in the ground straight in spite of jolts from rocks and roots. His communication was with the horse and every day they grew closer until words or lines were superfluous and they were of one mind. Winter crept in disguised as fall, and the ground sparkled with frost. Herds of deer arrived, grazing and browsing on their way to the lake where they would yard up for the winter. Fox, lynx, wild turkeys, Canadian geese and the wolves came and went, taking little notice of John and Nell as the furrows marched along even and open. John's mind became more clear every day as his fingers grew colder and the sky heavier. Like the earth, he felt drab and numb.

In John's absence, the exodus from the old barn had begun. The gate was opened into the freshly graveled yard behind the big new barn. The most curious cows ventured through all the way to the open double doors. They bunched up, eyes a-google, looking at the pristine hundred foot corridor. Sedate milking cows stepped timidly onto the white-limed floor, sniffing out grain in the manger. Then they turned into wild animals storming the stalls. Several wanted the same one, and often a scramble ensued with the greediest, hungriest or fiercest cow shoving her face through the stanchion first, leaving the vanquished to fade back and look for another home. Soon a third of the stalls were filled by round black and white bodies pressed forward behind speckled noses plunged into grain. To the sound of gobbling and smacking, they swished their tails back and forth signaling pleasure. After several days, and a little stall swapping, Lena could write names on wooden signs above each cow.

Mid morning, on some day in some month of late fall—John didn't know one day from another—he stopped plowing as giant snow flakes swirled over the sun, spinning plow furrows into glass and crystal and Nell into a shining white ghost behind a fantasy veil. John unhitched her from the plow for the last time that year. He swung up onto Nell's back and let her take him home in the blinding flurry—the magical prelude to an overture of winter.

Dan was about to sort the young bull away from the heifers when John appeared, a vision of white, as if the wind had blown a specter into Dan's barnyard. "Just in time John," he said, "I thought this storm would bring you home, and I'm glad you are here. How's she cutting?" He looked at John critically—a long careful look that told John he had better listen-up, straighten-up. He handed John a stick. "I'll be back John— I've something important to go over with you," and he disappeared into the big barn. John brushed the snow off his face, stomped his feet and swept snow off his jacket, trying to look civilized again. Dan, not sure of John's mental condition, came back with a pitchfork, brandishing it like a scepter, tines up to make his point. "Remember what I say now John," he said with authority as if commanding a squadron. John blinked the snow off his eyelashes and like a good soldier, stood silent.

Trying to get into John's mind, Dan spoke confidentially, starting out nice. "John, I see you petting the milk cows and soft-talking the animals. Certain sure you know about the good, but catch yerself on about the devil in the beast." Now Dan pounded the fork once on the ground for emphasis. "John, man to man, we must deal with our bulls, knowin' they think themselves to be kings. Always have a weapon with you. When I speak with Hannibal now, I am ready to blow up bigger then a cat does, and yell in his face if I have to, otherwise, I don't look him in the eye, and pretend I don't see him challenging when he glares at me. Lena raised him from a calf, and he loves her and follows her around like a kitten. He knows her to be female and I think he would protect her with his life, but she never tickled him on his head or played with him—cute little fellow as he was. A bull and a dictator respect only force. And, they know you to be male, and a threat to their throne."

John looked as impressed as he could, nodding in a sober fashion to acknowledge Dan's uncanny knowledge of cattle and men. About all the bovine species, Dan constantly advised to "watch out for the herd when the sun goes down." Convinced that some alien spirit entered with the fading of the light, and brown gentle cow eyes turned red with rage, Dan always skirted the pastures, or rode a horse if he had to pass through the herd at night. "Carry a pitchfork with you when you face a mature bull," he said, "be close to a fence just in case. Be ready to run—run like the wind itself, and don't look back lest you lose heart. If ever he gets you down, roll into a ball and play dead."

Dan never kept a bull very long, for dairy bulls were known to mature into fearful beasts indeed, often weighing a ton or more and becoming more protective of the harem with age. The milking cows were bred to the old herd bull which had been sold. Now it was time for Hannibal, the young bull to reign. He trotted obediently before the men, through a gate and into the barn where he announced himself to the cows. Soon he romped in his pen, pawing the yellow straw over his shoulder grumbling his throaty song. In the spring he would be the herd sire, the father, as his young wives the heifers, freshened.

Dan was full of jokes now that the bull was safely in his pen. He tried to cheer the day and jolly up John. "John, you wrote the poetry for the barn warming Whinn gave us—that tribal jingle bells he called a barn blessing. Lena brags you up too; so I thought I'd show you we Irish have our own special poetry for most every occasion. Here's a beginning one for you.

A limerick packs laughs anatomical
Into space that is quite economical.
But the good ones I've seen
So seldom are clean
And the clean ones so seldom are comical.

John tried to smile at Dan's limerick, polite as he was, and managed to say "I look forward to some more Irish poetry."

Seeing an opening in the clouds over John's head, Dan continued, "So, now that the snow has begun and the long winter lies ahead, Lena and I are taking up the invites of our friends. We love to dance and play cards. Our Finnish or Swedish neighbors also ask us to sauna, but Lena does not feel comfortable going; so we have never accepted. This winter however, Whinn has asked you and me to join him in his new makeshift Finlander Chippewa north woods sweat lodge steam bath. He calls it a Chippefinn Bath at Mule Sweat Lodge. The Irish surely invented steam baths, so I say "yes" to the idea. It gives me the chance to make him an Irish Blessing and pay him back for that jingle dress tomahawk thing supposed to bring luck from his tribe. I've even written my own poem to go with it and I thought we'd bring it up when we visit his bath. Besides, I'm betting old Whinn's been telling you stories about me. It's like passing behind a horse that kicks, you get close as you can to deaden the blow," Dan chuckled. "You know how you can tell a friend don't you now John? He's the one that stabs you in the front."

John was surprised. He agreed that a bath was in order, and that he could split some black ash wood for the fire as his gift for Whinn's new lodge. But he tried to beg off from participating, saying that he didn't feel like going, and that it was probably against his religious beliefs too.

Dan chided him some more. "John, you've been in the doldrums most of the fall; just the effect religion has on me too. Whinn and I might be able to sweat a laugh out of you—or else our humor might just put you out of your misery, you being an Englishman. You know, don't you, that St. Patrick drove the snakes out of Ireland using his serpentine crook that scared them all the way to England where they live to this very day?"

"I've heard that," John said. "And I've also heard that the English sent back fleas to drive the Irish out of their wits."

"Precisely why we Irish invented the steam bath," quipped Dan, "and we follow up a sweat with Northern Wisconsin's 40 below weather. The fleas don't like it here. Since both of us smell like old goats, I think you should be my date for this cleansing experience whether you feel like it or not. What say you about us going tomorrow night after chores?"

That night, John thought about the way Dan described his mood since the letter, as his "doldrums" and he mentally thanked Dan and Lena for setting him off to plow ground. He wondered if Dave had found it t0 be therapeutic, as he himself did. It was sort of a religious experience, he thought, and he decided to write about it. That night after chores, he sat down with scrap paper and pen. Rhyming words came easily and the poem he transferred into his journal seemed to him to express what he had been feeling. Writing got the doldrums out on paper, he thought, like turning over the earth, they were out where he could see them. He had written just a few words in his journal and decided to put poems in it. Winter was a good time to do this, time to cut down to the bare bones of meaning, a lonely quiet time when life sleeps, undercover. Poetry was like that too. He read over his poem, strangely satisfied with himself at saying how he felt. He called it

Plowing Doldrums

Hands on the plow
Breaking new ground
Glass, coins and bones
Treasures are found.

Rocks, roots unearthed
Steel turning clay
Heaving horse power
Wipe sweat away

Wind rain and sun
Colder each day
Seasons spin onward
Wipe tears away

What to hold on to
What to say's mine
Hold the plow straight,
Keep straight the line

Meadows from wasteland
My plow has turned by
A crop of fresh dreams
Where's mine, who am I?

Mule Sweat Lodge

Two nights later, Dan and John finished chores early, ate a hasty meal and walked out onto Moonshine Road toward Whinn's Forge. The moon shone on the snowy landscape turning night into day. It was still and cold. John felt and looked tired and Dan was talkative and full of energy.

"Ah John, what you are going to experience is not just a hot bath—though you and I could surely use that to clean up and warm up against the cold. Our Finnish friends tell us stories about what the sauna is to them, and Lena did some research before she decided *not* to go bathing with the neighbors." Dan's eyes filled with Irish mischief, hinting there was more to be told.

John was already wishing he hadn't come, for he was more comfortable alone with his grime and his gloom. Using questions, he pushed Dan to talk so he didn't have to. "So, you say Lena refused to take up the invitation to sauna. Why was that Dan?"

"Well, it seems she discovered that people stripped down in the bath. She said she didn't need to know the neighbors that well." Dan's chuckling faded as he took on a more serious tone. "Then, she said she found out it was a pagan ceremony. She said it was a place where the ancestors spoke to the bathers—sort of like a religion to the Finns. She saves her talking to God for church. We went to church together when we were first married. There is no Catholic church here, so we had to take a train to Superior, stay overnight and come home the next day. Church was filled with people who had been there so long they knew when to stand and when to sit—relics themselves they were. I don't think God goes to church much, probably likes the woods better."

John considered that for a long moment, then, agreed. "Well *if* there is a God, I'd like some words with him!" he exclaimed under his breath. "How did the Finns tell you so much about their saunas and religion? I've found them pretty closed mouthed."

"Since we go dancing in Brule next door to Oulu—where there's more Finns than anywhere outside of Finland, Lena learned a lot from them, and she can charm a rose into opening early, so of course she can get the Finns to talk of what they are most proud of. After Napoleon was defeated, and he ceded over the territory of Finland to Russia, the Czar of Russia tried to rule over Finland with a heavy hand, clamping down on any political talk. But Finland was independent minded and did not bow to foreign rule. They had a slogan: "Swedes we are not; Russians we can never be; therefore we must be Finns!" They wrote a poem about it called the land of heroes. Lena studied that poem. Just a minute, I'll remember its Finnish name."

John brightened up at the mention of poetry. He loved to be lost in poems, especially sad poems. "I know that Lena likes poetry, Dan, as she has brought me books of poetry that she gets from the schools and the library. What about this Finnish poem interested her?"

"She says it inspired Longfellow to write the Song of Hiawatha using it's sound. The poem is very important and long, like the one about Greece. "Kalevala," I think she said it was called, and it was about mythical heroes of Finland keeping who they were, their national identity, separate from Russia as they sat around the vapor bath. The sauna bath became a symbol of Finland, religious, like-you know, goin' to church; and political to boot."

By now they had reached Whinn's long drive. John was thinking about the Song of Hiawatha. He remembered only the opening lines of it; "By the shores of Gitche Gumee, by the shining big-sea-water." That was Lake Superior in the poem. He looked at the lake on the horizon and saw the lights of the Duluth hills twinkling across its western tip and the Milky Way above. "Shining big-sea-water" the poem said, and he was looking at that same sea-water, he mused. Perhaps Lena could get the poem for him to read. He wondered if it captured the beauty of this wilderness in the stillness of winter. For a moment he was in the poem, so absorbed with it he was. Suddenly, Whinn's mules exploded through the woods along the drive, breaking branches and dusting snow down from the cedars, startling John back to listen to what more Dan had to say.

"Whinneboujou has a whole library of books given to him by his father, and he reads every night. His grandmother, as you know, was Chippewa and I think he learned much about the sweat lodge from her. His name means "the fire wizard of iron" and if he lived with his grandmother's tribe, he'd probably be a medicine man, but he prefers the company of his mules and the counsel of his books. He says he reads to be sure I don't embroidery on the truth—can you believe that?"

Dan looked sideways at John-hoping to see a smile at least, but no—just a resigned grim expression occupied John's face, so he decided to spark up the conversation.

"Anyhow, I have my Irish story to tell when I give him the

gift Lena and I made for his sweat lodge. Maybe you will have a story to tell too. We will be our own heroes to ourselves. Ha! A half breed Indian, an Irishman and an Englishman in Mule Sweat Lodge—such a motley crew of heroes we will be, seeking identity in our own "pagan brouhaha" as Lena calls Whinn's Mule Sweat Lodge."

Whinn's old coonhound's baying beckoned Dan and John up the drive toward the shimmering light from the lantern Whinn had hung out for them. "Are ya trying to rustle my mules by moonlight?" Whinn teased. "They smelled you coming as soon as you left your drive-way; too smart to nuzzle up to farmers, they are. Come in and take a load off. I've mulled cider with rum if you like. It sets sorrows retreating and the tongue on the charge."

They stomped their feet to knock off the snow, and skimmed off mittens and hats which Whinn hung on a line nearby. The smell of wet wool mingled with apple cider, cinnamon, and cloves. Settled into chairs by the box stove, they warmed hands on the mugs, breathing deep of the aroma. With a little urging from Dan, Whinn began to talk about the sweat lodge tradition starting with the old ones, the Anishinabe, later called Ojibwe, who lived mostly around the Great Lakes.

"But you use the word Chippewa to describe your grandmother and Indians of the recent past. Where did that word come from?" John asked.

"Some say that it was an attempt by the French to pronounce Ojibwe. Anyway, the ancestors had the Algonquin idea of spirit in everything, and the great union of all spirit was Manitou. Big Manitou Falls, just 10 miles from here, is named for this connection of all spirits. My Grandfather was stationed at Mackinaw, named for the island where Gitchee

Manitou was said to live. The Algonquians were all over Eastern Canada and so the name of the Province Manitoba is also a form of Manitou. Stories about Manitou give him the shape of a man, who before humans came, decided the names, forms and ways of the animals, and declared that he would himself inhabit the earth upon which humans would tread. He is said to live in the sacred stones of the sweat lodge, where he waits."

"Waits for what? There is a lot of waiting in your stories Whinn—get to the point," said Dan.

"John, the natural state of an Irishman is talking, and Dan here, has no patience with listening or truth, for he suffers from being a politician along with being Irish. Manitou waits for fire and water to set free his spirit which comes in the rising steam to enter into those who seek his guidance. He takes away the pain of loneliness that comes from feeling alone, for he is the link to the divine. He enters in through the skin and breath. Some inflict wounds upon themselves so that they are more open to the spirit. Even when the rocks cool and Manitou goes back into the stone, he leaves enough of his nature to give power to those who are worthy."

"And how does one become worthy?" Asked John. Dan smiled at the question, and Whinn noticed and slapped him verbally.

"Indeed John, Sigmund Freud declared that psychoanalysis with the Irish was of no use whatsoever. Fortunately, you are of English heritage, like the officer my grandfather served, aren't you?" John nodded. "Well, your literature is all about that—the wounded King and the Search for the Holy Grail. Great philosophers have puzzled over that question. The Indians say that you are already worthy if you find who you are and are fully that person instead of trying to be another or live for another. And there is a way to do that in each tribe. They believe God speaks to them in signs and in dreams. The sweat lodge is a place to purify the body to receive the dream."

They sat in silence for several minutes thinking, a silence that Dan broke. He had been fidgeting, impatient to play his part in the inauguration, and present his gift. He began by telling about himself at his high school graduation.

"Deeds not Dreams" was our motto for the graduation of our class of 1916," he said. "They had it hung up in a 3 word sign above the stage and my buddies and me climbed up the night before the celebration and changed it around to read "Dreams not Deeds." Before the ceremony, while all our parents and friends were seated to watch, I was made to climb up a ladder and change it back."

"You made a political statement there Dan—'Dreams not Deeds' fits as your slogan," said Whinn with a wry smile.

Ignoring Whinn, Dan continued. "Well tonight, I'm telling my story about politics, religion and the sweat bath from the eyes of an Irish farmer—one of my ancient relatives—that heard the story from the blarney stone itself."

And so he began. Both John and Whinn settled in as Dan took charge. "Old Ireland is bone chillin' cold with nothing in the winter to warm you, so an Irish farmer, MaGee, invented the Irish sweat bath fired by bog peat and seaweed, turning stone cherry red. MaGee could not get it hot enough to dispel the cold of winter in Ireland even though he stoked and stoked 'til the stones themselves were ready to melt. They called out as stones do, according to Whinn here, and the devil himself heard and came rushing up to help. He thought he would show off, and show McGee up, so he invited him to hell to warm up since he clearly loved it hot. MaGee called for more heat soon after he arrived. The devil obliged turning his furnaces up, but never hot enough was MaGee. Finally, the devil made hell so hot that volcanoes were erupting all over the world and fish were poaching in the lakes. The glaciers were melting and the great flood happening and MaGee was warmer than before, but still calling for more heat in hell. So, the devil got embarrassed and mad as the devil. He sent the farmer packing back to Ireland with a curse on his head. "Out you go then MaGee, back to your own Irish sweat bath where I'll never again visit! From this day forward, I'm banning you and the like of you from Hell's fire and damnation!" Amen."

Dan had brought his story to a crescendo and ended with a flourish, like a proper minister of the truth, and now he pulled out his gift made to "one up" on Whinn's jingle dress blessing for the barn.

"Lena and I made a blessing for your sweat lodge that you could hang over the door—one of the little people who will remind you of the Devil's guarantee to those who love the heat of the steam bath."

Whinn opened the package Dan handed him and pulled out a shiny slab of wood embellished with the image of a leprechaun. Lena had cut the figure from her piano music for "When Irish Eyes Are Smiling." There was a poem, hand written on paper and varnished onto the wood along with the leprechaun. Whinn read the poem out loud.

He once was a burly lumberjack
Full of muscle, power and brawn
One hour in Mule Sweat Lodge
Shrunk him down to a leprechaun.

"How nice of you and Lena to bring me a Blessing for Mule Sweat Lodge, one that bans the devil from entering. It is fitting in ways you may not know. Let's go see the bath I've invited you to. I was hoping we could get into it tonight, see how it works and agree on our own rituals."

The path to the sweat lodge was wedged between refrigerator sized boulders. John had not noticed them before, and they looked to be set there with thought, to mark an entrance. They made their way alongside a little pond. The pipes that filled it from the spring above were covered in moss and branches. Whinn explained that he had only to remove the dirt and debris of thousands of years to uncover the natural basin for his pool. The sweat lodge was set nearby, into a niche in the rock face. It was made of black stones fit together and mortared. The tall chimney of companion stone was scarcely visible against the black basalt face of the rock hill while snow carpeted ledges and ridges beyond.

"Whinn, the rockwork here is just like the foundation of the barn. Did you do that too?" John's sad monotone gave way to enthusiasm as his interest was piqued.

"This whole area was explored for copper. There is a mine at the base of the hill near the still. The miner had blasted into the rock hill to fracture the basalt looking for mineral. I am not a stone mason, but the mules and I hauled loose rock from the blast site to Dan's for the foundation of his barn and then, at the end of each day, I brought stones home here for my own use. The Danes who built the barn fit the stones, set and mortared them. Working with their mason, I learned enough to make these walls and build them into my piece of the rock hill. The roof is made of slabs of sandstone covered with cedar boughs, dirt and then forest moss and sedum. The door faces east and is made of bog tamarack. I wanted this place to look like it just grew here and be a cave of sorts into the heart of our hill."

"You're over-tall for a forest gnome, Whinn, but you've done yourself proud and could be the king of the little people in this backwoods palace." said Dan.

"Better that than Town Chairman, Dan; and thanks for the compliment. You are right that the backwoods is not without culture. I'll hang the new sign over the door when we use the lodge—a guardian gargoyle to be sure the devil keeps his promise and stays away.

If you look inside, you can see the oil barrel stove, and a bucket of water to make steam from the rocks. I made the benches of white pine slabs from Conner's Mill."

Whinn opened the ornate cast iron door in the barrel, and the fire roared. John breathed in the smell of cedar and pine smoke drifting up, popping sparks, like sequins on a black velvet dress. The fire, fascinating, fierce and alive, licked at the drum. Whinn had made a brick chimney all the way through the ceiling and it was encased in stone above. The base of the stove was set onto bricks and rocks were piled all around. Round black rocks that sat over the stovetop glowed red-hot, looking, like wild animal eyes.

"I can tell you how the Indians respected the sweat lodge," said Whinn, "maybe use some of the language of mother earth in a way you will feel her." They seated themselves on the wooden slabs as the fire light played around them and over the stone walls of Mule Sweat Lodge creating patterns in shadow and light. Whinn left the entrance door open wide, for it was very warm in the lodge and the coolness and moonlight from the outside made a pleasant mix.

Listening to the fire snap, Dan said "fire sets yarns to spinning, but in this cave, it makes magic."

John leaned back against the wall watching shadows dance in the flickering light. "Its like being in a cave, alright." he said, and as he noticed some of the rocks seemed to have faces, he said "with spirits all around."

"Yes John, you're "right as rain" in London Town," said Whinn.

John gazed at Whinn in wonderment. Who is this man? He is speaking to me in the language of Old England, he thought. He remembered what Dan had said about Whinn— "he speaks the King's English... he reads every night." John decided to probe Whinn's mind a bit. "Whinn—you said that the backwoods is not without culture. As we walked here, Dan told me about the sauna baths of the Finns and how their poem about heroes gathered to bathe together inspired Longfellow to write the "Song of Hiawatha." I can only remember the first two lines of it—about the shores of Gitchee Gumee. You wouldn't have it in your library would you?"

"Yes of course I do John, and I'll loan it to you so you can enjoy its music. Thank you for the mention. I see that the spirits are giving us the perfect way to invite you both to experience Indian ideas. Whinn's voice took on the tone of a story teller— low, melodious and hypnotic at the same time. It was ageless, smacking of the earth and ancient knowledge. He began to recite the "Song of Hiawatha" out of the depths of his memory, accenting four syllables in each sentence so that it sounded like a drum.

*By the **shores** of **Git**chee **Gumee**,*
*By the **shining Big-Sea-Water**,*
***Stood** the **wigwam** of **Nokomis**,*
***Daugh**ter of the **Moon**, **Nokomis**.*
***Dark** behind it **rose the forest**,*

*Rose the **black** and **gloomy pine**-trees,*
*Rose the firs with **cones** upon them;*
***Bright** before it **beat** the water,*
Beat** the **clear** and **sunny water,
Beat** the shining **Big-Sea-Water.

Whinn's appearance was changing, the angles of his face and his coloration showing his native heritage. Add to that, in this light, he had the aura of a medicine man—someone who traveled into other realms to heal. Dan turned his head away, and Whinn saw, but didn't ask. John wanted more, leaning forward, eyes intent, and Whinn seemed to know their minds, and spoke. "What you just heard is the drumbeat of mother earth painting pictures with words—pictures of where we live and what we all know deep down. Those who feel this poem have hearts that beat to the same drum.

"Dan, tell us, why did you come to live in this place?"

"Because of the lake, the trees and the water falls and rivers," Dan replied. I liked to hunt here and wanted to raise a family to love this place."

"Ah yes," said Whinn, "and Longfellow writes that into his poem. He writes of Minnehaha, laughing water, and the waterfalls."

"And John, tell us, why did you come to live here?"

"I want to be who I once was," answered John, "before the war."

"Ah yes," said Whinn, "and that is in this poem too." He recited two lines.

"I can blow you strong, my brother,I can heal you, Hiawatha!"

"The sweat lodge uses herbs, charms, words, music, drums, chants and in this case it can use poetry to bring answers for what we seek.

"So tell me Dan, what do you ask of the spirit Manitou?"

"I want a healthy child. Lena is pregnant again and I am afraid for her—for us—we so want a healthy living child. There have been children that died." He again turned his face away so Whinn did not see the tears in his eyes.

"And John, what do you want?"

"I want my mind, my memory, and something to work for—I guess a new dream."

"I want something also, to see the way I fit into the tree of life," Whinn volunteered. "Since I belong nowhere, I want to hear my ancestors speaking, see visions—feel the oneness my Grandmother spoke of. I will tell you what I know from her tradition, and how I have tried, here, to keep it."

With both John and Dan fully engaged, Whinn continued, "some northern sweat lodges are of log, heavy bark and sod. Tribes that move around a lot or live in warmer places weave saplings into a circle covered with blanket or hide. They make a pit inside for the stones that are heated outside and brought in by "the one who tends the fire." Gifts are expected, never of money, but personal. Because of the black rock in this place and what I can do, I made this kind of lodge out of who I am and what I have here. In a tribal sweat lodge, natives too bring gifts of what they have—tobacco, sweet grass and sage. Herbs might be steeped into the water. Some use cedar to sweep over the living stones of lava spilled from the earth, and whip the essence into their bodies. The water is alive and so is the fire. Together they release the spirit of the stone people to speak across time to those being reborn in a safe warm place—the womb of the mother earth. A tribal ceremony is guided by a kind of hero, a medicine man, who will have had years of training, a vision quest, apprenticeships, has passed trials and suffered greatly. The ceremony remembers the four directions and the colors of each with all its symbolism. In song, chant or with ancient prayers, sometimes drumming, sometimes silent, they call forth the spirits. If you like, I can read from the epic Song of Hiawatha for it is of this place and we share a feel for it. Like sacred water over spirit stones, it is steeped in Native American legends and takes its form from the Finnish poem of heroes. We have a pool of water outside to plunge into and then can return to the heat and do it again. Traditionally, there are 4 rounds of this. When it is done, a phrase is used, "we are all relatives," "Mitakuye Oyasin."

I will go get the book while you strip and put your clothes outside on the shelf where the sign already stands. I'll be back in a moment." The men undressed in silence. They walked around the stove in the center, noticing that the 4 slabs to sit upon were each engraved with a direction. Soon Whinn rejoined them, disrobed, and sat down near the door. He had a lantern to read by and held the poem book.

"You can choose where to sit in this lodge by what you want or intend. I will explain how to choose. There are 4 winds of change coming out of the 4 directions. I choose the east to begin this sweat. It is of birth and new beginnings-—the place to set sights on something. The door faces east. I will read out of the book about the east wind for this first round. The south wind is about childhood and relationships, the west—the hottest spot— is a place of rebirth, the struggle where pain is released. The north is the place of our ancestors and descendants, of wisdom, quiet and gestation."

In a moment, Whinn had found the passage in the chapter called "The Four Winds." He read only a little, just enough to tease and flavor the mind before he would shut the door, douse the lantern and put herbed water to the hot stones.

Young and beautiful was Wabun;
He it was who brought the morning,
He it was whose silver arrows
Chased the dark o'er hill and valley;
He it was whose cheeks were painted
With the brightest streaks of crimson,
And whose voice awoke the village,
Called the deer,
And called the hunter.

NECKLACE OF WORDS

HOW TO MAKE SENSE OF IT? JOHN SAT IN HIS CABIN WITH HIS journal before him, and thought about writing down what he had experienced that night at the lodge, but he had no way to begin. Writing that 'Dan had invited him to clean up after weeks of plowing so they went for a steam bath to sweat it out together,' didn't express the experience. Something had changed. What was it?

He got out his scrap papers and wrote some phrases. First he wrote sensations from the evening, but deep inside his mind, a long ago barricade to painful memories had shifted. Thoughts tumbled out from behind it, tumbled and jumbled out uncontained. He wrote 'tincture of roses, cedar, musky,' and other words came to him—words he did not write: 'singed earth, burning flesh, gas in the trenches.' He wrote 'sizzle, popping, whistle,' but not 'incoming, stunning, explosion.' As he wrote 'dark faces, wet and shining,' they became ghostly and his memory showed him the whiteness of fog that contained numbness, palpable fear, bitter taste and choking pain. He heard colors and smelled sounds and couldn't distinguish anymore. He saw himself standing on the brink alone and then melting into his companions—sweating it out together.

John remembered that at the end of the first round in the sweat lodge, Whinn had thrown open the door and they rushed, radiating heat into the silvery moonlight and plunged into the pool water, immersed in cold, but not cold, only shocked to "now-ness" and then back again for another round of steam, sitting in silence as Whinn read of the winds of change. As if hypnotized, John fell in with the march of the beat—the shining big sea water, the beat of the heart of mother earth.

Now, as he recalled "The Winds of the Four Directions" that initiated the four rounds in the sweat lodge, as he tried to write something for his journal that expressed what he didn't know how to put onto paper, the drumbeat shifted and changed. A new but familiar beat was carrying him—where—where was he going? Hoof beats—the sound of a galloping horse—*"not since the war,"* he thought. He felt afraid and he didn't care, for he had tamed the wild beast to carry him. He was not alone but part of the animal. Oh the joy of it! How he had missed this feeling, this sound, this color of the wind. He felt clean and worthy. The dream was up ahead, he could almost see it beyond the terrible abyss, and the hoof beats resonated as he began to write to the sound.

Necklace of Words

The east wind breathes misty, playful, beguiling, bedazzling
        enchantment; mornings begun.
Hot drowsy south wind, languishing, lazy, sensual
        dreaming; flat out in the sun,
Wrestling the angel, the turbulent west wind, revenge,
        atonement; justice be done.
Dark howls the north wind, ice covers over,
        sequestered, protected; deep rivers still run,

And I sit in silence, pondering meaning, warm by the
    stove as the blizzard blows by.
Broken my heart, so heavy my sorrow, scarce can I
    breathe; longing to die
Yet something is growing, something inside me,
    something beyond me, of sun and of sky.
And I know if I rise up, if I live yet tomorrow, the next
    and another, someday I'll fly.

Lost in the losing, barren 'til springtime, 'til blossoming,
    birdsongs, fragrances thrive
Waiting for melting, expecting, exalting, longing,
    believing, I'll fight and I'll strive,
To write down the passion, to capture the moonbeams,
    to find words so rare, to dream and contrive
A necklace of words to present to my 'someone,' my
    pretty, my sweetheart, my love alive.

Jewels of the east wind, innocent laughter, beads of the
    south winds lingering caress.
Gems of the west wind, triumph, and anguish, strings of
    ice crystals from mountain snow crest.
Lights for the dark-times, shelter for storm-times, this I
    would give you, and I will not rest,
'Til you will know me, til you will feel me, 'til you will love
    me. That is my quest.

John put down his pen. He stoked and damped down his fire
and fell into bed and for the first time since reading the letter
from Ida, he enjoyed a deep refreshing sleep.

Up Jacob's Ladder

On certain nights, the siren of the overfull moon
Haunts this place with yearning.
Shadows gather to listen to her bittersweet songs.
Waving her wand of enchantment,
She tosses moonbeams on a magic trapeze,
To tumble entwined round lofty roof timbers.
And Jacob's ladder rises through high mow windows
Bejeweled in stardust; it leads to the gates of heaven
The gates of heaven
Siren
Soft as a melody
On sun sweetened hay
Jacobs ladder

As John forked hay down each day to feed the cows, he enjoyed the upper kingdom of the loft. The builders had installed a 100 foot long track that ran along the peak of the roof. During the hay season, a horse hitched to ropes over pulleys, lofted slings of hay from mounded racks. By the magic of real horsepower, rounded bundles of hay swung from chains up the front of the barn and swooped through the open double doors to career along the track until John signaled for the slings to trip. Leveling the hay was dusty work, often humid and hot. He sculpted the loose hay around the four openings to the concrete walkways in front of the cows below. Each opening had a trap door and a ladder from ground level up the inside of the barn that continued to the roof where four dormers streamed daylight. When full, the hay loft would feed an entire herd of milking cows and calves for the long, Wisconsin winter. At the front of the barn, there stretched a mezzanine level, which housed the grain bins and milling machines. Ladders in the loft gave ascent to the top of this level, which looked to John, like an altar bathed in light. Milky beams of light from the high windows mystically transformed heavy wooden beams into a gothic-like cathedral ceiling. The mow doors stayed closed for the winter to insulate the warm barn from the elements.

Like most Wisconsin farm kids, John had played games of daring and skill in a hay loft. As a boy, he used the pulley rope for climbing and swinging out further and further—maybe to escape an imaginary foe, maybe to show off to others, how far he could jump. Many a youth surveyed their world through mow doors. A barn loft provided refuge, a place to hide, and a secret place to make love in the soft and fragrant bed of hay. John had memories of all these things, but now he felt drawn to this high place to satisfy another need. He tried to write about it:

> Here—light somersaults over the rafters
>   gentle like
> And shafts through the gloaming
>   bright down.

Luminescent shine
Magically define
The reasons I am chosen to live on.

Smelling of the earth and sun
    mounds of hay,
Insulated from winter's cold
    this Cathedral loft,

Where birds soar and shadows play
A stair appears, perhaps to say
Ascend this portal to the divine.

If I could climb the crystal rays
    Jacob's dream.
Its source is where they've gone
    those I loved.

My heart deluged in bitter tears
Paralyzed by savage fears
Knows this ladder leads beyond the grave.

Electricity was installed soon after the barn was built. This state of the art dairy barn designed by Wisconsin architects was a model for the dairy state. Because of this, there were lights in the loft. John had a light installed at the top level for himself. He told Dan that he preferred to sleep there sometimes, close to the cattle. The plans called for a special maternity stall at ground level directly below him. John said in this way, he could hear a cow calving and be there in case of problems. True as that was, he also wanted to be in the loft to read, to write and for inspiration.

With laser-like precision, he chiseled and whittled a recess into a post big enough for his journal. He cut and fit a thin board to cover and fastened this box to a beam so that it looked like a brace. He kept his journal there so that he could read his poems over and write down his thoughts. No one ever noticed his hiding place, and his light, often burning late into the night, looked from the house like another star twinkling through the high windows flanking the mow.

Dan often farmed his plow horse out for the winter to a logging camp. With the mortgage to pay, and with a teamster like John to do the work, he decided to log some of the timber still standing on the farm, namely the black ash along a creek in the lake woods where he had dynamited and burned stumps in the fall. The Christenson brothers would pay dearly for that wood, favored as firewood. So it was that John spent hours each day horse logging with Nell. Compacted snow made a glazed road to drag the logs together. When enough logs were stacked, the Christensons came with their heavy team and logging sled. The men would then build a show load on the sled, and glide it home over snow-packed roads.

Nell was born and bred on the Christenson farm, sired by the same Percheron stallion that fathered their team horses, matched blacks of a "come or bust" nature. The mare that foaled Nell was of a different temperament—settled and calm and very intelligent. This made Nell the perfect plow and logging horse—one that knew when to shoulder ahead mustering might, and when to stand down and wait patiently, or stop when running into something immovable. She did not panic when branches hit her and tangled around her legs, and knew John's intentions, sometimes before he did. Nell was a dappled grey, the color of the carousel horse, that John had painted so long ago to win Ida's heart. Nell's color would change with her age to a flea bitten white, but now, in her prime, she was picture pretty sporting blue grey round dapples frosted in snow white, her coat pointed with raven black mane, tail and legs. John wore a red and black plaid mackinaw, and a red wool hat with earflaps to protect against falling branches and sifting snow. Surrounded by jade and hunter green cedars smelling like Christmas, and red brambles of wild rose all asparkle in Wisconsin white, they were an efficient and handsome team at work while the sun was in the sky. And then as shadows lengthened, they hurried home in the bitter blue cold to the warm and the bustling world of the barn.

John was uneasy with the bond of love that was developing between him and Nell, his work horse. He struggled to keep his heart contained while she called him out with the body language of horses, a nicker at his approach, the press of her nose against him, eyes watchful and protective, filled with devotion. When she sidled between him and the team horses, jealous and wanting him to herself, John tried not to notice. To him, love was like a gathering storm on the horizon.

One day as he hurried home pulling timber on a narrow woods path, snow and cold driving them to be swift about it, the load struck a glancing blow onto a dead tree which cracked, exploding its branches down over Nell. John worked desperately to free her. He was relieved when finally she plunged out from under the canopy, miraculously unhurt. But a mood came over John. It was as if someone was pulling a shade down shutting out the light. He tried to fight it, but a headache settled in, first dull and in the background, then pushing out rational thought. When he pulled her harness off and filled her grain box that evening, Nell nuzzled him and followed him with her great soulful eyes.

He wandered into the dairy barn to do chores. Lena saw his dazed expression and aimless movement. She brought sandwiches out from the house and offered John hot cider. He didn't eat. Dan turned up the music on the radio in the barn hoping to cheer him, but John took no notice. He had a vacant expression on his face and when they spoke to him, he didn't answer. He did not hear them excuse him from chores.

Like the tree falling out of the blue—virtual branches crashed down burying his mind in darkness. He sought to get above it. John climbed the ladder up-up into the loft of the barn, taking no notice of the cat clamoring up after him carrying a mouse as a present for him. He knelt into the hay, holding his head and moaning softly from pain and exhaustion. As if to hide from memory and winter, he buried into the hay and fell into a restless sleep. In his troubled mind, he continued to climb—climbing Jacob's ladder.

His slumber was troubled by storms of nature. Fingers of snow, cold as fear, crept in around the mow doors before the siren scream of the wind. The barn trembled in the assault, like the French countryside once shook with the boom of cannon. A white moon burst out from her cloud cover, lighting the intricate pattern of beams enclosing the loft, so like bursting shells once illuminated the battlefields of war, and a sealed door, its lock shattered in the barrage, burst open in John's deepest mind, releasing scenes he had vowed never to experience again. In John's dream, a younger version of himself climbed Jacob's ladder, up-up out of the depths.

It was 1917 in France at the Western Front of World War I. John was a farm boy who knew horses, and he drove a Yankee horse pulling a supply wagon. The horse was a mustang/Percheron captured on the Dakotas prairie where he had run free. John loved him for his spirit and so named him Uncle Sam. He was ragged and thin, shoeless and tough, and colored both tawny gold and silver black–a dark grullo. He worked for John giving all his best. The mud came sometimes to his belly yet he pulled his load forward while others quit or died in harness. At the moment they delivered the ammunition wagon to the line, a shell smashed into Sam, who served to shield John. Men tried to unharness the horse, cutting the traces away, calling for someone to bring up a new horse. John knelt and watched, and could neither help nor speak. He was frozen in the watching, as life ebbed away in the yellow brown bloody mud. It was several days before he could speak, and he never spoke of Sam. In his dream, he saw Sam again, but now unfrozen by time, he began to feel.

Sam was on the prairies with the wild ones. When John called to him he spun out of the herd and raced in a circle around John–tail high, eyes showing white, coat charcoal satin glinting gold. Unbridled beauty and power, he ran straight at John then slid to a stop and bowed his head in submission. John felt his breath kissing his outstretched hand.

Without words, Sam spoke to John.

"My master, I am forever yours and I have waited for you to come for me. Your heart is broken, but I know where the pieces are. Come–let me carry you back so that you can live again."

Like a boy, John leapt astride the big horse, and felt flesh against flesh. The joining of man and beast was the meld of body and mind, earth and sky, a kind of completion only felt with love, and he laughed with the joy of knowing it again.

They fast-forwarded through time. John saw scenes he had only imagined, for they were of Sam's capture and transport to France. He felt Sam's terror of losing everything familiar, of animal power contained in harness and rope, and the courage of the horse before the bombs and brutality of mankind. They lingered to watch Sam meet John for the first time. They saw John touch Sam and heard color rainbow out from the contact. Moving on again, they visited the trek to the front lines of No Man's Land, the stench and horror of the trenches and John's constant care to help ease Sam's struggle: John rubbed tar balm onto the horse's wounds made by the collar, John massaged the soreness from Sam's tendons, filled his feedbag with chaff, grain and seeds he beat from grasses. When there was no grain, John shared food and water from his own meager rations. They came at last to the time of the shelling that took Sam's life. John tried to turn away but Sam whirled him back to see.

"John, I chose this. I did not choose to die here so as to avert death on the killing floors where my kind that survived the war was later butchered for food. I did not choose to avoid the suffering of crippling wounds, I chose you. In the part of a second I had to move into the path of that shell, I chose you. As I have carried you—now carry me onward, for I have joined my purpose to yours. For I have joined my purpose to yours. Remember me."

John awoke to his cat placing her mouse by his face. He saw her waiting, watching him curiously—only the tip of her tail twitching—waiting for him to be delighted with her gift. He invited her over and praised her lavishly, drawing her to him and holding her tight. "*Remember me.*" Focused on the last terrible moments, death was the curtain he had not dared to push aside. Beyond it was connection forged in fire. "*Remember me.*" There appeared in his mind a fountain of water. Standing before it, was a man covered with blood. Plunging into the fountain, the man washed in its coolness and then

John saw that this man was himself. He lifted the cat, and buried his nose in her sweet fur, he breathed in her animal spirit. He brushed her body across his eyes, letting her fur wipe away his fear. Filled up with holding and feeling properly thanked, the cat squirmed, and John set her free. She proudly swaggered off toward the feed bins where the mice lived.

"Time to start our day" John reminded himself, noticing the first hint of dawn. He climbed down from the loft, visited the outhouse and went to wash-up in his cabin. There, he found a box containing half an apple pie, a plate of roast beef and potatoes, and a note with a badge. He recognized the badge at once. It was the First Calvary badge in the shape of a golden shield with a black horse's head facing forward, symbolic of the charge. He read the note from Lena. It said:

"Dear John, I bought a jacket at St. Vincent De Paul's for the wool, and took this off of it. I thought you should have it. The name of the soldier is on it."

John studied the badge admiring its design. He knew the gold stood for the setting sun over the prairie and the black stripe was diagonal– like the iron weapon he had carried. He fingered this wide black stripe of service. When he turned it over he read the name of the soldier whose badge it was, clearly printed in red ink, "Sam."

Lost in the Keeping

Spring warmed the days of April until ice-packed roads oozed red mud. Lena said she was so glad she did not have to walk home from Snowbound School where she had last taught. John agreed. He watched her struggle with chores as she became heavy with child. He offered to feed the calves and strip the last milk from the cows to give her some relief, but Lena would have none of it. She continued to cook and bake, keeping her commitment to the Betty Crocker test kitchen. The new recipes gave her the opportunity to comment on ways to improve the result, and Lena beamed with pride when she served a new creation. Neighboring women stopped in to wish her well and offer assistance, but Lena refused help and instead used those occasions to entertain, waiting on them, sharing food or giving away recipes.

Dan looked worried as the day of birth approached, becoming impatient with the animals, and putting his energy toward town business, especially the increasingly impassable roads. Lena refused to acknowledge the possibility of another child born disabled or dead. She never hinted to John that there ever had been a problem. Instead, she layered fresh white enamel on the threshold and new wallpaper in the baby's room. She asked John to repair, sand and varnish a cradle and crib she had stored in the woodshed, and played the piano while he worked, singing lullabies collected for the new baby. Lena used the full force of her mind to will the child well and told John what *she* would be like. Dan wanted a son but Lena had already named the unborn baby Lorelei and even described her—how she would look and act.

John watched, waited, and wove misgiving with hope into a verse for his journal. He did not understand what he wrote, but the words found the page out of some place inside him—prophetic words.

> Born from a dream of excellence
> Caught in the keeping,
> The caged dove grows wings.
> For beyond tether and fence
> Over loss and weeping
> Sweet freedom sings!

In mid-April, before the threat of a spring blizzard, Lena surrendered the farm to John. Chores had been especially chaotic that evening, as the cattle sensed the coming change in the weather.

"John, come up to the house and sit with me for a try-out of mincemeat pie. You deserve a rest and a special treat," Lena said as she untied the red bandana scarf from around her braided hair.

"Lena, you are the one that should be resting," John scolded. His eyes took in her swollen ankles below the long scar on her leg from the wagon accident. Exertion and the spring damp reddened the creamy porcelain of her skin. Leaving the barn's shelter, they fairly ran to the house before the bite of the wind, leaving Lena breathless and disheveled.

She coaxed John to sit at the table while she fixed for him. "Let me help you with the fire" he called to Lena, but she said it was started—soon to be hot. It was black outside, but light from the window illuminated the lilac bush. He looked at the buds covered in frost so like the lace of the table cloth. John sat thinking, remembering with regret moments like these between his lost wife and himself. He lit the candle in the table centerpiece of aromatic cedar and rose hips, wondering how Lena found the time and energy to decorate.

Moments later, she bustled out from her kitchen in her Dutch apron, having tamed her hair and splashed cold water on her face. She brought blue cloth napkins and cups of steaming hot milk flavored with chocolate, sprinkled with nutmeg over whipped cream. Setting a slice of mincemeat pie before him, Lena sat across from John, vapor from her cup curling around her smile.

"Dan wants me to go into the city to stay with friends," Lena said. "Dan will be spending much of his time working on town roads or visiting me. In truth, it will be an opportunity for him to attend county meetings. He says that he will not have to worry about me getting over these bad roads when the baby comes, and that he has talked with you about this. We are packed and ready and he will be here soon to get me; we leave tonight before the storm comes in." She now came to her point. "I hate to leave you with all this work."

John smiled back nodding at Dan's decision. He noted that Lena flushed when she mentioned the baby coming, and he thought that she was embarrassed to speak of herself having a baby. Realizing that she never wanted anyone to think of her as vulnerable, he thought how humiliated she must have been with her inability to have a healthy child.

"Now don't you worry about anything here, Lena," John

replied. He wanted to ask her if she was afraid, but he felt it was inappropriate. She seemed guarded, as if protected by ramparts in a high and remote castle, and he guessed that the Rapunzel who lived inside rarely let her hair down. He thought back to when she spoke of missing her dog Shep, and realized that for that moment he had known Lena–the hurt, fearful child; but now he looked upon a strong minded woman who shunned everything she judged imperfect in the past. He wondered if Dan took the time to take her into his arms and hold her until she felt safe enough to open her heart. But he was not sure Dan could deal with the anger and the flood of tears she might share. *Dan might be afraid of such intimacy, better to create his town park where families might go for happy times.* All of this came to John in a lightning bolt realization as he glimpsed his own fear of intimacy. He wanted to at least take her hand, but resisted the impulse. "Lena, it will be fine, and I believe God will smile on you and give you this child you have wanted. They say you must be careful about what you wish for. Are you ready to have your dreams answered?"

She sent him a look. In the spark of her blue eyes he read more then he wanted to know of loneliness, of self-doubt and strength born of pressing beyond endurance toward a goal. He felt the jolt of electricity between them. *The courage to hope*, he thought, and wondered how to find it–*it was not a treasure shining at rainbow's end, but perhaps like the Phoenix, it rose from a space forged of failure.* He didn't know how to tell her that, so he said instead, "Until later then Lena, when you bring your baby home."

John heard Dan's old truck whine down the drive. Moments later, they drove off in the blackness toward refuge in town—none too soon. The spring storm whistled in on Dan's coattails. A Saskatchewan Screamer, howling across the

Dakotas, heaped snows across Minnesota and the Wisconsin woodlands, winds sculpting drifts of new snow around each gate, against each door, over trees and buildings, swirling white over deep red clay sludge.

In the morning, over a cup of coffee, John surveyed a newly white world. *Snowed in,* he smiled with the knowing, warming his hands on his cup of bitter brew. He thought this storm would have been a white-out over wind swept North Dakota. Across the prairies, it was necessary to fasten a rope tight between house and barn in the face of such a storm. *Don't let go,* John visualized the farmer who must not loose his grip on the guide rope or wander blind and freeze to death. But John knew that in his own personal life, he had become exhausted from holding on. He had lost all that belonged to him, home, wife and family, and wandered blind without a guide rope. *Dan and Lena have left me to run their farm,* he thought, *me who could not run my own.* His lips curled in a wry smile at the irony of it. First light glinted off the iced weather vanes up top of the red barn. "*Nothing belongs to me here. I am alone in this world—* a startling new thought came to John—*and owning nothing, I am not lost in the keeping anymore.*" John watched diamond light shimmer down, outlining the eaves of the roof he had helped build. The storm was clearing.

Turning the Corner

Sucking mud. John had spent a horrifying night struggling, his dreams of the trenches in France, in yellow mud stained red with blood. That, followed by Wisconsin spring weather, rain, and snow-melt in red clay misted in vapor. This day, the remnants of an Alberta clipper mixed it up with April sunbreaks as he loaded heavy milk cans into the wagon, hitched the team and started out to deliver the milk for shipping. The horses navigated the impassable road, stomping through puddles and rivulets. The little creek of water off the hill had, over winter, been but a frozen dream. Now it roared awake overwhelming its plugged up culvert to flood the road. The team surged across this river, dragging the wagon, churning up ground. On the other side Dan appeared out of the fog, red ooze spilling over rubber boots.

"To a man idle and stuck a-foot in this mud, John, you are a prince driving a carriage! Work praises the man. I'll just ride along high and dry while our horses earn their keep slogging." Dan patted Tuck's round wet rump with appreciation as he scrambled up shedding clumps of muck, to sit alongside John on the wagon seat. The horses stood dripping and blowing, steam making a halo around them in a runaway sunbeam escaped from the fog. Just then a breeze softly drew back haze curtains and spring showed herself as a teasing tart a-sparkle with diamonds.

"Just look at the woods, John, see the buds pushing off on the new little trees," said Dan. He took a deep breath as if to draw in the smell of the warming land: a potpourri of loam, birch, poplar and aromatic cedar topped in moss and steeping in lake mist. "To mark the day, it needs an Irish blessing, John, of new good luck coming on green. Goes like this," he said:

Catch the moments as they fly
And use them as ye ought man,
Believe me happiness is shy
And comes not aye when sought man

John thought how he had judged Dan at first meeting almost a year ago; *this man could clear a cloudy day.* "Dan," he said, "is it that *you* look on the sunny side, or does *it* look onto you? Oh– and if you can bring out the sun, hurry home to the frozen swamp you are farming." Then came the question about Lena and the new child John had been afraid to ask. "So what new luck are we speaking about"?

Dan brought out cigars for the both of them and they smoked as they drove the horses on.

"I'm a father at last," he said. " It's a long road that has no turning, and so Lena and I have rounded the corner. We have a healthy baby girl. I'm forgetting that I wanted a boy, just glad for the getting, and glad for Lena. There's an old Irish saying: "A woman without, is she who has neither pipe nor child. Lena was not born to be a woman without. She is happy beyond words and making lists."

"Lists?" John asked.

"Yes lists," said Dan. "Lists of all this girl will achieve. I had to get out of there before she started on me. My Lena will teach her to love work, learning and religion, not a moment to waste—an idle mind is the devil's workshop she will say. Lena will teach her the skills of an accomplished woman—to paint, play the piano and read poetry. But I have a different list for her. I would teach my girl to dream. Maybe someday I'll crown my own daughter Dairy Princess at the County Fair. I'd like her to learn to be outside—oh and hunt of course. She will drive deer for me—flush out the buck hiding in tangle wood. I will teach her to fish so she will know the thrill of catching what's wild, and she will know every secret of my park, the mystery of the cave behind the waterfall and the scare of climbing sheer canyon walls. We will pick blueberries with the bears so she will learn the sweetness of danger, and I'll teach her common sense with my sayings and songs. Instead of religion, I will teach her enchantment. She will make bouquets of four leaf clovers and learn to read the wilderness."

John wondered what he could teach. The blue of the cigar smoke rolled around, swirled about and there appeared to him Ida's face. Surely he had influenced her life, taught her to ride horses and given her the wings to fly. He didn't mention that but instead, he said softly " I'll try to keep her safe for the learning. The world is a dangerous place."

"Ah Lena has that in mind too. She's named the baby Lorelei after a German rock in the Rhine. Guess she thinks a rock will endure. But, she has already told me she will be asking you to help watch out for the child in case she should slip out of her grasp. Houdini himself couldn't extract himself from all the foo-foo trundling Lena is putting around that baby. It makes me glad it's for her, and leaves me out of it. My horses have blinders on their bridles to see the work only, but I'd not wear them myself. And, as they say 'A wild goose never reared a tame gosling." The wagon creaked beneath rattling cans, big hooves smacked mud, while the men celebrated. Deep ruts filled with water behind them perfumed by a trace of smoke. Sunlit haze swallowed them up as they rounded the corner.

THE CIRCLE OF LIFE

SPRING UNFURLED LIKE A ROSE. EACH DAY BROUGHT A WARMER sun that stayed longer in the sky, and new life to the big barn. The calf pen filled with babies, licked snowy white, bedecked with spots of tuxedo black. They smelled of clean golden straw and the milk of mother love. At chore time there started to be a new "something else" nestled in padded satin, lining a wooden drawer in front of the calf pen. All the animals in the barn were aware of this curious little being. Baby Lorelei looked up from the drawer entranced. Soon she giggled and squealed at the calves, pumping her plump arms, setting them to romping around their pen. John smiled as he passed on his way to the milk house with buckets of milk. He thought: *Lena's little angel would be out bucking heads with the calf babies if she could,* but he didn't tell this to Lena, who dressed her new baby in downy pink flannels trimmed in lace.

Lorelei bounced, her blue eyes sparkling with enjoyment as the barn cats came and snuggled. Lena rushed over then, scolded the cats and seduced them away with a "Come Kitties" like the Pied Piper promising delight. At this, baby made a sour face, her lower lip all in a pout, behavior Lena ignored as she led the cats off on a safari in search of game. To accomplish this diversion, she set her milk stool under the wooden ladder on the white washed ceiling. Lena climbed up top, and Lorelei forgot to be mad and laughed to see her suddenly tall mother magically pull down the ladder and climb, flanked by meowing cats, up out of sight to the world above. In this daily routine, Lena played out a farm version of Jack and the Beanstalk and the golden egg, for she kept a trap-line all around the grain bins on the mezzanine, and gathered her mouse catch of the day for a fancy feast any cat would savor.

John could have pulled the ladder down easily, tall as he was, or he could have set the traps, or gathered the mice, but Lena never asked for help for what she might possibly accomplish. She scoffed at games of dependence other women might play, and had no patience for waiting. John thought to himself that that was a good thing, for she would have accomplished little if she had to wait for Dan to show up to help. When it came to caring for the baby, John sensed that Lena jealously guarded the task. But the task became increasingly difficult for Lena to do alone. Lorelei grew in leaps and bounds and it seemed that her intent was to break free of every type of restraint. Clearly, Lena had a problem.

One afternoon, Lena brought John a basket heaped full with a loaf of warm ginger bread and a jar of currant jelly covered by white linen. "John, would you take this over to Whinn before chores tonight, please? We owe him so much for his help dowsing for our new well, and I know he will be one of the men who helps dig it. Tell him we send thanks, and be sure he takes the envelope of money under the cloth."

John took one of the team horses out for the ride to Whinn's Forge. Whinn had lots of work this time of year repairing what winter had devastated. This day, a farmer was trying to barter with Whinn giving what he had for the work he needed done. What he had was a sack full of puppies. John couldn't resist looking at them. One little male snuggled against his big hand licking and squirming with joy.

"There you go John," said Whinn with a booming laugh. "That one is making all over you, with the look in his eyes like he'd just seen God himself. 'Getting a puppy is like catching up happiness,' they say. Take one of these little fellas then, for it looks like I have them to give."

"Thanks Whinn, I believe I will. Lena's old collie left her heartbroken when he died and she hasn't gotten a new dog. But this one could be perfect for her and the new baby, don't you agree?"

"Ah yes—for Lena and Lori, not for you my friend. Nothing for you—right?"

"The less I have, the less I have to lose," said John putting the pup in the basket for the ride home. "I'll tell Lena you exchanged the pup for the bread."

"Yes, and to seal the bargain, tell her it's because I'd almost starved, and was ready to eat this little varmint until she saved his life and mine with her bread and jam. You gotta be tricky with Lena or she'll give you back your gift, for she won't be beholding."

"Right you are Whinn; and she says for you to notice the envelope that came with the food. I think it contains some payment to you, and I am not to come back at all if I don't make you take it. Good luck Whinn—every man needs two dogs and a sack of pups to keep him company. Maybe you can trade the lot for a good wife!"

"No such thing as a good wife my friend—hang onto that pup—it's like burying a worm to keep him in that basket. Better tie him in," warned Whinn with a wave.

Whinn was right. The pup would not be contained in the basket, so John put him inside his shirt and buttoned his coat tight around the little warm body all silky wiggly and full of wet kisses. He held the pup firmly against his heart and felt him cuddle in, lulled to sleep by the sway of the horse, the sound of hoof-beats, heart-beats and the smell of Old Spice and sweat on the man.

When he reached the farm, John put the sleeping puppy back in the basket, covered him with the linen and brought it to Lena saying that inside was a token of gratefulness Whinn sent to her and Lori, for thinking to feed a starving man. Lena took the basket with hesitation, curious at its weight. She asked if Whinn had for sure received the money she had sent. "Yes Lena," John answered. "He said to thank you, and that he will keep the money if you will keep this small gift he sends to his girls." John left quickly, never seeing her suspicion turn to surprise when she found the pup.

"His name is Ginger," Lena declared at chore time. "He made a puddle right away in my kitchen and chewed some on my hooked rug. Then, when Dan came home, he yapped at him like he was a thief in the night. He already protects me and Lori and that's fine by me. He'll be our little man. When you see Whinn, tell him thanks and I'll be sending him jars of apple butter to pay for the pup." John nodded solemnly, inwardly smiling as he remembered Whinn's words, "she won't be beholding."

Maybe Ginger is a fox terrier, John mused to himself. As he grew in size, he grew in spunk, 'til he became a lion-hearted little dog that feared nothing. The girls indeed had a little man with them and because of his size and short hair; he was invited into the house to be a constant companion to Lorelei. When Dan picked up his little girl, Ginger growled and barked a warning, vigilant lest his charge be harmed. Lena relied on Ginger to sound an alarm as the baby began to get around. John made a portable fence across the aisle by the calf pens so that Lori and Ginger had a giant playpen while in the barn. As he worked at chores, John watched the child learn play from the animals, rolling to try to catch Ginger racing about in a teasing game of "keep-away," staying just out of her reach. With Dan, she giggled and bubbled with glee as he sang silly songs and tossed her up. Lena alternately corrected and praised the child, employing the notions of the day, and time tested German ideas to mold and raise her right, while John stayed on the edge of the circle, keeping it together, making it turn, respectful, but distant enough to see it all happening. He thought about it, and one night he wrote in his journal of his own game of "keep away."

Don't Touch

For you—pearls I make of needful things
Fashioned by my mind
Polished by my toil
Mirrors of my longing.
Wear them.
Let me watch you touch them with love.
But don't touch me.

The seasons spun like the carousel in John's memory, the radio in the barn played a kaleidoscope of the music of the depression. To the rhythm of the milking machine, Billie Holiday sang, "Love is a joy we borrow, payback in tears tomorrow, who wants love?" In late fall, the team horses marched through the barn pulling the stone-boat as John loaded it with manure from the pens, steaming in the river of cold coursing the long central aisle. As winter set in, John paused in his tasks, leaning on his fork to look out at the white world beyond the double doors, and listened to Irving Berlin's, "The Song Has Ended (But The Memory Lingers On)" and Gershwin's "They Can't Take That Away From Me." Soon baby Lorelei crawled, and climbed out of her pen, a toddler now, exploring the world of the barn, sure that John would come to her rescue, dashing against the shackled hind feet of the cow that kicked, splashing precious white milk out of a pail, throwing grain at the cows from the feed-room door. Lena shrieked her anger, Ginger barked, the child cried, Hannibal rumbled in his bull-pen, and "I've Got You Under My Skin" played on the radio. The circle of life was turning and John was being drawn in.

I Thought I Knew the Man

I read the next poem in John's journal. He didn't put a title to this one, didn't bother to rhyme it like he did with some of his poetry, but then a rhyme would have tamed it. I could feel his anger pulsing on the page and could imagine him writing to God in the loft of the barn.

God, I call you out
I would see the face
Of the One who knows
Here—in this cathedral of sticks and stones
Answer me!
What is your war plan, I scream,
For battlefields where innocence dies,
Dreams shatter—bodies break—life is consumed,
Tell me!
Why fight, why hold tight
When you rip all that is precious away
Take me too then
For I would see the face
Of the One who knows
GOD, I CALL YOU OUT

Before I began John's journal, I thought I knew the man. He was the one who saved my life—how many times I wonder? From the time I was two until I was ten, John was a guide to me on the road to becoming: reading to me, listening to me tell the stories back to him. Those stories shaped my life and, now I know, they helped him find answers too; for like any good teacher, he taught best what he most needed to learn. When I was little, we traveled on mythical journeys, sometimes as Red Riding Hood, or the Little Mermaid, or Alice in Wonderland. Much like the innocent fool of the Taro, we were accompanied by angels disguised as animals or unlikely beings, and along the way we met the wolf, the evil witch or the magician, all teachers too, and onward we traveled to the Falling Tower where things of value are lost—where we experience poverty.

Before reading John's journal, I didn't realize that John was on a painful journey, much like Odysseus, chronicled in Homer's epic poem "The Odyssey," who took 10 years to reach Ithaca, his home, in the company of fighting men. Soldiers paralyzed by the horrors of war often need the companionship of other warriors to recover, discover and undertake 'the road back'. While John worked for us, he encountered spirits in the sweat lodge and in dreams, grieved his losses, allowed himself to remember, and even to write down his rage over what he thought of as God's plan. The Bible speaks of wrestling all night with the angel. No one but a wild man would throw all that is himself away and call God out. Before I read John's journal, I really didn't know the man—but there are more pages to go, and now I am part of the story too.

GINGERBREAD MAN

"She owes you her life," Lena said as John wrapped Lorelei in his jacket. The toddler was shivering violently, sputtering water while babbling "waddy boo," her words for cold water; but she didn't cry until she saw Lena's face and then fell into a fit of sobbing coughs as fear set in. Lena sopped the icy water off Lori's hair and face with milk house rags, trying to control her anger mixed with gratitude.

"Ginger came for me," John replied, remembering how the little dog had raced barking thru the barn, grabbed his pant leg, and bounded back to the milk house where Lorelei had fallen into the deep cooling tank for the cans of milk. "Lets give all the credit to the dog—Lord knows I don't want to be responsible for the life of this child!"

"I know, Lena agreed, "I sometimes think she's possessed. I want to take her to see the priest. But Dan just laughs and says 'That's my girl.' Oh I'd like to throttle the both of them." Lena was trembling.

"Now Lena," said John, "the child is only two—she just has a pocketful of imps, Irish imps, the worse kind, all plotting trouble. She'll learn not to listen to them. Experience is a brutal teacher, but she'll learn. Bet she doesn't fall in the milk tank again. And all the animals know she's a baby—they all watch out for her."

But Lena grabbed up Lori in a flurry of anger and headed

for the house. Lori wailed and flailed her arms at John while Ginger ran alongside, yipping his concern. John watched all the way to the slam of the door, then hung up the rags and went back into the barn where the cattle stood silent, wide-eyed, flapping their ears to catch the last cries from the distant house. John buried his head against the flank of a cow, drawing solace from her, stripping milk into a pail with gentle hands. The milk made a swishing sound stroking into the pail, striking through the froth. When John went to empty milk into strainers to fill another can for cooling, he found Dan in the milk house staring at the cold spring water in the tank, his face as pale as milk

"Lena told me that Lori fell in here with the milk cans and you saved her from drowning. My thanks to you man." Though his voice was flat, devoid of expression, John could feel fear's grip on Dan. "My daddy used to say 'You can't learn to swim on the kitchen floor,' but on this farm, learning without common sense can be the death of you. Like I've always said, Lake Superior out there has an undertow, just waiting for the fool to fall in—just waiting to draw you under, it is. Twas a fair day when I found you John—better than any clover in the field, you bring me luck. Lena is in the house just now drying her tears. She's had a scare that one. I think Lena took it harder then Lori—the idea that God could just snatch away something so precious to us. Her God is like the undertow—out there waiting to be fed."

John began coasting along in a half-life, having negotiated a truce with himself, engaging somewhat with his chosen family, always looking out for Lori, who followed after him like a shadow, engaging sometimes with Whinn and other neighbors, but mostly staying to himself. He acknowledged his feelings best as he expressed himself with poetry or when absorbed in reverie in the safe and awesome loft of the barn. And so seasons spun along and the years went swiftly by: Daybreak—cold water, stiff muscles, sunbeams streaming through the barn's east windows, setting bright eyed calves to scuffling, scampering; sticky molasses over oats for the nickering horses; then the smack of pleasure, as wood smoke, whipped gold in the new light, rose up like a prayer. Afternoons— the in-between of chores—time to work at tasks of maintenance and building, plowing, harvesting and often, time for Lori. Evenings—time to think and write. And so, in this manner, time passed, and Lori grew.

If the years had legs and feet
I'd hear them marching by
Heartbeats marking life
Bells tolling time to die

On days Lena allowed it, Ginger arrived first to the barn, announcing an afternoon visit —ever watchful, ever proud. Then the little girl arrived with her entourage of cats and a special book for John to read to her. John noticed how she acted out the stories. After she knew the tale of Beauty and the Beast, she took special interest in Hannibal the herd bull. He grumbled and rumbled waiting for her to come close to him, and she would squat down by his pen 'til he lowered his giant head, pressing his wet pink speckled nose out between the steel bars for her to pat and kiss—hoping that like in the story, the beast would turn into her prince. Ginger allowed this, sometimes joining in with kisses of his own, for he did not read anger or aggression from the bull toward the child.

But when Dan saw it happen, he was horrified. "Never trust a bull—especially never trust a dairy bull," he warned Lori and everyone else within hearing. "It is his nature to use his power to kill what threatens him. Watch his eyes and you will see it. In every bull, there is a monster lurking. You will know it in his eyes when the monster comes out. And remember—always remember, the cattle are different in the night."

What did she take from that? John wondered. He hoped she would never see eyes aflame with evil intent—never face a killer. He shivered to think of it, for he had faced an enemy aimed at murder, and he knew, somewhere inside of him, there lurked a killer too—a monster he had never tamed.

In time, Lori brought the story of the Gingerbread man to John to read. She mouthed the words as he read them—pretending to read it to her Ginger who listened at her feet. As John read, she called out loud the words "run, run, as fast as you can—you can't catch me, I'm the gingerbread man," challenging the horses the cows, the chickens and cats to a race she would win. Ginger listened and believed. When the crafty fox, full of tricks, pretended he was a friend she fell silent. And she would sadly reach for the book when the fox snapped up the gingerbread man. Again, John wondered what she took from the story, for moments later, she ran wild around the circle drive playing Gingerbread Man with her Ginger dog.

It was a sunny day in May in the year that Lori was 5. This day, when he went out at dawn to bring the cows home from the lake pasture, John was surprised that they were already in the yard, the herd bull among them. He rolled open the rear doors and welcomed them inside. Later in the day, he noticed that Lori seemed different. She didn't look at him. She floated the wooden boats she had made herself from scraps, channeling rivers in the mud near the new well, filling lakes she had formed with water from the tank of water for the cattle. She hugged Ginger close to her and whispered her thoughts to the dog who listened carefully. John asked Dan if Lori was feeling well.

"Ah, its true enough John, yonder there, crawling in the mud, is Lena's worse fear. My girl suffers dearly from a double dose of original sin."

John looked where he gestured, and saw only a little girl wearing clean Oshkosh overalls kneeling in sticky red clay. She was building a new dam for her river out of rocks, ooze and straw—and she was singing!

"M-I-S-S," the song began," M-I-S-S," got louder, "M-I-S-S-I," and ended hopefully, punctuated with a glance at her father to see if he was impressed that his girl was at least smart.

Dan continued: "Before daylight in this swamp we live in, Lori got dressed and tiptoed mouse quiet out of the house to bring the cows home—and the herd bull with them—pretending she was grown up and helping you, John. She was strutting proud 'til Lena knocked her off her high horse. That's a lesson to bring down royalty she just had—no wonder she's kneeling—won't be sitting for awhile. Lena came after me next, and I was quick as a wink to tell her how I warned Lori about going near the herd bull—and the danger of the cattle. Lori thinks Ginger can protect her, but there's no protection from the fury of a German mother whose child will not mind. Heil dummkopf! Obey or die!" John nodded with appreciation, and went on about his work, but something inside was twisting, turning, and apprehension mixing with the strains of a rhyme he could not quite catch—was it the Gingerbread man?

It was later, in that afternoon space before the chores began. When he heard the scream, John stopped sharpening an ax in the machine shed—he dropped it, and ran out the door toward the sound, so full of anguish, like an air raid siren, an ambulance, the shriek of tearing asunder body and soul. Lorelei was running toward him down the drive from Moonshine road, howling hurt. In that moment, she entered in like a bullet to his heart. He did not think, he did not form words, for he knew—he'd been there—and now he only knelt down, opened his arms and caught her to him. Between sobs of pain, tears of anger, and self blame, she told the story. The little dog had chased the milk truck, speeding by on Moonshine Road near where they were playing. Ever her watchdog, he wanted to protect her from what ever came near. She called to him to come back, and he looked round at her. She had interrupted his attack because of her call and he didn't see the tire—he was looking at her, and it ran over him— just then. She saw his eyes—and then he was gone.

Lena came from the house. "You shouldn't have been playing near the road," she said. "Haven't I told you? Now you will listen." She was twisting her dish towel in her hands tighter and tighter. Dan came from the field. He stood for a moment listening to Lori, trying to understand what had happened. Then he walked up the drive until he could see the little crumpled form lying in the rut of the truck. He came slowly back, shaking his head. He crooned "Now, now Lori. Ginger is with the angels at heaven's gate." He reached down for his child. John said softly over and over "It's not your fault," as he let Dan pull her away from him.

"Lori, now you have your own guardian angel watching out for you forever. Come, your mom will make your favorite dessert, and John will take care of things here." He glanced at John, and whisked Lori away—still wailing in desperate grief.

John did not bother to brush the tears away—they came from a great river damned up long ago in the trenches of

France—the Mississippi in his deepest mind, and now the flood gates gave way. His tears washed over the little dog as he wrapped him in sacking for burial. He found wood for a cross and whittled a sign, Gingerbread Man.

Dan came and got out a shovel. He said he was going to dig the grave next to Shep's and to bring Ginger along. He didn't look at John, pretending not to notice John's grief.

"We've got a bloomin' death row in the yard, you know John—with all the dead pets. It's not big compared to the pile of bones out by the rock pile junk yard—a whole herd of our best animals lying tits-up in the rocks. What a war this farm is, and us workin' against fate to keep body and soul together while God is playing with us like a cat plays with a mouse. You remember Dave don't you—Dave throwin' things against the wall? I think he was aiming at God. Our God is useless as a lighthouse in the bog. Don't tell Lena I said that! She will pray the rosary over this, and make the child pray with her, and maybe they will have a funeral for this dog. He's only a dog, but such a brave one, don't you know? To Lori, he was her best friend. And this is her first goodbye. Ha! Don't we all have plenty of them? Well, the Irish say that "no one dies 'til we stop remembering them." And then there are those that say "never love anything that lives," but I say "love all in, for regret is sharper then death." What say you?"

"I'm like Dave without the throwing things," said John. "I think Dave's way was best for him and I don't know yet what to do with what's inside of me, but I am beginning to think there will come a day."

Dan spoke over the little dog, eyes directly on John, as he laid Ginger into his grave, "May your giant heart be tall as day." He stood and put his hand on John's shoulder. "Maybe behind all the poetry and kind ways, there is a lion ready to roar my man—for Ginger—for all those goodbyes, and for the man you are John."

WATCHDOG

IN THE LATE AFTERNOON, AS JOHN GAZED OUT ACROSS THE farm pastures, he saw clouds moving in over Lake Superior coating the lake in fog that shut out the sun. It was appropriate he thought, thinking of Ginger's death, shivering in the cold with the taste of anger bitter in his mouth, that the grey of the lake should darken to black. How many lives had been lost in those icy waters, snared by the watery tentacles of the undertow current, tumbled down into the insatiable mouth of the big lake? He thought about Dan's rant about God as the undertow. Though the cannons of World War I were silenced, he still felt its undertow. He likened it to a tsunami wave rising up to block the sun, curling, crashing down, and sucking back to satisfy the god of war. He felt powerless before it. Born of carnage, this blood vampire sobered his mood, and pounded his mind until his head throbbed and he could not function. It fingered his thoughts then seized them in a fist to feed upon. Helpless, robbed of reason, John only knew to retreat to higher ground, there to wait out the storm, curled around the fire light of his immortal soul.

He mechanically executed chores in silence, with no Ginger and no Lori. Then, much like Alice into the rabbit hole, John climbed up the ladder along the feed chute, navigating the tunnel to the cathedral of this upper world, to burrow down into the hay, seeking warmth and solace. He studied the timbers and light, and tried to think how he would talk with Lori should she come to him about Ginger's death. What would he say? But his head ached with the thinking and he let himself drift. From here he could see the swallows. They made their home under the eaves of the dairy barn, returning every year to raise their young and clear the skies of flying insects. Darkening sky, circling swallows swooping in and out the double loft doors.

A sort of interactive play came to him with voices and images. Memory reminded him that before he had come to work on this farm, he had disappeared from his home in Portage for five days only to be found by a posse of over 100 friends and neighbors, hiding in the loft of his own barn. This great shame had made the papers of course, one of the reasons he had left home. They said he was disoriented. He questioned. What does that mean—disoriented? Lost—yes, lost. Now he finds himself again in the loft of a barn. Finds *himself*? No— just a shell of himself—hiding. How to find your way when your mind stops? In the dark the lantern quits. Memory again: Well it hasn't always been like this. There flashed before him the image of his school picture above the caption "Handyman Sweetheart." The smiling oval face morphed into a target. Gun shots, cannon, and the image shattered like Humpty Dumpty felled from the wall. *All the king's horses and all the king's men can never put Humpty together again.* Sinking deeper. White sky, circling swallows in and out the double loft doors.

There was movement, high above him, a terror-filled shriek. He focused his eyes upon a scramble along the central timbers that supported roof and sling rail. The rise to aware- ness took too long—too late to yell "No!" The cat, claws deep into timber, had snagged a swallow out of the air—the swoop of the bird, the sweep of a foreleg, falling feathers and feline acrobatics, then balance regained. Turning carefully, containing the bird in her mouth, the cat began her slow descent along a lateral beam—the captor bringing her prize to John. John froze and waited.

Setting the swallow near John's hand, the cat proudly presented her gift, rolling onto her back, rubbing along in a patch of light, waiting for praise. John wanted to scold her, wanted to yell at her for taking this precious life. But, he shunned her instead, and picked up the still form, eyes closed, feet drawn up, limp, and still warm. He gently passed the swallow against his cheek—pressing the feathers into their proper position, fluffing the feathers of her breast with his breath. He willed the heart to beat. As if flown in on the wings of the swallow, a long buried memory transformed feather and form to canvas and wood. The circling swallows of twilight became the war-birds overhead in a day battle above the trenches. John held the swallow against his heart remembering the scene.

It was 1918 at the battle of Meuse. John, as one of the allied forces, was pinned down in a trench under intense fire from the Germans, fighting to hold the Meuse front until they had time to withdraw their troops from Belgium. Here, the enemy had concentrated the heaviest air force against the Americans that had ever been gathered together. The Germans were desperate to prevent allied bombing squads from reaching the Rhine towns dear to the heart of the Hun. From the trenches, it was sometimes possible to see the red nosed planes of the Richthofen Circus and the yellow bellied fuselages of the Loezer Circus engaging the French Spads flown by the Americans. The earthbound infantry and cavalry knew these flyboys had a life expectancy of three to six weeks.

Tim, John's machine gunner buddy was an expert on the war-birds. He had wanted to be a pilot himself and knew that it was the 147th Squadron that arrived overhead, causing excitement to ripple through the trenches. It was mid afternoon, an audacious time to launch a bomber attack. Flashing blue, white and red circles on their wings, the Spad formation flew protection for Allied bombers headed across no man's land. The name of the squadron leader —"Watchdog" Wilbur White, on his last mission before going home to wife and children, would be etched into the memories of all who witnessed what would happen next.

Telling about the planes flying above, Tim drew the attention of all who could hear. "The Yanks fly those Spads at 120 mph and fire their guns out the front. They don't have parachutes and will probably burn to a crisp if they crash. The German Fokkers, are better and faster, and they have parachutes. And look over there," Tim gestured widely and a hush fell over the trenches as the men saw the approaching tri-planes. "Here come the Huns flying their best and newest—like the Red Baron brags: "they's maneuverable as the devil and climb like monkeys." They have four guns that send tracer bullets in the air in a line that look like roman candles on the 4th of July."

The 147th formation separated away from the bombers to draw the fire of the Fokkers barreling down on them from their aerodrome at Stenay. Coming up behind, the German leader aimed his red nosed plane to gun down the rear plane of White's formation. The Watchdog—famous for his courage— instantly countered his move.

John was trembling now, remembering every detail as if in slow motion. From the trenches and from the cockpits, troops on both sides witnessed a sight so sublime the beauty and horror of it pierced understanding to simmer within, flavoring the remainder of their lives. White pulled his plane up and around, and hurtled full throttle headlong toward the lead plane. At the cost of his own life he would protect his pilot from certain death. Without firing a shot the American pilot rammed the Circus leader, their combined speed at 230 miles an hour. The planes encompassed each other—wings through wings, fuselage fused to fuselage in a firestorm that lit up the sky, and they fell together, a slow spiraling pillar of flame, disintegrating into a charred pile of metal, blood, and bone upon the banks of the Meuse. Time stopped. Wheeling away, the leaderless Boche planes flew back to their Aerodrome at Stenay, refusing further engagement with the American pilots. Silence. This lava hot memory in John's subconscious had been covered over by terror and shock, but now fully re-membered, it burned like a torch to the magnificence of spirit. "Thank you," he said to no-one.

John stroked the little swallow he still held, looking down at her sadly. Open eyes looked back at him. "So you're back from the war are you, my pretty. Are you disoriented, and how will you explain to the others?" He held her out resting on both open hands. She righted herself, arranging wings missing feathers, stood and flew. John watched her go—flying lopsided out into the twilight toward home. "Go home!" he called after her—for Captain White, for Ginger the watchdog. You are alive today, and this is your time to fly!" And more softly he added, "Show *me* the way to go home."

Hungry Eyes

LENA HAD THE SOLUTION. SINCE GINGER'S DEATH, LORI seemed inconsolable. Lena said that "work was the answer," and assigned a calf to Lori to raise. The herd bull Hannibal had sired a beautiful white calf with black spots around each eye and along her sides. Lena taught the calf to suck on a nurse pail with a lamb's nipple, feeding her colostrum, the rich first milk of the mother cow. Lori petted the new calf, scratched her forehead, and let her bunt and chase her around the pen. Ginger, had he been there, would never have allowed that game, but Lori thought it was fun and could scramble out over the fence to get away. She picked up ground-fall apples and Lena cut them into small pieces to feed to the calves, saving the most of them for Lori's calf which they named Hanna. Hanna grew fat and big and came to expect the apple gifts, gobbling them while watching Lori with hungry eyes.

Lori hung out around John when she came into the barn, and now he found her underfoot tagging along with him as he worked the horses. Dan had sold his good team to the logging camp, and bought another from the Montana horse traders who, in Whinn's words, "saw Dan coming." The truth was that Dan got a good price for his reliable team and when he was offered a new black Percheron team by the traders, he thought that John could train them up to be good horses. It was common practice to sell a team that looked to be matched, with one being a well trained horse, and the other being an untrained beast off the prairies. John worked the team together and the good horse, "Tom" did the bulk of the training for his half wild partner, Prince.

Lori begged to ride the horses, and John soon realized Tom was the perfect mount. He promised her a lesson when he observed her sitting on Tom while he grazed in the pasture. While she jumped up and down with excitement, he bridled Tom, and rode him over to a hayrack so Lori could leap up behind him. She hugged John with one arm, putting her face against his denim shirt, patting the big horse with her free hand, her strong chubby legs holding tight against the horse's muscular loins. John chuckled to feel her energy, giving her instruction as they rode. "Lori, I see you riding Tom all by yourself without even a bridle. How do you get him to turn and stop?"

"He just does what he wants," Lori admitted.

"Ah—it's time to use magic—do you have magic legs? John chided.

"Yes, John, I have. I can run like the wind," Lori said.

"Lori—you can use your legs to steer this horse—and make him go where you want him to. He will listen to you, too. Do you sing to him?" John asked. "Lori—the secret is in you already. You love this horse with your hands and voice and he will go where you want him to just to please you. A lot of people think you overpower a horse, but that's not it. If you learn the secret, this horse will know what you want him to do, even before you do," John said.

"Let's do it John! Show me John!" she begged.

John loved it. Years before he had shown Ida how to ride. He thought he had forgotten all that he knew, yet now it poured out of him. He showed Lori how to lean, how to press her leg against the horse and turn him around her leg, and best of all, he told her how Tom already listened to her. He showed her that Tom knew words, and felt the way the reins were held. Lori promised she would practice everyday and that she would brush Tom and feed him his grain so that he would feel like he was her "very own horse."

"Yes, Lori, that is the way to win him over, and you don't need sugar and treats for that. Some horses learn to nip that way—instead, use your voice and hands and he will know—love is like a magic key to unlock his heart. Animals want to belong and have a master to please. You must learn to master him—be a kind and wise master and thank him for his special love."

"I will John. You watch me! I'll learn to be a master just like you are. I want to be just like you!"

John caught his breath; then said firmly, "No, Lori, you learn to be just like you. The secret is inside of you. Remember that!"

Everyday, Lori brought her favorite book, Grimm's Fairy Tales, to John to ask him to read to her. The little green book contained stories of an unreachable castle atop a glass mountain, children lost in the woods, the golden goose girl, wicked witches, enchanted swans, Briar Rose and the last story—Iron Hans. She knew all the stories, and delighted in telling them to John when he didn't have time to read. Especially intrigued with Iron Hans, she loved the idea of a captive wild man set free by a child.

"And the boy got his finger and his hair in the magic water and they turned to gold" she said shaking her own golden hair and examining her own fingers covered with red clay. And then Hans said "You cannot stay here with me any longer, but must go out into the world, and learn the meaning of poverty."

What's that John—that poverty?"

There's more than one kind of poverty, Lori," said John. "People live in poverty if they don't have the money to pay for things, they live poor, and having little, they learn what is worth having and figure out how to get it. They become wise. But, there's the bad kind of poverty where people lose all hope and can't even dream." As he explained this to Lori—a thought came to him. *What kind of poverty had he been living in? And, if these fairy tales had life lessons in them, then would Lori someday have to learn the meaning of poverty?*

"Well, the boy dreamed a lot and got into trouble too, but Hans promised to help if he were called" Lori said. "Hans was really a great king, you know, only he was under a spell that the boy broke."

"How did he do that?" John asked. He looked hard at Lori.

"I guess cuz he married the princess and he needed the wild man to get her," Lori answered. You gotta remember John, that Hans was sort of like the boy's father. He got to come to the wedding... and they all lived happily ever after."

"Oh," said John. He thought of Dave who once lived above the horse barn, who became a raging madman in his timbered cell at night, who had it in him to save both Lena and her unborn child Lori, by destroying a monster. Now Lori's words, like a shaft of light, smiled upon the wild man crouched beneath hopeless waters of shame...in John's deepest mind.

Lori proved to be just like the boy in the story of Iron Hans. When Lena dressed her for school in long white stockings and patent leather shoes, she disobeyed rules, using recess time to climb the trees in the forbidden forest off school property. She was sent home soundly spanked, wearing her torn stockings, scuffed shoes and carrying a note from the principal. Lena, who sat on the school board, was mortified, while Dan, who had a history of making mischief and skipping school entirely, hid laughter from Lena behind stern looks. Lori spent more time outside, frequently punished, often disgraced, and banished from Lena's world. The next summer, Lori was given more work in an effort to keep her out of trouble. She now had the job of bringing the cows home from the hill pastures—a very important job, but one Lena no longer would do. Lena never spoke about the attack upon her, how her dog had been killed on that hill by the assailant hiding in those rocks, and she never again picked berries on the hill, and only shook her head "No" when asked to go there.

John was washing up for chores, having readied the barn to receive the cows, when he saw Lori skipping and singing behind the herd turning off the road, proceeding down the drive to the barn. Hanna, now a strapping big heifer, was lagging behind the others, and had turned to look at Lori. John stood still as he saw the girl stop, mesmerized before Hanna. John felt the danger like a bolt of lightning at the same time that Lori faced into it, and then Hanna charged. John was already running as Lori screamed. She did not have time to run, and Hanna hit her with the flat of her forehead tossing her up into the air and into the woven wire fence.

"N00000!!!" John yelled. Hanna had her head down, twisted to hit Lori with the stub of a horn, but when she heard John, and glimpsed him descending upon her, Hanna wheeled away and resumed her course toward the barn...as if it had never happened. John gathered up Lori white and shaking, but not crying.

"She looked at me and I saw what she was going to do," Lori said. "She was going to kill me!" Lori took a ragged breath. Her arms were tight against her chest—still protecting her body.

John pushed Lori's hair away from her eyes with a gentle

touch and looked straight into those bright blue eyes—full of shame and lost innocence. "Yes Lori," John said. "Now you know." She had recognized the look all vulnerable creatures fear when eye to eye with death. John too had faced an enemy intent on killing him. They breathed an allied breath of understanding. John helped her to her feet and when she was ready, she caught John's hand to walk. Before they stepped off, John asked "Are you hurt anywhere? Hanna tossed you like you were a clay pigeon—did she hurt you?"

"Oh John—you are so silly," Lori gasped. "I need to talk to Hanna about this—tell her not to do it again." Lori said resolutely. "She won't, will she? She was my baby calf to raise and now... John, she wanted to smash me with her head!" Self-doubt began to wash over her and she asked, with her lower lip quivering, "What did I do wrong? It must be my fault."

"Lori," John said, "look at me and remember what I say now. I saw what happened. Right from the time she was little, Hanna learned to chase you in the pen. It was a game, and she liked it but when she was little, you were her master—not any more. I've seen this before. You cannot trust all animals anymore than you can trust all people. Hanna is not your friend, she is your enemy. She knows she is big and powerful now, and can crush what is in her way, and she is not afraid of you. She wants to be boss. You must never trust her again. You saw the look she gave you before she came at you. That look comes from her mind and there is this thought in there. And you can't get it out. She is off her head, crazy, Lori. This isn't about you, it is about her and you have to realize who or what she is. I am going to tell your parents about this. I hope they will want to sell her."

"Oh no, John!" Lori pleaded. "Please don't tell them! I don't want them to sell her because of me. This is my fault. I taught

Hanna wrong. Oh, if only I'd had Ginger!"

John and Lori began to walk on down the drive. She was still a little shaky, but walked straight as she could so no one saw. John was thinking, a little smile coming to his face as he spoke.

"I know Lori. It's time we find you a dog—one that keeps you from flying off like a clay pigeon."

"Really John," Lori brightened, "can we really get another dog for me? I miss having a dog!"

"Yes, Lori, you shall have one and the best one that we can find," John said. And I don't want you bringing the cows home again on foot. I will go with you and you will ride Tom. Promise me you will not go on foot among the cattle if Hanna is with them."

That night John talked to Lena and Dan, trying to convince them to sell Hanna, but they both thought Hanna had just been playing.

"Lori must have caused it," said Lena. "She must have been teasing Hanna."

"Maybe this was just a fluke," said Dan. "John, you know Hanna is the best of all Hannibal's daughters. We need her in our herd."

John knew what he had seen and felt, and so he told them the idea he had ready. "I'd like a top-notch herding dog on this farm." John winked at Lena, "I believe a border collie would be just the best kind to have here, and such a dog would protect Lori or any of us. For now, Lori loves getting the cattle, but I've made her promise not to go alone. I'm teaching Lori to ride Tom, and I would like to go with her at first to be sure she learns the right way to drive cattle with a horse. Hanna will never bother her if she is up on Tom—she is becoming a very good rider. But, we need that dog. Lena, you have always wanted a border collie haven't you?"

Lena flashed a smile to John, for she had already shared with him her wish to have a border collie for the dairy farm. "I can get some addresses of kennels from the library," said Lena. "I'd like to order such a dog, but they are expensive."

"Well, let me worry about the cost," said John. "For all the treats, the apple pie and bread, the roasts and caramel rolls—all my favorite foods, its time I tip the cook. Let me pay for the dog you choose, Lena. I think a good dog would help me—would help all of us."

"I've got about half the price of a border collie saved," said Lena. "I'll let you pay for the shipping, for I think the best dogs are being bred in Illinois, and that's a long way from here."

"And I'll pay the rest," said Dan. "I want my girls to be safe and happy—eh John? And thanks for helping Lori out today. She needs to know some fear—that one—and not get killed in the learning. Ah, youth does not mind where it sets its foot."

"She does indeed, Dan," John nodded. "And that sounds fine Lena. I think this is a good plan," he said. Although he felt apprehension about Hanna, he was glad that he would have the help of a dependable horse and dog to keep everyone safe, especially Lori. Dan hadn't told him he would have that responsibility when he had been hired years ago, but he felt it strongly, and thought it was the most important of his chores. That night, sitting at his table in his little cabin, he thought of Lori's story about Iron Hans and realized that Dave, and he himself, had been prisoners in a cage made of memories too painful to touch; jailed there until they cared enough to break through. He thought he should write about it, so he jotted off a poem, and called it The Key.

Safe from hurt
Vowing never to care
Impoverished with nothing to lose
Try my gate? No one would dare
Leave me alone, I'm singing the blues.

My song looks inward
It sucks me down
"I don't care" turns people away
But a child has found a chink in my wall
And let in the light of day

My hardened heart
Prisoner of pain
Is opening, setting me free
Unlocking the door forged out of fear
Love is turning the key.

Then he sat awhile longer and wrote something simpler, not bothering to rhyme anything. It was not easy for him to do it, he struggled with every word and the finished work was spotted with his tears.

While wandering the graveyard, looking for my stone,
The no-man's land of "left behind and wondering why"
I found cool water, and waded into someone else's
    dream, keeping safe, by not caring.

I let myself float awhile, not expecting the current to
     catch me, the river of foolhardiness to take me
     over the cascade
To find myself loving a child hell bent and disaster
     destined.

To find myself.

I came to build a barn and run a dairy, not raise a child
Couldn't raise my own.
But when she vaults up, climbing mane to reach the
     back of a horse
unbridled and wild,
I know I taught her
And she lives because of me.

Sandy

"How long before they bring the puppy?" Lori had asked each day, and now finally, the day had come. Lena invited John for breakfast on this special day. She had decided to order a female tri-color border collie. Dan decided it would ride in his truck bed, and he would train it to flush deer, and Lori decided it was to be her dog forever and would be trained up to be smarter than "Lad the Dog." John knew Lena's unstated rule—animals sold or dead were not spoken of again. It just didn't do to be attached, but, he hoped the new dog would be lovable, long-lived and useful.

The men and Lori sat around Lena's birds-eye maple dining table set with the dishes she had collected from the gas company refracting clear and green in the sunlight streaming through the window. John noticed the purple lilac bush in full bloom framed by creamy lace curtains. He reminded himself that Lena created beauty around her—the wallpaper in the dining room was red roses set between ivy stripes above linoleum the color of jade; and hand-made rag rugs in shades of russet and gold which led into the living room thru a white enameled arch. Flanking the arch were open room dividers holding tall elegant vases of white lilacs and yellow daffodils. Spring was everywhere in color and fragrance. He inhaled smoky sweet smells drifting from the kitchen. Lena brought coffee to the men, a plate of banana bread and peach marmalade. Before anyone could eat, she led them in Grace:

"Bless us oh Lord in these thy gifts which we are about to receive from thy bounty through Christ Our Lord. Amen."

Dan winked at Lori noticing she was too excited to pray, while Lena's head was bowed, eyes closed in reverence. Back in the kitchen, Lena served up pancakes hot from her griddle, crowning each stack with butter squares that melted into puddles of gold. Lori ran for the pitcher of syrup. Bacon and eggs sizzled in cast iron skillets to be served sunny side up all nestled on a white turkey platter garnished with orange wedges. Lena poured German coffee around, filled her own cup and finally took off her Dutch apron to sit down to eat. Her day had started half a day ago when, in the velvet blackness and shivering cold of 4 AM, she had pulled her woolen work coat from its hook in the mud room, buttoned it over her dress, tied a scarf down and hurried by yard light and moonlight to the welcoming warmth of the barn. Jimmy MacKee, whom everyone knew as Mac, would soon turn his brand new milk truck down the long drive, load the cans, and leave empties to fill again during evening chores. The pup was to arrive by train, and Dan had spoken to Mac about picking up the shipment in Superior at the freight office when he delivered the milk in town.

Dan was loading the spreader with manure from the horse barn when Mac arrived. Lori had tagged along and was watching impatiently from the loft. "This is the day Mac; can you pick up the pup for us this morning?" Dan asked.

Mac glimpsed Lori watching from her perch up high. "How about it Lori, should I pick up your new pup for you? Or should I maybe give it to some other kid—someone that really wants it? I bet my daughter Charlene would like that pup. What do you say?"

Lori didn't answer but in a flash she was standing beside him extending her hand. She had a marble in it. "Here, Mr. MacKee, is a marble for Charlene. I want that puppy. Please, please, get her for me!"

"Oh—I didn't know you wanted that pup so bad as to give a marble for her. Not to worry, Charlene plays with dolls and wouldn't know what to do with a puppy, or a marble, and anyway, I will pick up the pup just because she's a real border collie and coming by train. Now that's special. So, what's she look like?"

"She looks just like Lad!" Lori said with conviction, sure that the pup would grow up to look like the famous dog in her mother's story book; she was relieved that he didn't want her marble.

True to his word, Mac returned, this time driving his old pick-up truck to drop off the crated puppy. Lori danced around the truck hoping to glimpse the Border Collie, barely containing herself at all.

"Please Dad, get her out! Let's see her. Hurry, hurry!"

But Dan took his time talking about Town of Lakeland matters with Mac, as if he was not the least bit curious. Finally, the two men set the crate down, and Dan slipped some money into Mac's hand, thanking him.

Mac did not immediately climb into the cab of his truck and drive away. "If you don't mind, Dan, I'll just stick around a minute to see the wonder dog that comes out of that crate. I can't recollect any farmer before this, getting a dog in from out of state."

John came from the machine shed carrying a pry bar and Lena came running from the house to receive the envelope of papers that accompanied the shipment. She solemnly read to them all: "Her name is Queen of the Sahara Sands. And yes, she is a tri-colored border collie, and you know, they are the best herding dogs." She let that sink in. Then she nodded to John to open the crate.

"Are you ready Lori?" John had to smother a laugh at her excitement. Then he pried off the wooden slats. Inside, was a cowering puppy. She was not cute, nor was she pretty. Pressed against the crate's far corner, she clung to the wood with her nails dug in, determined to keep all that was left of her life in Illinois. Her hair was dark bedraggled brown and black and she had white legs and a white chest and a white streak down her face. She trembled violently but did not whimper and cry, only turned her head, refusing to look, like she was waiting for her kidnappers to kill her.

Dan reached in and dragged out the trembling little bundle of fear, setting her down in Lori's waiting arms. "Here's your new herding dog Lori," he said, then, looking at Lena, "Haven't we paid dearly for every hair in her tail though." He shook his head and an Irish proclamation rolled off his tongue for one so puny: "The breath is only just in and out of her, and the grass doesn't know of her walking over it." He chuckled at Lena. "She looks more like sand blowing in the wind than a Queen of the Sahara Sands; and she bears no resemblance to Lad of Sunnybank.

"Her name is Sandy," Lori said. And that was that.

Sandy was a serious puppy. She was playful, but never in the comical tumbling manner of clumsy pups. Her play was like the wind through tall grass, wild, undulating and secretive. Never affectionate, showering wet kisses, or obedient; heeling alongside, her love was silent and her spirit illusive. She frustrated Lena with her willful ways, much like Lori's. She answered to John, but watched over Lori, running circles around her, darting close, then racing away. True to her breed she began to establish herself as a herding dog with the cattle. Nothing escaped her, nothing out maneuvered her, but she would not be caught and held any more than one could catch a moonbeam.

Almost a year passed, and with the promise of another spring, the men needed to roll up snow fence along Moonshine Road. Dan took Sandy with them in the back of the truck, so she could sniff out field mice while they worked— early training for her to flush game that he could hunt. Lori stayed at home to play in her spring playground; a place John had dubbed Lori's Thousand Lakes. Behind the milk house and between the barns, this was a sheltered area where the winds had blown in drifts and these last snows melted into streams and trickles. The water trough was set into the woven and barbed wire fence separating Thousand Lakes from the cow yard. When Lori stood on its rim, she could see boats on the Lake Superior horizon. The long ore boats sailed in empty and toiled out full from the ports of Duluth, Superior and Two Harbors. She mucked rocks with red clay for dams to make lakes, rivers and harbors to float her own fleet of work boats. She found red rocks like iron ore to put onto her boats bound for a new harbor she christened Mississippi Bend; but she still needed to find a board long enough to write out the name. She spied one, out in the cow yard. The cows must have ripped it away from the bottom of the woven wire flanking the tank, for she saw the space it had belonged in. The cattle were in the yard; coming up as they wished for a drink of spring water that gravity-flowed down from the rock hill's spring. She climbed the wooden ladder that served as a way over the barbed wire, mindful of the cattle. She didn't see Hanna.

Hanna had matured into the largest of the cows, properly placid, a serene monarch holding court with Lena and the men. She kept secret her intent to win the game Lori forgot they were playing. Hanna did not forget. She stalked and waited for Lori to be alone and vulnerable, and only then did she reveal herself as the killer she was. She was already charging when Lori saw her, but Hanna's sharp hooves sunk deep into the mud hindering her speed, while Lori ran right out of her boots, almost reaching the fence before Hanna hit her. Graveled clay and rocks of all sizes made wounds all over her, as Lori rolled to escape the thrusts of Hanna's blunt horns, ripping her jacket as she squirmed under the woven wire and boards into the only small space there was. Hanna might have smashed the fence and trampled the girl, but just then, Dan's truck turned down the drive. She stopped abruptly. From behind the wheel, John saw Hanna, ambling casually away to blend into the herd, as he pulled up with his load of snow fence. Before him face down in her Thousand Lakes playground, was Lori in stocking feet, bleeding and covered with mud.

John ran to her, calling out "Lori! Are you alright? What's happened to you? Here, let me help you." She rolled to her side and sat up. He was putting it together, seeing the tiny space under the fence and her muddy trail through it.

"I didn't see Hanna—I didn't know she was there. Honest, John!"

"Now Lori, you are without your boots," John said, looking around. Ah, I see them, stuck in the mud over there part way across the cow yard. If you are going to break your promises, you shouldn't leave evidence around for me to see. Now you just figure out what else you are missing—count up your arms and legs, fingers and toes and I'll get your boots for you."

As he retrieved the boots, John watched Lori brush off and stand. She looked fine enough; the blood was from scratches to her hands and arms. But then, she found the rip in her jacket and began to cry. John remembered Dan telling of the terrible spankings Lori got from Lena who was determined to civilize the child. *What would she be in for this time?* Clearly, she had a dilemma.

"Well Lori, let's go into the milk house and you can wash up while I get this jacket wiped down and the mud off your boots. We've got to wash those socks. Here, take them off and I'll just wrap a little cheese cloth around your feet, and then your boots will stay on better too."

As John scrubbed, he thought of an idea. "Say Lori, we can use some help with the snow fence. Would you like to ride back with me and help? I can leave a note for Lena so she knows where you've gone to. You're not too sore from crawling under the fence, are you? You remind me of Br'er Rabbit getting into the carrot patch. He had a problem sort of like yours—always going where he shouldn't go, doing what he shouldn't do."

"Oh yes, John! Please John," she said. "Let me go with you to help, and tell me about who is Br'er Rabbit?"

John told a Br'er Rabbit story about the carrot patch and the farmer, making up parts he needed, to make it come out right. He washed away the tears, the mud and the blood, making little bandages from the milk strainer cheese-cloth for bruises and cuts that had all but quit bleeding. He ended his story with, "And Br'er Rabbit never went back into the carrot patch; instead he took up eating clovers that tasted better and grew all around, and lived happily ever after." Lori sat in the truck thinking over the story while John unloaded the rolled snow fence, then they drove back to the fields to help Dan take down the rest.

Strangely enough, Hanna was the only cow drinking at

the trough when the truck returned with the last load. Sandy jumped out of the back, knowing it was almost time to herd the cows up to enter the barn. Hanna lowered her head and fixed her eyes on Sandy. Like a statue she stood as if in a spell, looking hard, while Sandy stalked her, eyes locked on hers. The hate between them was a living growing thing. John, seeing this tension, said nothing, but wondered to himself if Sandy sensed something of what had happened that afternoon.

After chores that night, Lena ran warm water for Lori in the tub. The ripped jacket must have happened on the snow fence wires. She scolded Dan for letting Lori be around that kind of work, getting scratched up, and tearing her clothes. Looking puzzled by it all, Dan shrugged, used to being scolded. These things happened when one worked around the farm and of course Lena could mend the jacket. Lori soaked in the warm water, never showing her mother her many bruises, never speaking of her foolhardy mistake, thinking about how Br'er rabbit learned to love clover. She thanked her guardian angel for saving her life and made Him a promise she would try to keep. In the morning, she began to practice the piano like her mother wanted her to. John heard piano music each day, gradually translating from scales to chords to strains of Claire De Lune.

Hanna grew older and fatter, Sandy grew in size, skill and courage, sparring with Hanna with increasing violence, and the piano played Chopin in measured time, and thundered chords of Rachmaninoff's Bells of Moscow.

THE ROCK GULLY FOREST

IT WAS A DRY SUMMER. EVEN THE FLAX FIELD, PURPLE BLUE IN the sun, was turning brown on the edges as each day dawned hot and hotter. The adolescent Holstein heifers honeymooned with the Black Angus bull high on the pastures of the rock hill. The bull and his harem were seldom seen out in the clearings during daytime, preferring to loll knee deep in ferns circling cool artesian springs in the shady green of the rock gully forest.

One day, Dan noticed turkey vultures circling above the rock hill and decided to check on his young stock. These black and whites, Hannibal's daughters, would replace and augment his growing herd. They were the promise of better times for his dairy. Hannibal had been traded now, and after this year, no more babies from him. A young Holstein bull of a strain famous for milk production stood in his pen, growing in size and majesty, waiting for his girls to mature to receive him.

Dan was worried, so thought to bring his 30-30 rifle with him as he ascended the steep hill, watching the birds, alert to the smell of death. Sandy accompanied him, running down wild scents along secret trails, scaring up deer, flushing grouse, then back to Dan as they proceeded into the deep woods above the river. When Dan heard Sandy barking and the moan of an animal, he crashed out a shortcut through the brush, fearful of the find. He saw the staggered path through the new little cedar trees, broken branches on the poplars, blood on a birch tree and then the heifer on her side, still thrashing, eyes rolled back, foaming blood from her mouth. She was sounding her crossing from life to death. Even if he had never heard a death song before, he would have recognized it from the depth of his being. He did not recoil from it, but listened to the primeval melody, holding his breathe so to hear the tones rise and fall.

Face grim, he aimed his gun carefully, and a single shot echoed against the canyon rock walls, all the louder for the silence that followed. He saw the black bull watching, a dark shape in the balsam fir trees. Sandy growled and stood protectively between them, and then the bull turned and disappeared like a ghost. Dan rolled the heifer around in the blood stained moss, smelling her musty, feeling her warm, looking in vain for what had caused her profuse bleeding. He could do nothing more, so he looked around, marking the place in his mind so he could find his way back, and since night was falling, he headed home to chores with the intention of finding the herd in the morning.

"John, I have a bad feeling about this," he confided as he motioned the cattle into their stalls for milking. "I felt it up there on the hill—the sound of her—the sound..."

The stanchions clanged shut, echoing Dan's gun putting a period on life. Hearing him stumble in his description, John met Dan's eyes, glimpsing there a memory that also haunted him. He respected the intuition of the man, but sought to disarm the foreboding. "Tomorrow we will know more, Dan. Don't fret over shadow play. We'll figure this out in the light of day. Get your big book out."

Dan cherished his copy of the Practical Stock Doctor. Its green cover embossed with golden scrolls held almost 900 pages of the best information known about animals in 1912 when it was written—everything from how to make a sling for a horse, to how to deliver a calf coming breech, as well as tips on breeding and emergency operations. John smiled to himself as he remembered how Dan had brought out his "big book" when they had to punch some cattle in the side to treat bloating. They had poured mineral oil down their throats and then tied blocks of wood into their mouths so that gases would escape as they were herded around. The wrong food or too much of it sometimes killed cattle, and Dan had lamented that he didn't have that big book before the war. If he had only gotten it sooner, perhaps he could have saved his first little herd of cattle; it would have changed his life.

In the morning after chores, Dan announced the plan. Lori wanted to go but since the bull was with the herd, Lena would not allow it. John said he would take Tom out and she could ride behind him. After some hesitation Lena agreed that was safe enough. Dan said he would bring his truck up onto the hill by way of the back road. They would find and herd the cattle into the corral to check for problems. Overnight, Dan had done research in his big book, and put the medicines he had on hand into his truck along with lariats, a pail, and grain. Sandy watched, waiting to be invited, then eagerly jumped up into the truck-bed, curling down alongside the bag of grain.

By this time, the riders had reached the summit of the hill, and John set the big horse to loping along the trail to the corral where they were to meet Dan and Sandy. He watched the woods on both sides, and Lori did the same, hoping to glimpse the black and white of the little herd. At the corral, the men decided to check out the springs first, for the cattle were most often there on hot days. Dan walked about setting gates, then filling the pail of grain. On horseback it was easy to find the herd at the big spring. Dan called the cattle to the corral by banging on the pail spreading grain in a trough inside an outer fence, while John and Lori riding Tom zigzagged behind, Sandy policed heels, keeping the young herd moving together. Two animals lagged behind, their heads down, weaving.

The little corral had a loading chute. Dan considered bringing sick animals home, but both he and John were afraid of infecting the milking herd with this unknown disease. The two stragglers were very thin, breathed with difficulty, looked anemic, as indeed they must be, for every opening was spotted with blood. The men roped and squeezed them against the corral boards with a special hinged gate, so they could work safely on each animal. Temperatures were taken, and then both were drenched with Dan's cure-all medicines of mineral oil and Epsom salts. Noting their lackluster and high temps, Dan proclaimed darkly, "When death comes, it will not go away empty-handed."

"We could call the vet?" John offered. "I heard that there are new sulfa drugs that he might be able to bring." He knew it was expensive to have a veterinarian out, and that both men were able to treat most of the conditions a vet knew how to work with; but new medicines? Now that was an idea long overdue!

Before he answered, Dan looked at all the other cattle. Some of them seemed to be unresponsive, a vacant look in their eyes. "Ah John, I tell you good luck comes in tricklets; ill luck comes in torrents. Yes, we had better get a handle on this. These two look determined to die, but maybe we can save some of the rest. Would you hazard a guess—what do you think it is?"

"I'd say it was shipping fever, because of the hemorrhages and high temps, but we haven't brought new animals in; so it's a mystery how we would get shipping fever into this herd. I just don't know, Dan."

"Let's leave these two in the corral then, John and go for a vet. He will want to vaccinate for shipping fever. Also, I know the State vet will be coming round soon to vaccinate for milk fever. He will be full of information on all the latest diseases—more so than old Doc Helvig."

Three weeks later, John found himself driving Dan's truck on a long trip hauling a different sick heifer. The struggles that led to this desperate trip to Richland were heavy on his mind, weighing him down. Four different vets had been called out; three convinced it was shipping fever. They had vaccinated and treated for that, but animals continued to get sick and die. Dan had used sulfa drugs, Lena had cooked up gruel made of bran and honey and first milk, and they had blanketed, poulticed, drenched and shot in medicines of every kind prescribed in the big green book, but in spite of all measures, every animal that got sick, died. The state vet, appalled by what was happening, had taken pity on them, filled out a form saying he didn't know what was causing the problem, and contacted the laboratory in Richland, Wisconsin, their last best hope. Richland labs were still being developed, but with the special referral the State vet gave, the staff there consented to receive a sick animal for testing. John then built a hood over the cab of the truck so the heifer they chose would be shielded from the wind, and late the night before, he and Dan had loaded her. "Better for her to walk on than be dragged on dead," Dan said. Whinn came over to help them load up.

Gripping the wheel, John's mind reflected on the events of the night before.

"I tell you boys, death is the poor man's doctor," Dan said as he dropped a loop over the listless head of one of his prettiest heifers. "I'll just donate my best heifer to be a fresh specimen for this new laboratory—public minded as I am. Or do you think they will be miracle workers in Richland? Can they raise up the dead, do you think John? We'd have a whole herd to donate for that experiment."

John received the end of the lariat and set himself to ratchet her into the truck.

"Now Dan," Whinn said, as he joined arms with him to shove the young animal up the chute into the truck, "its sad sure enough to sacrifice a good heifer to the gods that watch over politician farmers, but maybe they'll shower you with some Irish luck for this. You've gotten through things like this before, and I think you'll prove out what they say about your countrymen—after misfortune the Irishman prospers."

Grunting, edging the animal on, Dan replied, "Well Whinn, you must feel truly sorry for me with saying something kind about the Irish. I should have thought you would say something like "Ignorance is a heavy burden."

"Yes Dan, I thought it, but being thoughtful and caring, I decided to keep still about that," Whinn said. The heifer stood shakily in the truck and they put a barrier behind her, slammed the tail-gait closed, and drove the truck back to the farm to park for the night.

The next morning, relieved to see the heifer was still alive, Dan gave John a four leaf clover to put in his hat, and the "send off he used for bad times." "John my man, it's an ill wind that blows no one good. Drive carefully and we'll be waiting." John saw him standing alone in his rear view mirror. Lena and Lori waved from the porch of the house, and the little truck groaned up the drive bearing the young animal on her last trip.

A bump in the road jolted John back to the present as he drove South along Highway 53 on his way to Richland labs.

Crossing over the Fond du Lac, Dan's favorite river, that coursed through his park, John thought of the great Wisconsin waterways and their French-Indian names. The Bois Brule flowed into Lake Nebagamon that birthed the Eau Claire and the St. Croix Flowage fed by the Chippewa coming from the Flambeau River. He had traveled through the logging towns of Gordon and Minong before he noticed his rising excitement. He slowed down to cross the Nemakagon River, breathing in the familiar pine needle scent, feeling warm all over. He was in the sand country he had grown up in. The bus that had brought him North to Superior had traveled this route—how many years ago? He tried to remember.

The heifer shifted her weight—scrambling to keep her feet, jarring John back to reality. He chalked up his exhilaration to the novelty of the situation. He had never visited a state lab before. There weren't any. Some bureaucrats in Madison had secured funds to grease pork barrel projects to modernize agriculture. The state vet had told him about the Wisconsin Idea of Higher Learning, which was to teach beyond the boundaries of campuses— indeed to extend knowledge to all peoples of the state. Madison's veterinary school was targeting the Richland labs as the newest and best diagnostic lab for the dairy state. John looked forward to this visit, except for the gravity of it.

Back at the farm, Dan would be using Tom in single harness to pull the carcasses of all the dead heifers out onto the road, and then he would haul them with the Oliver 80 tractor, and pile them for burning. Nine of Dan's beautiful Holstein heifers were to be burned up on this day. The way they had discovered sick animals flashed across John's memory. The black bull had met them at the gate to the rock hill each day, and led them to more heifers dead or dying in the rock gully forest. John tried to put that out of his mind, glad that he didn't have to smell burning flesh and see shattered dreams going up in smoke.

Shattered dreams. He saw the sign for Portage, his home town, laying just off to the right on Highway 63. A part of him wanted to drive through the town and look at where he used to live. Going on 63 was a longer route to Richland however, and mercy decreed he put need before curiosity. He felt relief as he put Portage behind him, and still the strange surging excitement. Driving through Rice Lake, he was struck by how it had grown—new stores, houses dotting the rich farmlands; and now, Highway 8, with Weyerhaeuser on the left and Richland on the right. He felt the truck tremble as the heifer struggled, almost falling, as he made a slow turn. "Not long now my sweet girl, hold on pretty one," he called back to her, his voice heavy with foreboding.

His directions were good and he pulled up in front of the office. One quick look at his load told him to hurry, and he briskly entered in. The woman behind the counter rolled her chair to face him. John was silhouetted in the early morning light which flooded the office, turning her golden.

"Hello Sir, you must be Mr. Daniel Moyer—right on time, even a little early. You had a long drive, all the way from Douglas County by the lake. I am Eva Nielson." She stood and extended her hand to him.

John caught his breath. She looked Nordic, blond hair caught back to the nape of her neck. She moved with the grace of a willow wisp, her sky blue skirt flaring around her slender form, provocative yet proper in her long sleeve white blouse. He swept off his hat, the four leaf clover still in the band, and took her hand as he introduced himself. "Ms. Nielson, I'm pleased to meet you. I am John Chapman, workman for Dan Moyer. He stayed back on the farm with some sick livestock, and sent me with a Holstein heifer loaded in the back of his truck for your laboratory. She is living still, but not for long. Can we get her off this truck as soon as possible?"

"Of course! My brother will be helping you—he's been watching for you to come. When we got Mr. Moyer's request for help, he insisted our team try to diagnose the malady infecting your herd. It seems he once worked for your boss." With a nod of her head, she invited John to join her at the window to see the man inspecting Dan's truck outside. "See, he's by your truck already looking at your heifer and the best way to unload her." In the moment John stood next to the lady, he basked in her presence, inhaling her perfume, feeling like he had stumbled out of the depths of the rock gully forest into a sunlit clearing carpeted in wildflowers.

"I'd best get out there and help him," John stammered, tearing himself away, and out the door.

Three steps out the door, and John already knew the man. Coming round the back of Dan's truck, Dave smiled broadly, calling him by name. "John! Remember me?" he asked.

Indeed John had never forgotten him. Dave was the symbol of rage who lived just beneath the surface of John's memory—an eerie silhouette in lantern light bombarding the walls of the horse barn. The secret they shared was their bond. And he remembered again how Dave worked to stitch Lena's leg using the tools of a medic and the skills of a healer. Of course he would be here—it all made sense in the cosmic way.

"Dave—how are you man?" John said. But he already knew. Straight up pride was in Dave's handshake, the ease of honesty was in his bright blue eyes, and his smile lit up his handsome face like the sun through a rainbow.

"Good, John! And better than that! And if it wasn't my friend Dan who came driving up from my cloudy past, then it pleases me that it is you instead. I have always wondered—did you fill in for me with the plow, John? Ah well, let's talk of that later. We must get this poor animal off this truck! I'll show you where to go with her, drive along behind me."

Dave walked ahead opening gates so that John had access to the unloading ramp complete with sling and pulleys to swing an animal into the facility. He and Dave backed the heifer down—a great effort for her. When she stood inside, she stumbled around once and fell to her knees breathing heavily. Four men surrounded her, drawing samples of blood and other fluids, taking her temperature, listening to her heart and lungs. Dave suggested John go back into the waiting room while they attended to the animal. He said they would do what they could to save her. John guessed that wouldn't happen.

"Have a seat Mr. Chapman, while I brew coffee for us," Eva invited. "Soon we have another animal arriving, but for now this lab and everyone in it is working for you. Dan and I spoke at length over the phone about the symptoms exhibited by your sick cattle, but just a few questions to fill in the blanks—OK?"

"Please call me John—never, in the years I've worked for Dan, did anyone call me Mr. Chapman." John relished the idea that he would have Eva to himself for a few minutes. His heart beat a little faster, and he wished he had combed his hair. "May I use your bathroom to wash off Lakeland County mud Eva, and then I will tell you everything I know." He thought he would like to do just that, and wished he knew more to tell.

"Yes, of course, John. Do you take sugar and cream?"

"No, black, and I thank you." He noticed the counter held a bouquet of roses. "This office has a woman's touch. Did you grow these?"

"Yes, I have a fondness for English roses, sunny little faces with petals round and round like a cup of fragrance."

"My mother loved English roses too," John said. "I grew up pruning her favorites—let me see if I can remember— she loved the Victorian Castille , but her favorite was called the Sweetheart rose. It just exploded with little pink blossoms like fireworks on the 4th of July."

"You have a way with words, John." I'd love to hear more about your mother and her roses, especially since I also grow the Sweetheart rose, Cecille Brunner is the proper name some say, and now I have a new way to appreciate her."

John looked at himself in the mirror of the washroom. His hair was flattened beneath his hat, so he combed it back 'til it fell soft in a wave. His dark hair was mostly grey now. Time had softened his face, troubles had furrowed his brow, but his mustache was thick and his hazel eyes still had a spark. His heart was singing, and he had to remind himself of why he was there, and calm down for the business he must tend to. He took a deep breath and walked back into the room, standing tall, smiling, and self controlled. "I am ready for your questions," he said, and sat down facing Eva.

"John, our team will be trying to determine if your cattle are dying from anthrax, tic disease, shipping fever, poisoning or something else. We have had so little rain this year, plants that are already toxic, have a concentrated effect. Tell me more about the pastures your cattle graze, and I will relay that information. Because of what the men have observed so far this year, our team has already a suspicion that the answer to your plague lies there."

"Ah yes," John replied. This year is different, so dry and hot, that the cattle spend more time by the springs in the rock gully forest." The name Dan had given the woods at the top of the rock hill rolled off his tongue like poetry, and she seemed taken by it.

"So, there is water there—in your rock gully forest?" she asked.

"Yes, large springs bubble up from the hill, but no pasture to eat, only ferns."

"Only ferns," she repeated. Thank you John. Enjoy your coffee and some sweet bread to keep body and soul together after your long drive. I'll be right back."

John watched her without her seeing, all the way across the room and out the door, taking in her womanly curves, thinking the sweetness of her body was food enough to keep body and soul together. Dave and his sister were both lithe and graceful, maybe like their mother, like his mother too. He thought again about the roses, and in his mind's eye there floated a watercolor vision of a lady by a rose covered trellis—frail—ethereal really—and she spoke to him from his long ago past. His mother's voice speaking one of the verses she loved: "Tis at the edge of the petal that love waits."

He tried to keep her—but the vision floated away as softly as it came—on the scent of the roses. He approached Eva's bouquet like one intoxicated, as names he once knew, came flooding back to him. The Cardinal de Richelieu, the Empress Josephine, Celestial Musk. He touched the red rimmed white Leda, the painted Damask Rose, as his gaze fell on the dainty Sweetheart Rose dancing among the rest.

"Perhaps you recognize your old friends," Eva said, breaking his reverie.

"Yes," he said.

"I have certainly enjoyed meeting a man who loves roses! Indeed, the time was too short. Our team leader, Dr. Martin wants you to join him for consultation about the findings of our team. Please follow me to his office, John."

Down the hall they went—she, showing the way with a gracious manner, and no ring on her finger, he—hoping her warmth was flirtatious, knowing full well that he would follow her anywhere.

"Thank you Eva. You and your roses have added grace to what I feared would be grim news. I did meet Dave on Dan's farm years ago and I would like to visit with him before I drive back. I hope that you and I meet again."

"As do I," she said. She gestured at a chair in the empty room, smiled, and walked back to reception, leaving him wondering if she wanted to see him again—or wanted him to see Dave. Leaving him wondering—and the room all the more empty because she wasn't in it.

Alone, and with time to think, John wondered at what had just happened. How strange it was—this vision of his mother—the memories of her flowers—just then. It had been years since he thought about the roses, and indeed, felt the love he had for his mother. Instead, he had entertained memories of the war, bursting shells, fragmented bodies, deadly gas spreading through the trenches. It was like his memories were in layers and the lovely had been covered over by the hideous. And for the first time, John understood his love of poetry, his need to write the words so they spoke beyond their meaning, across time, as his mother had just spoken to him. With a start Dave's words sobered him. "Did you fill in for me with the plow, John?" Shaking his head, John thought it is all too much for me.

Just then he heard men's voices in the hall and the door swung open for Dr. Martin. With a quick introduction, the doctor presented his report. He had submitted it to Eva to type up, but delivered it orally to John.

"Mr. Chapman, first I must tell you the bad news, that in

spite of our best efforts to save her, the heifer you transported to us died minutes after arrival."

John nodded. "Yes, I expected that. We did the best we could on the farm she was raised on, but could not save a single animal that got sick," said John.

"You are not alone in that. It is virtually impossible to save animals once they show symptoms. Blood platelet transfusions, and injections of thiamine are possibilities, but prognosis is poor due to the huge dosage required, and on farms, it is not a practical option. The good news is that I have a reliable diagnosis to what is killing your cattle and a way to stop the dying."

"Many people do not believe this kind of news," he continued, "for cattle can get sick and die weeks after being moved to pastures without ferns. The poison is cumulative in the bodies of horses, sheep and cattle that ingest bracken fern. Certain animals, like this fine heifer you brought to us, become addicted to the fiddle heads and green fronds that flourish around wet lands, especially on dry years when pastures are dry and brown. It takes at least three weeks to build a deadly dose, causing internal hemorrhaging and anemia. Literally, the animal bleeds to death. Sometimes, there is difficulty breathing because the larynx swells in some animals and that makes people think it is phenomena or shipping fever.

If you stop at the front office, you can pick up a typed report to take with you on your return to your farm in Douglas County. Do you have any questions for us?"

"Yes," said John. "How do you kill the ferns?"

"That is the same question farmers have asked all over the world, for indeed the Bracken Fern is found in most climates. In Scotland, farmers will graze cattle heavily on ferny pastures for 2 weeks, and then remove that herd and bring in unexposed livestock to continue to overgraze the ferns. Spraying is dangerous, and not practical in the glades where the ferns grow best."

"Thank you," said John. "We will move the cattle off the high hill pastures immediately—especially now that we understand they are not going to spread a disease. And, I'd like a word with Dave since he used to work for my boss Dan Moyer. Dan always spoke well of him. Dan was a veteran, knew Dave was, and I am one too. I just want to be able to tell Dan something about how Dave is."

"Yes, well we were all in the great war were we not?" Said Dr. Martin. And Dave has finally made it home. He has a break before the next animal arrives, and I'll ask him if he will come by to chat—just give him a minute or two."

Before John could think what to ask Dave, there he was, saying the next client had arrived, and he must get back to help. "But John, I may have a mission in Superior, and I'd like to see Dan and Lena again. Send them my love will you? I've been promising my sister a diversion, a time away. She has had a tough time being alone after Walter dyed, and would love to see the farm with the pastures growing green that I plowed so many years ago. When you pick up your report, ask her when we could schedule a visit. She does all the scheduling at this lab. Until later, then!"

Eva had just finished typing the report when John reached the reception area. A man and woman sat on waiting room chairs looking anxious, and the phone was ringing. John waited with the others. When she had a moment, he approached Eva's desk, received the report with thanks, and then posed a question to her in a confidential manner.

"Eva, Dave said he had plans to come to the Superior area, and I was to ask if there was a convenient time for him to be away from the labs. He said he would like you to accompany him, to show you the farm where he worked for a time—Dan Moyer's farm in Lakeland County. He said you were the keeper of the calendar and would know the lab schedule."

"Yes, he knows we are soon to have time off." She indicated a calendar with notations. "We are not making appointments for half of next month because the doctors will be away in Madison for training," she said. "Dave has been speaking to me about a trip. He thinks it would be good for me to get away. I have an idea. I write articles for the Hoard's Dairyman Magazine. This would be the perfect opportunity for me to take pictures and write about your Rock Gully Forest—maybe call it Fern Gully Forest, telling about the bracken fern, its habitat and the dangers it poses to our livestock. Do you think Dan Moyer would allow me to do that? And, if he approves, would you show it to me John?"

The Day the World Ended

One day he just wasn't there. Lori was used to animals disappearing suddenly, only this time it was her big black work horse, Tom that was gone forever. She knew better then to ask, but Dan noticed her hanging around the horse barn looking forlorn. He confided in John that he had been offered a price "just too dear" and had to let Tom go. Out of longing, Lori began training Patches, a heifer, to be her riding horse, using just a halter and a rope for a bridle and reins. John made a surcingle from old harness leather, adding a handhold and he put it around Patches' girth. The training kept Lori busy, so she didn't seem to miss Tom so much.

One evening, while she was out in the pasture where the young stock were grazing, Lori surged with the excitement and joy animals feel when they are young, energetic and possessed by a playful spirit. "Beware of cattle at night," Dan had warned her many times, but Lori loved being wild like the animals. And wild they were. One look at Lori on top of Patches and the whole herd stampeded. Patches bucked and kicked up her heels, and Lori catapulted through the air like a missile, landing hard on unforgiving ground. Sandy warded off all the cattle that circled round to see why Lori was lying on the ground and not frolicking across the meadow. Protective of the very sorry little girl, who kept looking in disbelief at her mangled right arm, afraid yet knowing she must tell her mother, the dog stayed by Lori's side all the way back to the house. Lena was angry and upset, loaded Lori in the car and left for town. When they came home, Lori got out of the car sporting a cast on her right arm and complaining that she didn't know how she could play softball now, for she batted right handed. Lena summed it up for John, "just a broken arm," she said with a deep sigh of relief as she slammed the car door, and stomped toward the house. "Lori, your arm won't fit into your costume for Halloween," she tossed over her shoulder in a disgusted voice. "Its time you grow up anyhow. We will make some candy to hand out to anyone who stops by, and you will stay home and learn something about cooking and cleaning and leave the wrangling to John."

It was the evening of the 30th of October, 1938. John turned the radio on and proceeded to milk the cows to the enduring music of a noted composer of the day, Tchaikovsky. Music helped calm him, and the cattle liked it. He went to pour the milk into a can and when he returned, a dance band was playing. He paid little attention, rehashing in his mind the events of the day.

A weather report from the Government Weather Bureau; then back to the Meridian Room in Downtown New York Plaza, the orchestra leading off with the loveliest of all tangos, "La Cumparsita." John turned the radio up on his way to empty another pail of milk, just as Dan came in to help.

A special bulletin on the radio, interrupting the music, caught their attention, breaking the rhythm of their work. From the Intercontinental News: "Strange flares on Mars," said the Princeton astronomer, "like a jet of blue flame shot from a gun." The men paused to listen, but just then the music resumed, and Stardust Melody drifted through the barn, filling every dark corner with an ethereal bliss.

A car pulled up outside and Dan went to greet the Hakolla family from a neighboring farm, returning from a day-trip to church in the city. The Hakollas had heard rumors of an accident on the farm and said they had come by on their way home to see if everyone was alright. Dan related the story of how Lori had broken her arm while John stayed in the barn to finish up the chores. Their happy conversation and laughter drowned out the radio.

Lena came from the house, with Lori in tow, dressed nicely in a red corduroy skirt and white blouse, her arm in a cast. In her left hand she carried a bag of goodies they had made ready for trick or treaters, and she dispensed chocolate turtles to the two Hakolla children, Elias and Sophia, while Lena chatted with Esko Hakolla who, she knew, loved astrology. He was a great teller of the old stories and could have you believing that the northern lights were the reflections of the shields of the Valkyries racing across the sky on their way to their resting place, Valhalla. "We were listening to Edgar Bergen and Charlie McCarthy on the radio," Lena announced, "and they stopped for commercials, so I tuned to CBS and caught the news. Something strange is happening to Mars, and a Princeton astronomer, Dr. Pierson, was explaining it. He calls it a 'phenomenon'."

Esko Hakolla looked interested. "How grand it is that the radio brings to us the finest music and the latest advancements of science. I read that on any given day, there are 32 million people listening to radios in this country. I wonder how many other people are hearing this." Esko was warming to his subject. "Just think of it—we are able today to know about the goin's on in space! It wasn't long ago people thought the planets were gods. Mars was the god of war."

Esko turned his head toward the open barn doors. "I think

that's the report we are hearing now." He climbed out of the car and started for the barn—let's listen for a bit—Dan, do you mind? It looks to me like the chores are done, so can John, join us?" Lila Hakolla and Lena stood back, whispering between themselves and enjoying the entertainment. The children examined the cast on Lori's arm, petted Sandy and then Lori brought out her marbles and they began to play in the long hay aisle in front of the cows.

The adults gathered under the brown Bakelite radio that sat high on a whitewashed beam as Professor Pierson explained theories of the mysterious rings of Mars and what he thought the strange explosions signified. He called Mars 'a red disk swimming in a blue sea.' As he spoke, they heard the ticking of a clock in the background, which was the vibration of the clockwork in the Observatory. Breaking into the interview, came the report from a Dr. Gray of the National History Museum in New York, claiming that the seismograph there had registered a shock of almost earthquake proportions within twenty miles of Princeton. Professor Pierson thought it must be an asteroid—but probably not tied to the explosions on Mars. Bulletins came in from the Intercontinental Radio News in Toronto Canada of more explosions on Mars, and then came the news that a huge flaming object had landed on a farm in the neighborhood of Grover's Mill, New Jersey at 8:50 PM. The flash in the sky was seen for several hundred miles. A special mobile unit was dispatched to investigate. Carl Phillips, the eye-witness reporter described the strange sight as straight out of a modern day "Arabian Nights."

The Arabian Nights was a widely read book of 101 stories, and with its very mention, fans entered the realm of imagination, flying off on storyteller Scheherazade's magic carpet of fantasy.

John and the others listened spellbound as the land owner, a farmer, said "there was this greenish streak and then zingo! Somethin' smacked the ground. Knocked me clear out of my chair!" he said. Dan laughed appreciatively. Carl Phillips painted the picture of people pressing in around what looked like a yellowish metallic cylinder, half buried, and emitting a hum. The crowd was silhouetted by the lights of cars spotlighting the enormous pit, listening to scraping sounds growing louder. And then, as the top turned off the cylinder, the reporter's voice rose in horror. There were sounds of the crowd crying out, and his description shot through with fear and emotion poured across the radio waves, deluging listeners in a grotesque portrayal of an indescribable face, tentacles wriggling up and out, black eyes above a V shaped mouth, rimless lips dripping saliva. The state police brought forth a flag of truce. Carl Phillips bellowed in response to a high rounded shape rising out of the pit, topped with a mirror spewing flame that struck the men head on. The crowd screamed and he shrieked the word "fire!"-as a towering inferno caught the woods, the barns, the gas tanks of automobiles, everywhere in sight, in blazing whistling thunder, and then, an eerie silence.

Admitting to circumstances beyond their control, CBS broadcasted explanations from scientists around the world and then came the sad news that over 40 people lay dead in the field at Grover's Mill, burned to a crisp, including Carl Phillips.

In 1937, a year earlier, the great Hindenburg dirigible burned, and the newsreel commentary recorded the disaster. Now, a year later, this calamity, was even more horrifying. General Montgomery Smith announced the deployment of the New Jersey State Militia and declared Martial Law. The office of the Red Cross announced they were sending 10 units, and firefighters in several counties combined their services to quell the flames. Piano music was broadcast to fill in between bulletins. Captain Lansing of the signal corps, attached to the state militia, reported that eight battalions of infantry surrounded the crash site. Seven thousand armed men closed in on the tub in the ditch as low lying smoke crept up from the woods bordering the Millstone River, as the soldiers donned gas masks. The entire broadcasting unit of CBS arrived to cover the battlefield.

John stepped closer to the radio, his face was white, his expression fierce. Esko gave Lila a hug and Dan embraced Lena, hugging close his little girl. The men moved closer to John at the radio, to listen. Lena reached over and took Lila's hand. "We should pray," Lena said in a firm voice. "Come children. Lila and I are going to start praying right now and you men come join us, when you've had your fill of blood. We will set up our own little church right here in this barn!" The women scattered straw by the calf pen, and laid out a rug kept to drag calves on. Lena set horse blankets out for the children tucking them in, humming softly to "All Through the Night." She sent Lori to the house to get her favorite book of fairytales while she sang what she thought would be calming.

Guardian angels God will send thee,
All through the night

Sophia was suspicious. She wanted to go home. But little Elias loved to hear about Snow White, as Lori read to the children, while the calves behind her, already laying warm together, snoozed away. The little children soon were fast asleep. Lena sang the last two lines

I my loved ones' watch am keeping,
All through the night

Then Lena knelt down with Lila and they petitioned the Lord to have mercy on them. Lori wanted to go listen to the radio with the men, but Lena told her to stay with the women and pray hard for peace in the world.

In the center of the barn, the three men tried to absorb the devastating news. Despite the overwhelming odds of the infantry and the helplessness of the Martians in Earth's gravity, the battle turned deadly as an alien fighting machine reared up on tripod legs from the pit. With the militia obliterated, the news sank in that the world now faced an invading army of Martian war machines from multiple cylinders. Emergency response bulletins gave way to damage reports and evacuation instructions as millions of refugees clogged escape routes.

Sandy's barking brought Dan away to welcome in more neighbors. He, as Town Chairman, was the official that would make decisions for the safety of the local community. Other women joined Lena and Lila in prayer. The talk was of protection and survival. All the families had guns and knives with them. The barn was to be the place of last refuge as they planned to make their stand.

Meanwhile, John was left to listen alone to the grim news on the radio. Three Martian fighting machines, with the help of others from a second cylinder, flipped power stations, toppled bridges and destroyed railroads, tossing engines like toys. The Secretary of the Interior, sounding to John much like Franklin D. Roosevelt, urged calm resourceful action. He spoke of what must be done: "confront this adversary with a nation united, courageous, and consecrated to the preservation of human supremacy on this earth."

It was all happening so fast! John had no time to examine his feelings, but there was about him the air of a warrior. As he listened to the gunners of the 22nd Field Artillery located in the Watchung Mountains—heard the firing of the big guns and the last word, "fight" as the black smoke overcame them, he was living again what he had lived through in war—all so familiar. There came the transmission from the army bombing plane, V-8-43, Lieutenant Voght commanding eight bombers, reporting to Langham Field—planes circling, ready to strike. A thousand yards—eight hundred—six hundred, and the arm raised from the machine below—a green flash spraying flame—two thousand feet and the engines gone—diving on the enemy machine." John stood with eyes downcast, jaw set, as the reports of carnage continued to pour out over the airwaves.

Dan came back to stand by John. They heard a news reporter broadcasting from atop the CBS building describing the Martian invasion of New York city—"five great machines" wading across the Hudson River, poison smoke drifting over the city, people running and diving into the East River "like rats," others "falling like flies"—until he too fell victim succumbing to the poison gas. Dan turned away, swearing softly, hastening back to report to the men outside. He wiped his nose on his sleeve, his eyes moist with tears. "I can't listen to this anymore," he said to Lena as he passed her and the other women on his way out to the brisk air of the October night, leaving John to stand alone with the war. He heard a lone ham radio operator calling "2X21, calling CQ... Isn't there anyone on the air? Isn't there anyone on the air? Isn't there.... anyone?"

There was silence; long enough for John to feel the despair in the voice. Then, just when he thought it was over, a commentator identified the broadcast and the network:

"You are listening to a CBS presentation of Orson Welles and the Mercury Theatre on the Air in an original dramatization of "The War of the Worlds" by H. G. Wells. The performance will continue after a brief intermission. This is the Columbia Broadcasting System."

"An original drama—a presentation," repeated John. He turned away from the radio, and for a long moment he stood, stunned, as the meaning settled in. "It's a play! It's not real!" He spun around and sprinted up the aisle calling to the kneeling women. One of them leaped up and ran outdoors to tell the men. They came in and gathered round as the play continued. The women, wiping away tears, gathered with the men to listen. No one believed it was a hoax at first. But, as they listened to the monologue following intermission, and realized it chronicled the recollections of a survivor over time, they knew for themselves it was a Halloween concoction, the equivalent, as Orson Wells himself said at the end, "of dressing up in a sheet, jumping out of a bush and saying, "Boo!"

Dan switched off the radio, disgusted. He turned and faced everyone. "Guess they fooled us," he said, "and we should be glad it wasn't real; but I for one, am mad."

"Yeah—they should sue that CBS. I could have had a heart attack over this—this bad joke!" exclaimed a blue haired grandmother. Lena's cheeks flushed red, she gathered up Lori and stomped off for the house saying she was too mad to talk, "what if John hadn't heard the part about it being a play?" She just shook her head when someone offered, "Praise the Lord for answering our prayers—surely a miracle!"

At that, Esko said some Finnish swear words under his breath for which Lila gave him a sharp poke in the ribs with her elbow. Mostly, the men just shook hands with Dan and went back home in embarrassment, saying they'd see him at the town meeting next month. One man said this was the most excitement since the buck deer attacked his wife last year, and that he'd start target shooting in case of a real invasion.

"Let's call it a day, John," said Dan. "Be sure and turn off the lights when you leave, would ya?" He left muttering to himself that he should have known.

John switched off the lights in the barn leaving the starry night to illuminate the velvety blackness. On the way back to his cabin, he looked for Mars in the sky. He saw a thousand twinkling lights and the Halloween moon—God's lights. When he looked toward Lake Superior, he saw it, crowned in the lights of Superior and Duluth—the lights of humankind. He breathed in deeply; glad the air was fresh and cold, untainted by deadly gas. On this unlikely day, he had relived a war of the worlds. The radio program teamed up with his imagination and his memory, to trigger once again the desperation, futility and grief, until he was empty of war. It was as if the poison gas in the trenches of his memory had blown away before a sweet Chinook wind and he relaxed into it, letting the illusion of control slip away. As he visualized the prayer meeting, the men plotting survival, and he by the radio; there came from some unused place, a rusty chuckle. Unchecked, it sprang into a tentative laugh. He did not stifle it. Soon, he was doubled over with the ridiculousness of the scene in the barn, and of his own serious nature. It was Halloween and the trick had been played, and the treat was this insane hilarity carrying him away. He surrendered to it, and laughed until he cried, and that night he woke several times laughing. Later that night, reliving the unlikely day in his dreams, he thought maybe he heard God laughing too.

A North Woods Welcome

Grey bottomed clouds tumbled themselves black and blue in a wind-swept swirl toward the big lake. It was just at that moment that the low sun lit up harvested fields turning them amber set among emeralds. Smacked with sunburst, the wind stopped, and there—just then—the Nash Rambler emerged out of wood smoke, crunched flame-colored leaves, and a fog of burned oil to park, unannounced in front of the horse barn. No barking dog, no friendly greeters. Dave the driver gestured toward the loft above, explaining something to his passenger, Eva. They both sat awhile, Dave taking in what the farm had become with the passage of ten years' time, before he jerked the door handle and flung the door open, asking Eva to wait in the car. He heard Lori singing before he saw her. She suddenly burst out of the machine shed screaming unheeded commands to the lamb chasing after her. The girl and sheep buck had been playing "climb up, balance and get pushed off" on a pile of planks, terrorizing mice out of their homes, to be snapped at by a collie in full hunting mode. Chagrined and embarrassed by her dereliction of duty, Sandy charged to Lori's side, and managed a small woof. The unlikely trio stood staring at the man who seemed to have dropped in from nowhere.

"I might need to make up to your guard sheep here," laughed Dave. Bucky was making little head butts like he was practicing to charge. Clearly, he considered this girl his and didn't want to share. Sandy was looking the situation over before making up her mind. She sniffed. Dave was a blend of English Leather and lavender soap, gasoline, gravy, sweat, tobacco, and motor oil. Manly he was; he knew how to court a gal, and he set to winning Sandy over "slow handedly."

Lori looked up at him and took in his hat—the very one the Lone Ranger would wear, and she was as impressed as any nine year old would be. At 15 she would have thought he was cool, like John Wayne, or maybe felt the reckless bravery in the man, like that of a marine raising the flag over Iwo Jima; at 20 she would have likened his blond good looks to Alan Ladd playing Shane, and at thirty, she would have melted in eyes so like those of Paul Newman. As he straightened up, his over-sized silver and gold trimmed trophy belt buckle caught Lori's attention and she drawled in awe: "Wow—are you a cowboy?"

Dave smiled a toothy smile that deepened the furrows framing his mouth. "I'm here to find real cowboys. You wouldn't know where there are any would you?" Lori motioned toward the Dutch doors by the milk house and sped off to show the way. Dave kept a wary eye on Bucky who lowered his head to show his horn buttons as he trotted by. Finding a treat at the feed room, Bucky soon forgot all about the stranger on his heels who was now entering into the other-world of the dairy barn.

Excited, to see his old friend, Dan set down two pails of foamy warm milk and ran to embrace Dave. "Man you look great! Good is never late they say, so you're just in time for us to celebrate!" Dan exclaimed, clapping Dave on the back. "Come up to the house for a bite to eat. Lena has been fussing all day to bake your favorite bread." Casting his eyes about he asked, "And where is your sister? You promised to bring her, and we all want to meet the lady who took you in—you rascal you!"

Dan gave Dave a meaningful look. He then turned to John who was standing nearby watching this warm reunion. "John, would you mind finishing up—get Lori to help you, and then come on up to the house. Lena wants you to come to dinner."

John nodded. "Lori, you can go on up and help your mother if you want to, and I can feed the calves," John said.

"No John, I'd rather help you." She was already running to get the calf buckets as the men headed out to the car where Eva would join them. When she returned, John was more firm. "Lori, your mom will want you cleaned up and dressed for dinner. She will want to show you off to Dave's sister, Eva. Skedaddle now—and save me a place at the table," He called after her.

John was glad to be alone. The calves bunted each other, frisking in fresh straw, so eager were they to slurp down their evening meal. As John finished chores, the bustle and smell of the barn surrounded him in familiarity like a downy quilt on a cold night. He levered the stanchions open and let Sandy usher the cattle out to the night pasture while he stood quietly by Goliath's pen watching them go. The angry bull demanded to be let out. He rubbed against the massive boards, shook his head, and bellowed threats to John. Sandy raced back to provide protection to John, and he spoke to her, ignoring the raging bull. "He doesn't like being a bachelor, does he girl? Ah well, I know how he feels, but what to do about it? Shall we see, my pretty girl?" He hastily rolled the barn door shut, threw some hay to Goliath and headed to his cabin to wash up and change clothes.

A short time later he emerged from the cabin a new man. Walking briskly past the outhouse and woodshed, along the tree lined path to the main house, John admired the last bit of sunlight across the fields, now dotted with deer. He smelled Lena's red rose bush blooming again. *Of course-a bouquet*, he thought. He cut roses, daisies and buttercups, adding some cedar sprigs for the color and fragrance of the deep woods— then up the steps with a bound; letting himself in the screen door to the mud room entrance. Lena spied him from her kitchen— steeped in the aroma of roasted wild game, fresh bread and cinnamon apples. "Come in—come in John! Oh what a lovely bouquet. It will be perfect for our table." Lena produced a cut glass vase, "from Germany," she said with a nod, arranging the bouquet expertly as John watched, suddenly feeling clumsy in the white enameled kitchen. He noticed fresh rosebud wallpaper and remembered Dan telling him that Lena tried to wallpaper over stains on the wall for she would not tolerate imperfection. Yes, one area was darker, maybe in a different light. Shifting from one foot to the other nervously, he thought of important things he should probably do out at the barn, and was about to excuse himself when Lena called for Lori. "She'll show you into the screened porch. Go right on in and join the others"— handing the bouquet to him— "and put this on the coffee table, will you John." Lena gave him an encouraging hug sensing his shyness as she shooed him out of the kitchen. Lori, freshly combed and wearing a dress, bounded down the stairs into the living room. She grabbed John's hand. "Come on John—see, I fly my planes from up here. My favorite one got all the way into the dining room," she announced, as they passed by the white enameled staircase. I'll show you later. I make them myself." Lena's piano, a Baldwin covered in burl wood stood near the entrance to the screen porch. Lori whispered, "Mom says I have to play the piano for everyone while she gets coffee served out here."

Misgivings fell away with Eva's animated greeting. "Roses—please set them here by me," she said. "John, these roses are the final touch of welcome to the north woods. Dave, you never told me about the brightness of the flowers! Do you suppose Dan, that the lake has something to do with it?"

Dan laughed. "When Dave worked here, the only flowers we had were white clovers. Truth be told, it's only lately that Lena got a rose bush. 'Roses are the smiles of prosperity.' Dan quoted from some mythical unknown. Lena has a rose bush 'cuz she nursed a sprig given her by a friend. The big lake breathes on the flowers here, and they hurry to make a grand show of themselves before they are covered in snow. Colder by the lake, they say. Yes, the lake changes everything."

Lena brought in her blue enameled percolator and the room warmed with the smell of her strong coffee. "Let me help you, Lena." John said, jumping to his feet. He felt better being of service than being waited on. He passed around a platter of braided raisin bread drizzled over with powdered sugar icing. Everyone broke off a piece, still butter-melting warm. In the living room, Lori was playing Fur Elise on the piano. Mosquitoes covered the outside of the screens as the night edged in—chilly black bewitched to silver by the full moon rising. "Its good sleeping weather," Dan said. Eva excused herself to help Lena in the kitchen leaving the men to man-talk. John watched her go, memorizing her grace, the flounce of her skirt, the smell of her perfume, enchanted by the magic of the evening, as the words "good sleeping weather," like the moon, lit up his imagination.

Dave smiled at John, as if reading his thoughts. "Eva is looking forward to touring the rock hill with you tomorrow John. She wants to take some pictures of the woods knee deep in ferns for the article she is writing. And, I think she wants to learn about this place where I found work before I came to Richland. I was lucky she took me in—me being on the run and in the condition I was in."

"Yeah Dave, well it must have been the horse she saw was worth it." Dan said. "If you'd like to tell it, I for one, would like to hear your story—how your life took a turn. You left here hell bent."

Dave rose to the task. He stood and walked around the room, looking out at the yard. His blue eyes took on the look of Lake Superior's deep water and his voice rang rich with meaning.

"Hell bent you say Dan. When I came to you, that was my intent—my hope was with the fires of hell—that there, maybe the memories would burn away. You set me plowing with Nell. Every day I kept that plow buried in the red clay ground, focused on the curl of earth over the shear. I sweated buckets and Nell spattered the ground with her lather; me inhaling the scent of dank, new ground, covering over, covering over in neat straight furrows. But the ghosts were in the trees of the Lake Woods—stuck dying in the branches I dragged away, reflected in the water of the marshes I drained—oozing out of the clay. Was it blood that made the waters red? And after a day of it, could I get tired enough to sleep? I would cinch that with some booze from the still. Could I drink enough?"

Dave sat down and looked right through the listening men to something beyond. "But with night, they found me—the faces—the body parts—the screams. So, I threw things at them until I couldn't anymore, and I'd finally fall down in a drunken stupor that let me rise up in the morning and do it again. Sometimes, when I got quiet, I'd hear Nell in the horse barn below me. She would be nickering to me that she was there. Lord how I loved that horse. Solid. Calm. Trusting.

But she was flesh and blood, muscle and bone. The stench of dead horses on the battle field reminded me 'it's foolish to love something that bleeds and dies. What could you depend on— what lasted? Was it all quick sand? Yes, hell was welcomed—or maybe blessed nothingness. What would that look like—nothingness I mean? Would it be colorless?"

John listened gratefully. He had never heard a man talk like this—put words to his own tortured existence after the war. Somehow, Dave knew this and set his gaze on John now as he continued.

"So, it began here on this farm— in the woods eating berries, venison and Lena's bread, working to exhaustion each day with the horse, letting animals and the good earth sustain what was left of me. I was clearing land, breaking ground for a new crop and now I know—for my own new life. There was power to change things for the better in every red furrow. I made a difference—had a purpose. But at night I slid backwards until I could see the open gates and hell's fire calling for me. I was thinking more and more of putting a bullet in my head and just marching in, like you said Dan, 'Hell bent.'

"Then, one night, I shot a deer, dressed it out and hung it to age from a tree. You know in the northern chill, a deer hangs a week before it's cut up. Every day, I saw it hanging there and it began to speak to me. I thought I was crazy now for sure—but I listened—like I listened to Nell when I got quiet in my mind, and I began to think somehow that that deer was called to me, the hunter. Like magic, the knowing came through that deer that I was going to be leaving soon and I must be ready. I brought you the meat Dan, remember? And I ate some of that deer. His soul was in me now—the wild wanting to live. So I cleaned my gun, packed my gear, and that medic bag I got to use on that last day here. I was ready however it came down. On that day, I no longer wanted to be dead with my buddies and my enemies, and I chose to carry it forward—life I mean. Like you carry forth the flag or the torch—or like a deer flags it's white tail as it bounds off into the wilderness. I had it in me, and when I joined together with something—like that roan horse I rode out on—I felt it, that *something* that is not lost, cannot be destroyed. Call it spirit. Do you know what that feels like—spirit I mean?"

John thought about that and the image of his beloved Sam came to him—service impelled beyond endurance—by a love beyond comprehension, all wrapped in silver and gold. But of course he said nothing. It was not easily told of, such a thing as spirit.

Lena and Eva came into the room inviting the men to the dining table. John was hungrier than he had thought, not for the food but for a full helping of Dave's words. Dave graced him with a smile. "Later," he said. "We'll talk later." John was seated across from Eva. She sat next to Dave and it was like a family coming together or a circle being completed that had been missing a piece. Lena said the grace and they ate the gifts from the bounty of the Lord. So good, so filling. Amen.

"Tonight Dan, are you making me throw my roll down above the horse barn like in the old days or, with John agree-ing, might I try out a real bunk house?" Dave asked. "How about it John—want a room mate?"

"Dave, I'd be honored." John replied. "And I'd like to hear more." He bit his tongue before he said what about. He knew Dave knew.

John watched Dave and Eva interact. He saw her touch his arm sometimes, including him in what she said. Lena in-sisted on waiting on everyone, bustling back and forth from the kitchen, bringing out the foods she and Betty Crocker had created. She too, touched Dave on his shoulder as if she was being sure he was real; and she served him before the other men as if he was her miracle man.

Dave expressed his deep gratitude to both Lena and Dan for welcoming him into their home and for giving him a chance by hiring him years ago. Then, with farm family zeal they devoured wild partridge in raspberry sauce, buttery mashed potatoes pooled with onion gravy, spiced apple chutney, green beans and white bread. Dan praised Lena enthusiastically for the meal saying, "Food is a good workhorse!" "And Dan is a good shot!" She added.

"I'm glad that I worked for you as you were finishing the big barn," Dave said. "My space above the horses was cozy enough while your little dairy herd shared that barn. But the writing was on the wall for me. I knew you'd be moving the cattle into the dairy barn when it was finished and I'd have to move or freeze. Although, if I'd stayed longer, I might have spent some nights above the cattle in the finest dairy barn in all of Wisconsin—right John?"

Lori, displaying the manners of the day, had joined them at the table quietly, and was managing to keep still.

"How old are you now Lori?" Dave asked.

"I'm almost ten," she said.

Dave looked over at Lena who blushed and excused herself "to bring more gravy," she said.

Looking thoughtfully at Dan, Dave said "I've been gone from here over ten years. The Richland labs took a chance on me for sure. Of course I'd never have been able to get that job without Eva's help; for she worked there from the beginning. My first duty was cleaning the barn—whatever needed doing that most of them didn't want to do. When Eva saw how I lived, she insisted I should go with a friend of hers to a group meeting. The guys there were mostly vets, and all drunks, like me. That's where I began to get beyond just surviving. Tomorrow, I'll be going to Superior to meet with a group forming there. That's how I am staying sober and getting sane—by taking in help from those who've been there, and giving back to others what I've found to be true for me."

Lena came back with more gravy, saying "leave room for cherry pie." Dave whistled appreciatively.

"Tomorrow, I'm leaving Eva here with you Lena. Can you teach her to cook like you? She's an artist with words and pictures, not so much in the kitchen like you Lena, huh Ev?"

Eva elbowed her brother playfully. "Dave has been living on burned toast and deer jerky, barely managing on my food, Lena. If you spent full time teaching me, you'd soon be discouraged, for I love tending my roses, writing and photography with little talent in the kitchen; but like Dave, I do love to eat and this meal was a feast." She slid back her chair. "Cherry pie? Let me help you serve it," she offered. "That I can do" She rose and began picking up dishes. "Shall we make room on the table Lori?"

John thought how smart it was of Eva not to compete with Lena. In her kitchen Lena was the queen. As the women cleared the table for desert he stole looks at Eva and imagined she glanced at him too.

After dinner, Eva spoke to Lena volunteering to work in any way helpful, adding "and then I'd like to take some pictures on your rock hill." She turned to Dan and asked "May I borrow John to show me the areas where the cattle found bracken fern? Last summer, when he brought in your sick animal for diagnostics, he told me ferns were plentiful around the springs on the hill."

"Eva, we had a pistol hot summer that burned our fields,

but the springs were overflowing green on green. Its no wonder the cattle took to eating ferns last summer while they cooled their feet and drank the sweet water. Like you said in your letter—maybe pictures from our rock hill in the Hoard's Dairyman can help other farmers from losing cattle to the fern. Besides, John you could use a holiday, right? What good is the pipe if its not played upon!

Lori my girl, would you like going to the Park with me?— Eh Lori? You can look for dinosaur eggs in the cave behind the waterfall. Want to come Lena?"

"No thanks," Lena replied. "I've got a new recipe to try, and shopping to do."

"How about if you come with me then, Lena, and you can drive my car shopping in Superior while I have my meeting," Dave suggested. "OK with you Dan if your bride takes the day off between chores?"

Dan chuckled at being asked. "Lena'll not be kept asking permission of me to do anything she wants." You do have all those bundles of things to give at St. Vincent's don't you Lena? And you know you like to shop there too."

Before Lena could decline, Dave delivered the deciding argument. "Lena, I don't know my way to the part of Superior you are speaking of; but I think our meeting is next door to St. Vincent De Paul's. Please come along and be my navigator."

With plans set for the next day, John thought he should excuse himself and let everyone visit. But Dave wanted to join him. "John, I'd like to have a walk around —especially, I'd like to have a good look at the big barn. When I wasn't plowing, my main attention went to stumbling my way to the still on the hill. I'd appreciate you walking with me."

"Yes, go you two," Dan said. "I've got a speech to work on, with elections coming up soon. Besides, John knows this farm better than I do—don't know what we'd do without him. See you in the morning for breakfast. John—you come too."

As the two men stepped off the porch together, Dan snapped on the yard light, saying "Welcome back to the north woods Dave. Enjoy the night."

THE POEM OF THE WARRIOR

THE YARD LIGHT WARMED THE FACES OF THE BARNS IN A SHIM-
mering golden circle as the men, walking round, first looked in
at the machine shed, to admire the Case tractor, the combine
and bailer. Across the courtyard stood the horse barn with
its loft and lean-to enclosure now occupied by young stock.
Beneath the vast star spangled sky, it looked small, overshad-
owed by the looming dairy barn before them, it's massive form
glowing dark red and white. Above and behind, the harvest
moon made a diadem of the cupolas and cedar shakes, playing
"Misty" over the gambrel roof, as if it were a keyboard, and
on the horizon, shone the lake, pulsating to the lights of the
Duluth/Superior harbor, dancing in the fog in a silvery dress.
Dave took a deep breath of the damp chilled air, pulling into
himself the magic of the night.

"So now its later John, and we can talk man to man, like
I promised" Dave began. I always felt bad that I never got to
know you when we lived on the same farm. Let me tell you
best I can why that was. I've figured it was 'cus I always knew
you. You had the look—like army surplus was stamped across
your forehead—only it would read war surplus wouldn't it?
Did you know I watched you? Maybe 'cus you resembled
someone I knew from then, in the trenches, wary, waiting
for incoming, like the whistle from the train pulling into the
depot two miles from here—remember? Couldn't it set your

hair up straight and your hands to trembling though? Yes, you were too much like my buddy from back then for me. Everything was too much for me. I needed cover. It was like holing up behind a wall that had been shot away and "they" were coming for me. How to hide? Where was I safe? I kept the animals with me and worked in the woods and far fields—but that whistle, it came through everything like a bullet through body armor. How about it—you had to hear it John. Did it get to you too?"

"Like the wails of a banshee," John agreed and instantly felt a little embarrassed. He wasn't used to talking about these things, but Dave had flung off the lid on a trunk full of memories, and spoke unashamedly of his fear. "Yes—well a banshee is the Irish hag of the mist." John explained, "I thought Dan's Irish tales had got to me—you know—the Irish live in shadow lands."

"Ah—and so do I," said Dave. "And I'm thinking you too, when you've seen too much and can't get back to the before."

"Can't get back to the before," John repeated and looked straight at Dave.

"No—there is no way back, you are not the same."

By now they had entered the barn. John flipped on the lights and they walked the limed center aisle to the sliding rear doors. Above them, Whinn's Chippewa charm tinkled alive as the herd bull Goliath lurched his shoulder against the wall in his haste to rise. His mean little eyes glared at Dave who dared intrude upon his domain. He began to paw up his straw and shove along the floor to cover his head in war paint.

"Once you've crossed over—its like you are in no man's land between the living and the dead. You can stay in that place or follow after those of us that died, or find another kind of way—a back way forward to live again. It's hard to explain, for we are soldiers, you and I, and fighting is what we are trained for. We learned to kill, and to hide from being killed, but no one trained us in how to surrender, give up hiding and come out." Dave was about to roll open the doors to look toward the lake woods where he had once worked, but he stopped in surprise hearing the jingle bells above his head. "Tell me about this decoration Dan has hanging here," he said. "Those are Indian tomahawks aren't they, and what are they doing hanging above the rear doors of this dairy barn?"

"You remember Whinneboujou don't you Dave? Did you ever meet him? He is Dan's old time friend—the blacksmith who helped him move the house down off the rock hill with his mule team. Whinn found the old tomahawk on the hill and he made the other one from stone and wood. He made them into this charm. The one tomahawk is the fighting kind; the other is for digging up the dirt like a hoe. And you hear that sound? Whinn made tobacco lids into a hip bracelet for Lena. The Indians would sew these into a jingle dress and dance for children and rain for crops. The tomahawks are for Dan, since he was in the Great War, and also was trying his hand at farming. Whinn knew the materials to make this barn came from the rock hill so this was his barn warming gift—a kind of blessing from the tribes who worshipped on that hill. Whinn said it was for fertility and good luck to counter all Dan's bad Irish luck. 'He needs all the protection he can get' Whinn even now is fond of saying. And I made the fastening to put it up. I am thinking I should give it a once over to be sure its still up there secure what with the bouncing around it takes from this big bull."

Dave rolled the rear doors open, then stood silent before the sight framed and set off as it was—with Indian symbolism. Goliath, who had so recently been peacefully bedded down, now rubbed against his four walls growling his anger, sending belligerent roars out into the blackness to the cows in the night pasture. Jingle music jangled a warning as the barn shivered before the bull's power. "I'll just shut the doors again and let the bull settle down. Sorry to disturb you big fellow. John, I'm glad I don't have to deal with him. He looks big as a tank and just as deadly. Show me the loft. That would be my favorite place—safe from the bulls of this world—high above it all—a great place to hide out."

John switched on the lights in the dairy barn loft, and motioned for Dave to climb the ladder up through the tunnel of hay. They stood quiet, then headed across foothills of hay to the mountain-like platform that formed the ceiling to the mezzanine grain storage rooms. Another ladder and up-top Dave turned a full turn, looking up, down, and out, and whistled in appreciation at the massive landscape of hay he had just crossed, the illuminated courtyard before him, and the tracery of beams, doubly intricate with the shadows from the lights.

"Ah John, this barn is a piece of art and to think you had a hand in finishing it. Do you spend time here or just come to level the hay and fork it down?"

There it was. John could have dodged—the escape was a given. But, he answered Dave with the same kind of honesty Dave had displayed as he shared his own story.

"The truth is Dave, I could just as well move in here. It's my own cathedral and feels more like home than any place I lived since the war. I think it's the opposite of the trenches and here—well if there is a God—I can almost hear him speak to me. Or maybe it's the wind around the cupolas setting the weathervanes to spin. And in a storm—not even the battlefield (flashing white and cracking-the booming canon pounding through—armed with fear that blasts the gates) not even the battlefield can equal the show from this place."

"Yeah—I get it. After living in the trenches, I get how you and me would climb up to be above it all. The smell. Remember the reek of the war over there: rotting carcasses in the thousands. I heard there were over 200,000 killed on the Sommer battlefield alone, the latrines that were always overflowing, even the smell of our poor dirty feet, and always whiffs of poison gas, the stench of stagnant mud and rotting sandbags. And the stinking antidote was creosol and lime, and all of it was misting in the muck. Yeah—I'd climb up high in that loft above the old horse barn, like you here, to get away, somehow get above it. The rats. How I hated the rats—some big as cats. I saw men go mad trying to kill those rats. A single pair could produce over 900 offspring, so what was the use of it? But a man'll start shooting or use his bayonet and go berserk to try to kill off the rats."

Dave stopped talking, and turned to John. "Ever go off your head John—you know—lose it—go wild?"

"I don't know. I got headaches—couldn't remember anything—just like my head was about to bust open—and that's how I went crazy. I embarrassed my wife and family when I would disappear not even knowing where I was. And then, if I got angry, I scared them—even scared myself. I finally left home and came here. It was better here, less pressure (safer, quieter-so I never jar open the cage where the Wildman lives) just work. And, she found someone else."

Dave glanced at John, saw his face illuminated by the yard light below, and they shared a moment of silence that summarized years of isolation. He decided he would tell more of his story.

"John—I told you I had been trained as a medic. My job

was to go out into the combat zone, do what I could to pull together the injured for travel, and somehow get them to the field hospital. Down in those trenches, the fire-steps kept the guys on the stretchers dry when they got flooded, but try to get one of those stretchers full of hurt up out of a six foot deep trench without having your head blown off, and then across open ground all in the dark. You remember how the shells lobbed in. Random shots—and one moment you were talking to your buddy and the next you were talking to where he'd been. Well, I took to fighting back. Want to hear about it? I mean—do you want to hear how I got friendly with ole Crazy Dave?

"Sure Dave—go ahead if you feel like you can. I'm a good listener."

"Yeah—I can, for I tell this story in my groups. It gets easier each time, others hear how I have surrendered to who I am, and they get freed up to do it too.

It began on one of those trips back with a load of wounded. There was this tree—or it seemed to be one. I hadn't noticed it there before, but there it was spread out onto the trail and a man was lying there in the rubble. I stopped for him, did what I could for him. He was a sniper working out of that fake tree and he had hit a German officer before they gunned the position. He was dying, and at the last, he gave me his gun and a poem. I have them still. I learned that it was written by Julian Grenfell, a sniper and a poet, who trained many snipers before his death from wounds in battle. I memorized some lines from the poem—for they were written just for me, I thought. Now I know, it was written for all of us—all of us. And though I kept it all these years, it was only when I shared this poem that the words found me, and I felt safe with myself.

And when the burning moment breaks
And all things else are out of mind
And only joy of battle takes
Him by the throat and makes him blind

I practiced with his gun, and found the soldier in me that kills. I became a deadly shot perhaps better at killing than at saving lives. In battle, there is certainty. Afterwards, it drops away. Afterwards, nothing makes sense. Except that the last lines of this poem—when I shared these lines with others who know, like you, John, the words gave me peace and the strength to live with that side of me.

Through joy and blindness he shall know,
Not caring much to know, that still
Nor lead nor steel shall reach him, so
That it be not the Destined Will.

The thundering line of battle stands,
And in the air death moans and sings;
But Day shall clasp him with strong hands,
And Night shall fold him in soft wings.

John said the sniper's poem made sense to him. He gave up his bunk house to Dave and spent the night in the loft of the barn where he thought about the evening and planned the day ahead. Finally, he wrote his own poem, thankful for a journal where he could put his thoughts out where he could see them, change the words around, control the meaning, and finally acknowledge what he feared was true.

Wildman

I keep a monster in a cage
The lock is caked with rust
Hefty bars enclose its rage
The key lost in the dust
It reeks of war, will not be tame
I loath to set it free
'Tis awful but it calls my name
I fear the thing is me

Mother Carey Will Be Plucking Her Chickens

"If I could only write the words to catch this view," she said.

He nodded. "I often climb here just to see the whole of where I've been living and working these last ten years. See—the barn is like a castle don't you think, and below her the feudal lands where her peasants slave."

John and Eva were walking the trail up along the face of the black rock, breathing in the splendor of the morning. It was the last feast of nature—a grand Thanksgiving festival. Fall laid out yellow-gold poplar, flamboyant maple and purple maroon sumac, on a bed of amber, russet, and forest green, while overhead charcoal clouds tumbled in an azure sky. A bittersweet melody swayed the slender white birch and danced through red berried mountain ash. The pine scented air had a bite to it, the winds sang a warning—WATCHOUT—gather wood and lay in matches by the stove, for winter is coming, the time of withdrawal.

They walked briskly. He wore his best shirt; the one Lena had ironed for him, and gallantly carried Eva's camera equipment. She, wearing a white blouse with rosebuds stitched on the collar, had a notebook to record her impressions. When they reached the twin white pines at the top of the hill, the last remnants of the great forest that once covered the hilltop, they stopped to look back.

"I think the farm looks like a patchwork quilt from up here. See its calico, velvet and silk pieced with homespun, all tied and embellished. And see each piece is joined in to the center medallion. I'd call the quilt "Bountiful" and it would win first prize at the state fair in Madison. I'd like a picture of it from here for my article, John."

John handed her the camera, his mind a-flurry with sensations she had stirred up. He tasted satin, heard tassels, and there flashed before his eyes, scented brocade undulating to a woman's swaying hips—other women—other times— lusty appreciation for a woman's company? It was intoxicating, so he sat down on a mossy rock to watch Eva at work.

She wanted facts, so he sobered up from his reverie. "What crop did you grow in that long rectangle along Moonshine Road," she asked. "It looks blue around the edges."

"Ah well, the blue is the flax we missed cutting—an early crop and pretty. They use flax for oil and linen and Dan likes to mix it into his dairy feed. He read everything he could get his hands on about what could bring up milk production in his herd. He said he was out to make a record."

"And I think flax blue is as close to divine as is possible— one of the only truly blue flowers, and cultivated for 5000 years," she informed him, but he was dazzled by her eyes, sure they were even more blue and divine than a whole field of flax in mid-summer sun.

"Look John, the cattle are like black and white toys from here, marching along in a line toward that woods—and am I right that the fences are all of stone?" She sounded impressed.

"Yes," he said, glad she was interested in a subject he knew something about. "Every rock was hand-picked off the fields to be built into walls for the half-mile lane from the night pasture gate to the Lake woods. Dan wanted his herds to access the white clover pastures he'd cleared there. We grew peas on the bordering field, a bumper crop this year, which we hauled off to be processed by Wilderness Foods."

John got up and touched her shoulder lightly as he pointed to the various squares below. "That's the field Dave, your brother cleared. And left of that is our best ground, limed, fertilized and planted in alfalfa with timothy as a cover crop so to stay hardy longer. The cattle grazing there are our young stock, knee deep in the 3rd crop. The other two crops were harvested and stored in the barn. All the fields and what's in them feed into that barn down below. I am proud to have helped build her."

"And well you should be," she demurred.

Her fragrance drifted over him, and he retreated to his rock, tipsy over Highland Lilac, and pleased by her appreciation.

While she busily put her camera in its case Eva began to fill John in on a little of Dave's history from before John arrived. "It wasn't like that when Dave first came here. There was just the old barn and the land was all stumps, rocks and bramble. He tried to work in the timber camps but his drinking made him a danger. He told me that he owes a lot to Dan who hired him and gave him space to live and work and fight his demons. He even credits the plow horse! But when he came to live with me in Richland, he still drank and went a little crazy sometimes."

She paused, considering her next words. "Did he tell you about the group—mostly veterans—that he meets with? It was like a miracle when he found them. He finally found some peace."

John sighed. "Peace. We fight to get peace—strange—I

never thought of it that way—this warring to get peace, and then, for those that fight and even kill for it—for those soldiers there is no peace."

Eva examined the blackened stump from an ancient white pine, commenting on its massive size. She spoke as she caressed the old wood. "Can you imagine what it must have been like here before they cut this forest, ghost walking on pine needle paths under the great canopies? What stories happened here—who can tell them now?"

She sighed. "The logging companies made a kind of 'no man's land' of the virgin forests, a bit like the remains of a war here. Dave likens his group to Dan's stacking and burning the slash; then turning the earth over so the sun could shine in, warming the soil, growing crops. He says that's what the group is for—those who know and suffer from the horrors of war, lay out the memories to those who have the kind of experience to hear them, and the energy burns away the pain—the sun shines —like love remembered, and the crop that grows is peace."

John looked up at Eva, a little sad, and rose to stand beside her. "Dave says I should come to his group—that it would help me too. But, Richland is too far to go and I am needed here."

She acknowledged the farmland below with a sweep of her arm. "Yes, it's hard to leave what you have created." Then, with sparkling eyes, she presented words like a gift. "But, maybe you will change your mind. Our farm in Richland could use a real manager. I confess, I have let it go since Walter died. I work away from home now, and only grow roses in my yard."

Gazing off into the distance she seemed to be speaking her thoughts aloud. "Writing for Hoard's Dairyman gives me the chance to meet people, like you John. People doing real work, dairymen mostly, who love to build with their hands and are after the latest science for the industry. The Hoard's Dairyman is a gathering of ideas and personalities put together into a guide for Wisconsin and the world. I like to think we're impacting farms for the future."

She whirled around and exclaimed, "Aren't we lucky you and I? We get to enjoy our best efforts. I can have tea among my roses as I read over my own article in an international magazine. And here we stand to admire your work, your art, lucky and grateful for the chance to use our talents and see the fruit of our work."

John took a deep breath. Lucky was not a word he would have chosen to describe himself. This woman was spinning golden threads all around his world, gossamer bridges back to his mother's rose gardens, and rainbows, arching to possibilities he had not dared to dream.

As they walked on, he turned the word "lucky" over in his mind. Images of luck flashed: Dan's four-leaf clovers, Whinn's jingle dress, and an image from some deep dark place he had buried with his friend from the war. The medal of St. Jude that Tim wore around his neck. He hadn't thought about Tim in all these years—or maybe the memory was heavy on his mind and he had not entertained it out of fear of the pain. Strange—that pain was worse than any wound. Undaunted like a worm, it tunneled up, this image from his memory. He knew the time was coming now, the medal danced before his eyes. It would not go away. When they stopped by the spring where fern's grew, Eva took pictures and John sat on a rock and held his head while the medal, freed at last, teased at his perceptions.

Eva came to sit on a log facing John. She looked at him closely before she spoke. "You seem a million miles away," she said.

"Eva," sometimes I get fragments of memory—" His voice

drifted off.

She didn't speak right away. What she would say called for her best thinking. When she replied, her voice was gentle. "Do you want my theory about that?" she asked.

He looked up at her—her face softened in empathy around blue-violet eyes that called to him. "Yes, please," he said.

"First of all, John, I don't deal with the mind straight on—in stories, poetry, song, visions maybe, for the way I find to get in, is around back or from the side. So humor me for this round-about way I want to talk to you."

She began with a question. "There are many rivers near your home town—right?"

John thought about the elation that rose in his throat as he had crossed over them on his trip to Richland. "Yes." He recited a litany of names—all music to him: the Nemakagon, Flambeau, Eau Claire—"Yes of course, and I loved to canoe them when I was a boy."

"Well then, picture canoeing the Nemakogon—her sandy shores, deep fish-filled pools shaded by the trees and the sun sparkling on the blue waters. Then, around a bend, you are drawn into bad rapids where you run into a rock that breaks your canoe, spilling you out. You wash downstream, almost drown, but manage to crawl up on shore. The prettiness of the river above the bend is forgotten—only the terror stays. Like a dam on the river, fear stops the normal flow of memories. And you sit streamside, alone, and paralyzed with not remembering. Only, over time you begin to wonder where the river goes. The dam begins to dissolve and bits of your canoe sneak through, floating down to you. Like fragments of your past they wash down to you. You catch them and begin to put your vessel back together to go on. But do you trust enough to push off?"

"Safer to stay streamside" he said, waiting for more of the story.

"Yes, safer. Only a fool would leave, says your mind." But you told me you loved to canoe, not sit streamside." They say there are only two emotions—love and fear. To get back to what you love, you must trust again. That's where others can help—others that have learned to do that. They come drifting downstream just in time to help you float your canoe and push off. The river brings them drifting along with the memory fragments. Together you have the heart to go on."

John, thinking that his solitary life best fit the man he was, all but dismissed the tale Eva had conjured up for him. "I'll remember your story, at least," he said. He stood and extended his hand to help her up. "Let's walk down to the corrals where Dan and I treated the heifers poisoned by ferns. We lost 11 of our best Holstein heifers last summer. Dan has lost heifers other years, one or two, not many at a time, and never knew why. It has to have happened to others here in Wisconsin, but our local vets were not aware of the actual cause. The article you are going to write can make a real difference."

As they toured around the corrals, John described how they had isolated and treated the sick animals, all to no avail. Eva took pictures there, and they walked on toward the river as John continued. "Those were terrible days, losing so many cattle—not just that they died in spite of all our efforts, and having to bury them not knowing why they died, but it all took a big bite out of Dan's dream for this farm, and I don't mean just monetarily, though that was huge, but it wore on Dan that somehow, it was all his fault; caused by his wanting to set records and have his cattle be the best.

"The heifers, all the finest we raised, were here on the hill to be mated the first time with a black bull so as to calve easily.

And then they would be mated to the new herd bull Goliath. We came daily to look at the cattle, and most times, the black bull was waiting at the gate to lead us to where heifers from his harem were sick and dying. Dan said he was the messenger of death, and like 'Mother Carey plucking her chickens,' he was the petrel of bad times ahead."

"What do you mean, Mother Carey who?"

"Ah, Dan from his Irish ways, told me of Mother Carey, the name came from Dear Mary, the Virgin Queen of the seabirds, and all earthly creatures. So it was that the Irish credited her with plucking her chickens when the snows came, and the storms right after. Seabirds, thought to contain the souls of dead sailors, were long sacred to seamen, for they showed the way to safe harbors on land. Birds called Stormy Petrels found along the Northern shores, especially in Ireland, gather before a storm. They, like their namesake St. Peter, seem to tiptoe across the water. Mother Carey's chickens, the petrels, signal bad times, and that black bull, a petrel to Dan; like I said; the messenger of death. "In the barn," Dan would say, "bought and paid for by greed, there stands in Hannibal's bull pen, the new bull Goliath, the golden calf, the cause of it all, the image of evil." "So much worse than a financial and emotional loss, Hannibal's daughters dying, here on this hill was a bad omen to Dan, and I confess Dan's superstitious nature must be contagious for I also worry about the mature cows and the calving season to come. Dan had such high hopes and now they have turned sour and he wants to sell the big new bull. Strange how things happen."

"Do you think things happen by accident John?"

John didn't answer for awhile. They had traversed the top of the hill all the way to the river and now stood to look down at its canyon cut through red shale at the edge of the black rock. A deer with half grown fawn twins stood motionless hiding in the river cedars below—watching and waiting—as if for an answer.

Eva glanced at John, wondering if he had heard her.

"I don't know," he answered. "Dan would say everything is planned out, and he would find signs all around him to the way things would happen. Lena would be sure God was pulling the strings and bolster-up her praying for favors. Lori—well she is full of fairy tales. Me? I don't know anymore, though I did once sure enough. What do you think?"

The doe slipped away without a sound, her fawns bounding after her with only a flash of white tails. Eva watched, and answered with a question, "Does the deer find her way by accident—sure footed even at night through the brambles on a whisper of a trail, jumping fences she doesn't measure? And the swallows! I watch the swallows around our barn at home, diving after mosquitoes and missing each other or some solid thing by a feather. It's a marvel to be able to think that fast. Our best pilots in our best planes with all the best instruments can not maneuver as well as the swallow. So how is it done? Its 'built in design' I think. Don't you guess we should have it too? And coupled with our animal brains, we can scheme away with plans we think out. I do wonder where does the desire that fuels those plans come from? I don't think it comes from having everything good and easy. Poverty and strife might be reason enough. Hmm, it's something to ponder; but for me, one thing is sure. It's not by accident. Its like a big play and we all have a part in writing the script if we follow our director out onto the stage."

John liked her answer, and a thrill ran through him tasting of excitement flavored by fear. He liked standing there with her; felt like they were in a theater and the curtain was being drawn open. He could almost hear the curtain call. He wanted to reach over and wrap her up. Of course the music would propel them like the swallows in a dipping, diving dance. He didn't care where the desire came from; he wanted to act on it. He was about to reach over and take her hand when a sharp breeze blew up the river canyon, rustling leaves, setting the birches to sighing. Showers of golden leaves filled the air and tumbled down around their feet. "We should be getting back," she said, and she reached for his arm.

John and Eva walked the trail down along the face of the black rock, breathing in the splendor of the day together. The world around them swirled with fall's colors. Overhead, a long V of geese sounded their way south to a warmer place. John wanted to go with them. As if she knew his thoughts, Eva took her cue from their summoning song. She said, "Do you think Dan could spare you from the farm for a weekend with us? The farm house has room, my roses need pruning and are begging for your expertise, and Dave would love to bring you to his group. I'll tell him I asked you to come back with us."

John caught his breath. Hadn't he been a good soldier—marching along to the drum of someone else's tune? But suddenly now, the chance to slip out of the ranks and set his own course had been offered to him. More gaggles of geese flew over, headed for the Mississippi flyway, disappearing into the rolling grey clouds, some so high only their excited voices told of the journey they were on. He looked ahead at the face of the barn and noticed the swallows were gone for the winter. Departed. Soon Mother Carey would be plucking her chickens. Unfamiliar ideas were forming up in his mind—a new configuration led by a new thought. He wanted to leave. He wanted to go South.

THE NEW SONG

DAVE WAS AT THE WHEEL. JOHN SAT IN THE SEAT BESIDE HIM— "the guest and the man," said Eva as she settled herself in the back seat. The engine started and Dave switched on the radio. John sat still, listening only to his mind racing. How had he let himself be convinced to leave the farm? Now, it was as if someone sat on his shoulder reminding him he shouldn't leave, reminding him of his responsibility, and the easy way he fit in there. John looked back once at the barn as Dave drove onto the main road—saw her "widow-alone" on the horizon, and he felt guilty, like he was leaving a wife for a lover. Panic swept over him. He had become set into the landscape of work, and now he was stepping out—being part of something new. He could feel it happening. Like someone takes a root bound plant out of a pot and replants it into one that is too big for the old familiar space, and now the plant is going to have to set out roots and explore fresh soil, and forge new life, or die.

They had seen something in him—these people. Dave had come back for him like any good soldier, and was expecting he could fit into a group, but John feared he had kept his own company so long, it was too late. She—what was she seeing? John felt her presence washing over him in waves; he caught a glimpse of his face in the window and remembered trimming his mustache that morning looking critically at the face he had almost forgotten. Off to one side—just beyond, he heard the girls that were his long ago classmates giggling, making eyes at him. They thought he was handsome; he knew he was—then. Ida drifted across his mind, she warmed him in the sunrise of her smile—Ida who he loved at first glance. She had wanted him—then. But, he recalled disgust and fear in her eyes as the love clouded over. Panic. He could almost hear something calling after him—back there by the spirit rock, he heard "come back," the call of an old love "where you belong."

Listen— the whir of the tires up off gravel onto concrete, picking up speed going south, leaving the land where whispering reeds grow tall through cushions of moss, thick with brambles. The highway follows the trails of the voyagers thru the great north woods, river to river, along paths so deep in pine needles, that moccasined feet once stalked shadow silent like haze amid ghostly sentinels, or cedar incense adrift over the red rivers. Breathe in the mist off Lake Superior. And look there—a deer stands in yellow leaves watching from a grove of white birch. Hear the wind through almost bare branches, "time to go."

Look—now the rivers run clear between banks of sand; see the heavy arms and crooked black fingers of the live oaks tumbling rusty copper leaves onto flat green fields, squared out and cultivated. Beyond are hills all tamed and civilized with fences and cross fences holding cattle basking in fall's last sun.

Hear the tires speeding south, and with each mile, the call back dissolves more and more in a melody hummed by the tires, and the scent of the woman in the seat behind John spins his senses, until he can't remember duty.

And then, as if she read his mind, Eva reached from the back seat and touched his shoulder as she said his name. She had that about her—that she touched when she spoke some-times. It was a kind of contact he had forgotten, or maybe never knew, but it made his heart sing. It was as if he was surfacing from having been stuck in the cut-over swamp of desolation. Utter loneliness sucking at him, like the unre-mitting mud of the trenches in France. And then—with that touch, in that moment he knew—she was pulling him out and up, into the light. He took a deep breath of courage before he answered her, then turned to see her behind him, giving her his full attention.

"John—there's the new song on the radio. Listen. Lena gave me piano music for this song. Dave, turn up the radio please."

"Somewhere Over the Rainbow" lilted from the small tinny dashboard speaker of the old Dodge. Eva was singing along when she suddenly stopped short. "That's the lead song from the Wizard of Oz, and it's playing at the theater in Rich-land right now. Let's go tonight!"

Dave teased Eva. "I have an idea; you can make dinner for us instead. You know— practice cooking—improve your do-mestic skills? And then you can play the rainbow song on the piano in place of me spending money to take us to a movie. Besides, I don't have time anyway. John and I are going to the Richland group tomorrow so I am working tonight. I've got to get pens ready for cattle coming in tomorrow to the lab. Seriously, why don't you and John go?"

"John," Eva put her hand on his shoulder again, sending more shockwaves. "Are you a fan of the movies, John?" Dave winked at John supposing he would not have had the opportu-nity to go to movies; and at the same time curious to hear how John would get around going to see a children's film.

"Dave, the last movie I saw was "Torrent" with Greta

Garbo—a silent film! But this one— "The Wizard of Oz" —
what a story! Little Lori asked me to read all the Hans Chris-
tian Anderson and the Grimm's fairy tales to her, and told
me the stories herself as we did chores. I read Frank Baum's
book, Wizard of Oz to her! Eva, I'm primed for it, and I know
that this year, the movie won the Academy Award along with
"Gone With the Wind." I would enjoy it if you would like to
accompany me—my treat. Dave, I could help you with your
work and you could still get to the movie on time I am betting."
John's sudden burst of enthusiasm was surprising—even to
him; but he couldn't seem to help himself.

"Nah," Dave chuckled. "Now if it had Scarlet O'Hara
instead of a Kansas farm girl, well let's just say Vivien Leigh is
worth the price. Nah, you go John, but take care Eva doesn't
get you to following some yellow brick road lined with roses."

Eva bubbled with trivia about Judy Garland, the star they
would see that night: that she was one of the Gum sisters but
changed her name to Garland, and that she had been born in
Grand Rapids, Minnesota, a small town to the northwest. The
lively conversation about books and movies, alternated with
Dave telling more about the group he would be introducing
John to. Anxiety began to descend upon him but John steeled
himself against it and determined that he would not allow
tomorrow's worries to rob him of the enjoyment of this day.
And since he was not driving, he let himself settle into his
role of 'the man and the guest' as Eva had called him. There
was little he could do about it anyhow, being the passenger
in Dave's car, but when they pulled onto the drive of Eva's
farmstead, he saw quickly how his role could change.

John looked first at the barn which seemed to be just as
Walter had left it 5 years before, the side door was ajar and it
was leaning a little in that direction, as if looking for someone

to come back and care. The old roof had a dip in it and was missing shingles. Its red color was never the shining mahogany red of Dan's barn but had been cheaply coated in a russet red matte that was now silvered and threadbare. Out dated machinery sat haphazardly about, deep in weeds. Ancient history contained the better days it had seen. There was no grand drive leading up to the barn; just a path—a bit meandering—as if whoever made it was not keen on getting to the chores needing done in a barn. They pulled up in front of the house just beyond. It was a blue haired Victorian, transparent white with age. Wisteria barged up a trellis and draped heavily over the porch, threatening to take over the entry. Rose bushes lined the brick walk, and John thought of Dave's warning about following Eva's yellow brick road. He almost mentioned it, but thought better of joking about what might smack smartly of truth.

While Eva made dinner, Dave took John on a walk about the yard beginning with the apple orchard on the stream bank where startled white tailed deer, at first wary of the stranger, soon went back to stealing apples, standing almost upright to reach the sweetest ones. Dave picked up an apple as they walked on to approach the barn from the other side. John saw the horse barn lean-to with an upstairs loft apartment. An old roan horse came running to Dave nickering, nosing his jacket for the apple he had hidden for him. "That's home for me," said Dave, gesturing toward the loft. "I never want a big house and as you can see I've never taken much to farming. I worked for Walt and Eva when I first came here, but I was still pretty messed up; doing a lot of drinking; so I lived out here. After he died, I straightened up some. Eva had to get a job, and when she landed one with the labs, that was when I began to get back to doctoring. That was when I started to meet up with some of the other vets, having in mind more than just getting drunk."

Dave hesitated, weighing his words. He looked at John straight and said, "Eva's made up the guest room in the house for you, but if you feel like you want more privacy, after the movie, come out and switch on the light here by the stairs. When I get home, I'll see it and stay in the main house. If the light's not on, I'll know you are snug and good with the guest room over there. Whatever you decide. Eva has had a long alone time, and maybe you too, so you can talk the night away as they say. I have a friend of my own on the other side of town and know what its like." Dave grinned at John who said nothing but noted the positioning of the light switch should he want to use it.

THE GROUP

Dave introduced John to the group and each of 9 men acknowledged him. They exchanged the briefest comments about where they had served during the Great War. Most of them had been with the American forces while John had fought with the British, so it was unlikely he would have seen any of them before. John's service was the longest. Place names, battle names, like old songs drifted into memory, and looking around, John did recognize each man. Twenty years ago they could have been the boys he had known come fresh into the horror that was routine. Trench warfare was a kind of reality that aged them overnight—a wasteland filled by feelings too big for their minds. They knew the slipperiness of the duckboards in the trenches that kept them from sinking into bottomless mud, the fat rats in every shell-hole, and the thunder of the guns setting up for attack. They all knew the relief of a bath and a change of clothes only to find that lice eggs buried in every seam, hatched out after clothes were warmed by skin.

Dave had gotten training as a medic and joined in with the Canadians at the end of 1916. John doctored the animals, Manny set explosives, Joe was a sniper, Allen was trained with the Lewis gun, Jack cooked for his men, Ted maintained the howitzers. They held jobs of vital importance over there, some twenty years ago.

When they arrived home, people shrunk away from them—from the vacant eyes, and the ghosts on the shoulder of each one. They were mangy, missing limbs and teeth, some dressed in animal skins, some slept with their rifles, and they didn't talk about the war, but wandered, lost, like aliens in the world they had longed to come home to. Stalled in the mud of isolation, each alone struggled to regain faith in anything that put meaning to their lives. With these groups, Dave was playing on the brotherhood they had known, to which all else paled. They were joining up again in a new kind of war that survivors fight, finding a way around the mountain of death onto sacred ground, guided by the love and respect of fellow soldiers.

The group met for 3 hours every week. They had been forming up for two years now and had discovered a way to include a new member. John was only visiting, and that was the way most of them had entered in. He had to tell a little about himself and then could sit back and speak only if he wanted to. No one was required to talk—in fact Joe had not said a word for most of the two years. He sat looking off toward the wall, only his eyes indicating he heard and felt. Allen seemed to tear-up almost immediately, and his shirt collar was wet the whole three hours. They are like different ways a person reacts—each one functioning as a part of the whole thing, John thought. He wondered what part Dave played and guessed he was the heart of the group. Another man, Manny, saw the humor in things. John guessed that was the only way to survive setting charges. John thought he might share his memory of the way men like Manny had helped win the war.

"Manny—were you there when they blew the tunnels under Messine Ridge? I got to see that and I'll never forget it."

Manny brightened "Tell us John," he said. What was it like?

I know they said the blast was heard all the way to London.

"Yes John—what was it like for you? asked Dave. "All of these men except you and I came into the war after that time."

"I saw it," John began, "well, and felt it too—we all did. The German trenches were made so well—heavy reinforced cement that we couldn't budge with years of shelling—but budge we did that day. Well, the trench life had been going on for years and not much movement forward, but at Messines, they planned to blow the German trenches so we could get past them. And so the tunnelers began to dig in January. The sappers dug a warren under the ridge. They told me later there were maybe 5 miles of tunnels under the Glory Hole. That's what they called the place below Messines Ridge."

John had not planned to talk, but he could not contain the memory, and the words flowed out of him—words he had never found the place to share in two decades.

"They were sappers from the coal mines mostly—come from New Zealand and Brittan, Ireland and Wales. They were special to have the nerve to be underground, though some said it was better there, quieter at least, but the Germans were digging too and trying to blow up our tunnels. Some tunnels were combat tunnels where they met the enemy face to face fighting with bayonets and guns underground. Some of the shafts were down 100 feet. The sappers had special ways— like they put a water barrel into the ground and then, with an ear in the water, they could better hear the Bosch above them. Then, in June—I'll never forget it."

John stopped talking—the hush brought the attention of the whole group to him as they sensed the intensity of the experience. No one pressed him, but it was as if every man held his breathe. John began again—his eyes looking at something across the room. "It began in May—our heavy guns bombarded the ridge for 18 days. Day and night the thunder, the deafening roar. When they stopped firing, the quiet fell on that place, louder than the guns was that stillness. The Germans were sure we were going to attack and set off flares to light up the battle field. For 20 minutes, it was like daytime though it was still dark. Jerry had been gathering for weeks to repel the attack they were sure was coming. When the guns stopped, they rushed to get into their bunkers to kill us storming their ridge—like they always had been able to do before—like they slaughtered our horses in a wall of bullets and target practiced on the bodies of our soldiers caught on their wire. And there they waited in that terrible silence."

Unknown to John, tears coursed down his cheeks as the spectacle unfolded. "The charges were set to go off together and they sandbagged the tunnels so the thing went up under the German lines, under the bunkers filled with troops. It began with a rumble and the earth trembled like a quake. I couldn't believe it—it was beautiful and terrible—first it was like a great fist pushing up the ground and then a tower raising up —maybe 300 feet high, all of sticky earth, and the blast up its center making shells of the ground itself, exploding mines—the force beyond my telling of it. It was like the sun and moon came together, and the brightness was hell's fire in the sky. 10,000 German soldiers and the whole top of the ridge went up." John's voice dropped and he looked back at the group—no shame in his voice. "We stormed up the ridge after that, the tracks of our tanks filled with gore, and we moved the line forward. For Germany, I think that it was the beginning of the end. I had my friend's medal on, and took the hill back like I promised—I fought for him. Didn't we all fight for our friends..."

John dropped his eyes, his voice trailed off. He had mentioned the medal and his friend—things he never talked of. He remembered, in another kind of explosion that took his breathe away—the dog in the trenches. The men were never to touch or disturb the dogs that carried messages. This one had raced by him on the way to the dug out headquarters and shortly afterwards came back to him the medal and the note from his friend. The eyes of the group brushed across John though no one looked at him, no one spoke and everyone knew. The memory was consecrated in silence. John would share when he was ready. It was the code of the group.

When the three hours wound down, Dave ended the group as it had begun—with a prayer for peace. They disbanded to their watercolor lives, the tamed reality of fashion and pretty people, where they must keep the beast asleep in his cage, rough feelings in chains. But they would meet again, and John knew he would be back—he knew he belonged with these men. He was not alone after all.

REFLECTION

EVA DROVE JOHN TO THE BUS STATION, LAMENTING THAT their time together had literally flown by. Lingering until the last call to board, both of them loath to say the final goodbye, Eva impetuously leaned forward and pecked a kiss on John's cheek. John let go his bag and caught her lithe body to his own and drew her face to his, eyes penetrating deep into her soul. All the longing, all the loneliness, and all the heartache of his self-imposed exile flamed forth desire and he pressed his mouth into hers, savoring the sweetness of it, recklessly drawing her tenderness into his manliness; mingling, kindling and bursting into a new thing that defied his comprehension.

"All, aboard!"

They were jolted back to reality. Abruptly he pulled away, picked up his bag and giving Eva one long, emotion-filled look, swung up the steps of the waiting bus. He hesitated and turned before the doors swung shut and shouted "I will write to you!"

"And I will write back!" she promised, tears wetting her lashes.

His eyes were locked on her slender frame; skirt billowing, one hand pressing the crown of her hat with its wide brim fluttering; the other raised in farewell, until her image blurred and disappeared from the unwashed dusty window. He sat back in his seat, glad there were few people riding the Greyhound that day. He didn't want to talk to anyone; instead he wanted to sort out what had happened—what was happening. He felt so happy—like someone had brought him a bouquet of flowers and he had inhaled the fragrance and it left him powerless and giddy. He let his memory play over that first evening with Eva. On the way to the movie they had talked and laughed as young couples do. The movie, he realized, summarized his life after the war, and he pondered that a bit. But soon his thoughts drifted back to Eva. They had wanted to talk about the film so they went to the President's Bar and Grill for a bite and a drink. She wore a black skirt tight over her hips with a flounce at the hem and a red blouse open at the neck. He ordered a whiskey sour and she an Old Fashioned. She asked if he was glad to see the end of prohibition and he said it made no difference to him, except that it changed the traffic past Dan's farm. The dance hall at one end of Moonshine road had been painted yellow by the Ku Klux Klan and the still at the other side was mysteriously destroyed, meaning traffic back and forth between the two entities had finally ceased, as had robberies and unsavory conduct. John said he was glad enough (but what he was really glad about was the spellbound expression on her face as she sat opposite him, her lovely face like fine china in the lamplight).

In good spirits, they headed home; John driving. When he helped her into the car, her skirt fell away showing shapely legs and delicate ankles. John held Eva's hand all the way to the door, and of course he was invited in. They had coffee spiked with rum and laughed a lot. When she carelessly brushed against him as she served his coffee; he couldn't help but notice the creamy whiteness of her breast that his hand could just fit around. When she bent to pick up the napkin that had fallen off his lap he was further enticed by the curve of her hips and instinctively took her in his arms lest she fall. From there, it would have been easy to drift off to her bedroom where he would slowly undress her, and they would explore each other's hidden mysteries. But standing between John and Eva was Ida; reminding him that he was half a man, good for nothing. He had left his post. And as much as he wanted—needed Eva, memories and the labyrinth of trench warfare barred his way. He had to reconcile himself to his past before he could have any future. Oh, he was on the right road. He knew that he was, but Eva was not a way station, she was a destination. He was bound and determined to get there; and that meant walking out of that house and out to the barn alone. So, with every ounce of resolve he could muster he backed away, pressed her hand to his lips, and said "You give me reason to hope." She thanked John for the wonderful evening, as he picked up his hat. Knowing everything had changed, they stood a long moment lost in that space in between called bliss, before he let himself out the back door, trudging heavy feet the short distance to the barn.

Arriving home later that night, Dave saw the light on and stood for a moment, gazing up at the stars and remembering his own way back. John still had a ways to go, Dave knew. And deep down, grew an even greater respect for the man who thought enough of his sister to hold himself in check.

Bits and pieces of meaning infiltrated his reverie, and John tried to catch on to them, as impressions of Eva ran in trickles between thought like rain washing over an upturned face. Still, he needed to get to the place where the pieces came together. The group of veterans, it was clear, were all trying to get back to being themselves—like Dorothy in the movie wanted to get back to Kansas. How strange that Eva had suggested they see that particular movie, where everyone, The Tin Man, the

Scarecrow and The Lion all had the same shortcomings that
he thought he had too; and they all possessed what they were
seeking all along, but they only found that out by joining up
together on that yellow brick road.

John let his mind wander undirected for awhile, and gazed
out the window at Wisconsin spinning by—a blur of colors and
images and sounds, the turn-off to his home town Portage, the
road sign already passed, now the whir of the wheels on the
bridge crossing over the Namekagon River; see the silver arc
bending below him, and now only the road out ahead going
north. The yellow brick road; in the language of fairy tales—
was that life, do you suppose? For a little, he put himself on
the yellow brick road and thought of each of Dorothy's companions on the way to Oz.

I am The Tin Man, John thought, alone and abandoned,
immobilized by rust. Yes, he had walled away his heart, trying
not to feel the pain that comes with love, keeping his salty
tears inside where they rusted him solid. (An image flashed
of the veteran in the group, his tears oozing out unbidden.)
But on the yellow brick road, The Tin Man got oiled up by his
friends and could hit the road with them. That oil—was that
love do you suppose?

I am The Scarecrow, John thought, remembering how he
had scared his wife and children and disgraced his family. Yes,
his mind was blown before the force of feelings too strong to
think around; his thoughts scattered like straw in the wind of
the civilized world where his actions and experiences made
no sense. (Again—images of the group, their knowing arms
outstretched to receive with compassion, the shameful and
secret burdens that blocked the minds of their fellow travel-
ers).

Follow the yellow brick road. Arrive in Oz—where everyone wears green glasses to protect their eyes, from what? From flesh and blood reality—the kind of rawness that is too frightening and needs to be sanitized, from death itself—the illusion of loss, and the need to think for one's self. Better to depend on Oz to do the thinking, and stay off the road—it's just too dangerous.

His mind turned to Lori, startled to realize he had been traveling for quite a while now with his own farm girl from Kansas; and every childish tale she had shared with him had taken him toward truths he could not only teach to her but learn himself. Ah, the wisdom of the stories! Even as old as he was, he was still learning what they meant; like in Grimm's fairy tale of Iron Hans when he tried to explain poverty to Lori and realized he was living a life of poverty himself. That story still haunted him; there was yet something more that he needed to learn from Iron Hans the Wildman. He thought of the third companion on the yellow brick road, The Lion.

I am The Lion, John thought, the beast who desperately wanted courage, while his nature contained something wild that made him king of the forest. That was the very thing that had scared him and Ida—the uncontrolled streak of wild deep down inside of him— was that about courage or just about being crazy? Was the way forward to embrace the monster as a part of him—even call him out if need be? Far from the battlefields of France—was there a task needing that savagery? Did he, John, have the courage to fight for what he loved; or for that matter, even dare to go after a new life?

John sat back looking out the window at the changing landscape as they entered the realm of Lake Superior. The rivers ran red, the birches waved from islands of bright yellow leaves, a "welcome back," and the fields became clearings where he saw deer browsing. Filling the horizon ahead, the lake held the ghostly purple hills of Minnesota curled in her fingers of fog, and, as he fell under her dominant spell, John also felt his dreams being captured and contained. He sighed the sigh of a man who knew freedom was something you claim—not just earn. Soon he would be settled back on Dan's farm with its big red barn full of those needing him—wasn't that what home was—being needed? Or was it somewhere over the rainbow? And did he need to go looking for it? Did he need to follow his expanding dreams out onto that yellow brick road that Dave had teased him about? Silently he replayed the melody, halting at its last line. "Birds fly over the rainbow—why then, oh why can't I?"

THE SPACE TO MATTER

LENA GAZED OUT A FROSTY UPSTAIRS WINDOW AT THE DAIRY herd huddled together in the fir trees trying to stay warm. Still stewing about the argument she'd had with Dan earlier that day, she quickly donned a mackinaw over her dress, wrapped her head and neck with a wool scarf and braved a bitter wind. She neglected to put on boots, reasoning she would make quick work of bringing the cattle in. "She fussed to Sandy about the weather turning bad, stoking her anger with Dan for his having neglected the cattle in John's absence. Propelled by impatience, she slipped and slid along on her way to the barn. "Sandy," she said, "Dan took off for another County Board meeting and left his work undone. John's gone and Lori's in school—no one left but you and I. Doesn't that just beat all, Sandy? We have to do everything ourselves. We would freeze to death on this farm if we waited for them to show up. Let's go get the cows! I'll bet they're anxious to come in and they'll come a-running."

Lena hated things left half done. As she hurried, she thought about John's budding romance with Eva. This was his third trip to Richland to spend time with her and go to Dave's group. He brought gifts for everyone when he returned, but it was hard to have him gone, hard to replace a good worker like him. He was due back today, but who knew when? He would be catching rides out from town and probably would end up walking home. It's just like Dan to be gone when things need to be done. Sandy trotted along with her, sensing her mood, but so overjoyed that Lena had come outside to see her that she made wild crazy runs in circles and figure eights, with snow on her nose and a feral look in her eye. "Oh to be young again like you, with your energy," Lena said to her, smiling at the dog's antics in spite of her self.

"Snap" went the lights shining down the long white-washed aisle, illuminating the great barn. There was hay in the mangers. At least Dan had done that before running off to deal with other people's problems, she thought. "Yeah Sandy, where are our men? Courting and politicking; and that leaves us to do the work! You can't depend on men Sandy, mark my words." Goliath the bull rumbled around his pen telling her to hurry—that he was cold. And Mineva, her cat, rubbed along her bare legs purring and meowing hungrily, reminding Lena to climb into the mezzanine to gather the mice trapped in the grain bins.

"Oh all right kitties, I'll feed you first," Lena said. She set the milk stool in place under the ladder, as she had done countless times before. Lena called out "Here kitty, kitty," and other cats showed up, anxious for the feast soon to be presented. She stepped up onto the stool and greeted each cat by name, enjoying the meowing chorus surrounding her. Lena had been listening to "Queen for a Day" on the radio, and as she reached to pull down the ladder she said "and now my lovelies, I will grant all your wishes." It seemed impossibly high, so she rose on tip toes—up—up—fingers touching the coarse white wood. But her shoes were a little icy from the road and one foot slipped to the side flipping the stool, plummeting Lena onto the pitiless concrete. Her ankle twisted and strained incongruously, and her head thudded against the

stool as the cats dodged and ran in panic. Sandy barked her
surprise, then yipping encouragement; she tugged at Lena's
jacket, nudged her nose under her arm, and finally lay close
alongside, her eyes fixed on Lena's white and motionless face.

Lena became conscious of Sandy licking her hand. Straight
above her the ladder she had reached for came in and out of
focus as waves of pain swept over her. She rolled to her side
and testing to see if her arms and legs still worked, pushed
herself to a sitting position. She saw that her right leg was
bruised at the ankle and already swollen. Her head hurt so
that she could hardly think. What to do? If I can get up, she
thought, I can drag that leg and get to the house. She had to
try. Each movement was excruciating, but she fought her way
across the aisle and pulled herself up on the pipe pen divider.
She worked her way along to the barn entrance door, holding
on to whatever she could. How impossibly far away the house
looked. She wanted to stay in the refuge of the barn, but it
was too cold for her—she had to get to the house, and she
needed something to lean on that would not slip. She thought
of Lori's skis and poles, but they were standing in the machine
shed, too far away. Dan kept the pitchforks on the other end
of the barn now, handy to have with him when they handled
the bull. How ironic that she would be defeated by her own
mandate—a place for everything and everything in its place.

"Go get your stick Sandy," she coaxed. The dog bounded
off and came back with a stick—not really big enough, not
stout enough, not sharp enough, but better then nothing.
Sandy dropped it in front of Lena who took a step out of the
door to get it, slipped and fell. Swallowing back waves of pain,
she seized the stick and speared it into the ground using it to
pull herself along, not what she had in mind, but it worked on
the icy surface. Well, this way she didn't have far to fall she

reasoned darkly. As long as Lena's energy lasted, she could move forward. She was so cold and tired, she wanted to stop to rest, but no; she had to keep moving. Sandy jumped around and over Lena, excited, wanting to play, but unsure. Lena wasn't throwing the stick, and the sounds Lena made were hurting sounds. Sandy answered her in whines and barks like a mother dog comforting her pup, and when Lena finally stopped to rest, the collie rolled over alongside her, then snuggled close, trying to stave off the cold with her body.

John waved goodbye and began his two mile hike from the highway. He had hitched rides all the way from Richland and felt fortunate. This walk, cold as it was, gave him time to decompress from his dive into a social life. Many thoughts and feelings danced through his mind and it was overwhelming. He needed the solitude of the loft to sort them out—was that why he was hurrying so? He smiled at that notion. The body has a mind of its own, he thought.

He tried to capture and file away his thoughts so he could get above them. He had his journal, and he wrote on scrap paper. The file was another technique he had developed to handle the way his memory and feelings got jumbled when he was stressed. The first file folder he imagined was labeled "Eva." With every step, he filled it: the perfume she used—was it lilacs he smelled when he brushed against her? The way she touched him when she talked—light expressive gestures that transported her words deep inside of him. And her voice, low, modulating, almost like a song—what song—"Ah, Green Sleeves," he said to himself.

He had covered a mile already before he created another folder for what he was headed to. What to call it? "Work?" "Responsibility?" "Family?" Thinking about responsibility he picked up his pace. Who was watching to make sure Lori hadn't roped a calf? He remembered how she had gotten tangled in the rope and he'd had to rescue her from being dragged. And Dan—was he taking care of things or had he gotten his dreams and deeds mixed up again? What might Lena be cooking up in her Betty Crocker test kitchen? He realized that he loved these people. He wondered how he could leave this place, this way of life that had given him the 'space to matter.' He turned the last corner and there, still a half mile away stood the barn. "My barn" he said to himself admiring her lines. "My space to matter." Now, he imagined another file folder and he called it "John." But, he did not have the time to fill it. There was something happening at the farm. He could feel it. He realized he was almost running now, his heart pounding in his chest.

Sandy met him as he turned in at the drive. She was barking—why was she barking at him? Then he saw Lena, lying half way up the sidewalk to the house. "Lena! Lena! What happened? "What's wrong?" he called out as he ran to her, dropping to his knees beside her. Her legs were bare and he saw that her ankle was bruised and swollen. She had a stick in her hands. It was apparent that she had scuttled and crawled all the way from the barn. She looked at him dazed and said simply, "I fell."

Teeth chattering, she mumbled in a ragged voice, "John, could you please help me get up these steps; I have some cookies for you." "You're freezing!" he exclaimed. He knew she would be embarrassed by her frailty. Bundling her up in his jacket he soothed, "You can treat me to your cookies soon enough." Preserving her dignity he said, "I hate to see you dragging that leg—looks as though your ankle is likely sprained," while in one fluid motion he reached an arm around her shoulder and lifted her to a sitting position. "Let me help you sit on the steps, Lena, and we'll take a look, see how bad it is. She flinched when he gingerly touched the swollen ankle, already showing some lovely color in spite of the freezing cold. "Ah yes, I think I should just carry you into the house, Lena."

"Oh no John—I can walk," she protested, but he had already scooped her into his arms.

"Yes, I know you can walk Lena," he said. "You're my can-do girl that can do anything. Maybe after I get you warmed up and settled, we can have cookies together if you don't fire me for mutiny. But for now, I am the boss, Lena, and you will do what I say."

"Well, all right then John, I'm sorry to be such a burden. And there will be more money in your paycheck this month," she added resolutely, steeling herself from the pain in her dangling leg, leaning her aching head against him.

John smiled at that, remembering what Jake said about Lena, "she won't be beholden." Once in the warm house he set her onto a kitchen chair and took off her shoes. She turned her head away from him, embarrassed and not wanting him to see tears of pain. He turned on the faucet and ran the water warm, soaking towels and putting them against her legs, frowning at the bruises, his eyes taking in the thick scar from the gash made by the wagon years before. "Lena, you've got to take better care of these legs of yours." He said.

"I'll never be Miss America anyhow," she retorted.

"You are to me, Lena. You are Miss America to me! I've always thought so; but you'll have to get over being black and blue for the contest—eh, Lena?" He was trying to make light, to keep her mind off the pain but he realized that she really was his Miss America and he cried a little inside, to see that along with her legs, her dignity was black and blue.

"And what were you doing out in this weather——it's not

time for sun bathing you know," he teased as he wrapped her ankle tight with a scarf from the mud room.

"John! You've got to stop fussing over me and get out there and get the cattle in. Dan left them out and they are cold!"

"All in good time, Lena. And where is Dan, by the way? At a meeting, I suppose?" They exchanged a look of understanding, as he snugged up her scarf in a final leg wrap.

"Yes, he has no use for this farm really," she admitted.

"Ah, and its hard on you, Lena. I've always thought you should be living in the governor's mansion playing the piano and entertaining friends—maybe servants bringing you tea. Not that I would make a good waiter—but for you, I'd try. But instead, you are a nursemaid to cattle."

She tried to toss her head, but the movement brought a wave of pain; and a slight groan escaped her lips. "I can do it." She said stubbornly.

"I know you can, sure you can Lena; but do you want to anymore?" He asked.

She didn't answer and he realized he was now the one on slippery ground.

"I'd like to take you to the doctor and get this leg looked at—your poor head is all bruised too. I can call Whinn and borrow a car."

"No, I can call the Swensons. You get those cattle in," she said with authority. "But, I'll wait a little to call—I hate to ask them to take me when Dan may show up soon. He can take me to the emergency room."

John had water boiling on the stove. Knowing better than to argue he instead asked her, "Lena, can you tell me where you keep your tea? And do you have some aspirin somewhere? Better yet, maybe a little swig of alcohol to deaden the pain?"

"The tea is over there," she gestured toward a cupboard by

the stove. "But John, we are not people so soft that we need alcohol as a crutch. That's what God gave us sticks for. No siree, there's no alcohol in this house. Now, Lori should be home from school soon, too. If I need anything, she will get it for me, and then I'll be sending her to you to help with the chores when Dan gets home and takes me to the hospital."

"Ah yes, of course Lena. I'll be getting to my work soon enough." He brought a blanket from the living room couch and tucked it around her like a robe. "Stay warm then, My Lady," he said with a wink.

His hand was reaching for the kitchen door, when she called after him, "I'm so glad your back home," and realization dawned on him that it was going to be impossible for him to leave.

Pulling Together

"I'll have the best dairy in all of Wisconsin", Dan said when he bought Goliath to be his new herd sire. Dan had traded Hannibal for him, looking to breed in a strain of milkiness making headlines in the world of Holstein cattle. He wanted the ultimate moneymaking bovine machines standing in his barn, and so sacrificed temperament, and ease of calving for the promise of huge productive udders on his milk cows. The bull, at first a brawny big calf with indifferent eyes, grew daily, his heavy neck bulged with muscle and his massive face took on a combative look, as he became focused on obliterating his surroundings. Goliath's roars thickened the air. Like ink spreading across parchment, a penned up storm was a-brewing, gathering strength and spawning fear, darkening the sun.

John began to fortify Goliath's pen. He used half-inch carriage bolts through 3 by 8 inch timbers, sistering in boards to strengthen the middle, and new head boards along the top. Goliath pounded the boards, polishing their edges smooth and shiny with his head. His onslaughts shook the dust from Whinn's Indian charm above the wide rear doors. As Dave had noted, when Goliath rampaged, the tomahawks rattled, the snuff lids jingled, and the barn trembled.

Dan nailed a hook onto an upright and hung a pitchfork alongside Goliath's pen. Then he had a talk with John. "Stand here with me a moment as I've something to share, man to man," he said. "Remember when I followed those vultures up onto the rock hill and found the first heifer dying and calling out; do you remember I talked about the sound? It was her death song, and it set my hair up on edge; like after a battle, don't you know, when the screams and blasts quit, out of the eerie hush there rises the lament of souls departing! Well, I've heard it again from the barn itself. I tell you my friend that something is out of kilter.

"All my life, I've not cared about money. I've wanted to live the hard life of a farmer in the wilderness to be close to hunting and unbroken land while scratching out a living from my wilderness. And I've traded and sold horses and cattle to keep shoes on our feet and hay in the barn—sold my team, sold Nell, sold Tom, devoted creatures—hardening my heart to get what was necessary to keep this farm running. But this time, trading for Goliath, I had riches in mind. Was I wrong do you think? What does this moan in the night mean? Is there a curse upon us? Have you heard it?"

John thought a while. "When you witched up your water well Dan, I envied you your Irish magic. I heard stories of holy springs in Ireland and those special people drinking those waters. I wish I had that blessed gift of discovery but I think it brings with it a shadow of doom. That's a heavy price to pay for knowing ahead of time. No, I haven't heard the barn moan. I've heard it crack in a blizzard under heavy snows and high winds, but never did I hear it moan."

"I think it's this bull, John. And me, well Whinn would say I'd be in the field when luck is on the road. I hate to admit it, but I'm afraid of him and I'm warning you to be also. A man not afraid of the sea will soon be drowned. He's not like Hannibal who was Lena's baby all dressed up big.

"Just have a look at him, John. He is so wide in the head

and shoulders, I fear for the ability of our cows to have his calves. And to think we bred Hannibal's best to this mammoth. Soon, they will be calving, beginning with Bell. I've ordered a new calf puller, it should be handier to use then our old wire stretcher."

"Dan, can't say that I ever used a calf jack. I have used a 'come along' when we needed more heft, but for the most part the calf can be turned a little or the legs alternated so the shoulders slip better through the birth canal. Lena is a good midwife and I've found myself helping her. She says proper calving is an art."

"Yeah, well Lena isn't going to be helping for awhile what with her bad ankle and cracked head, I'm forbidding it. And I'm not around often enough to depend on, so I told Lena we should let Lori help you. Lena didn't want Lori out here helping with calving, it's not proper for a young girl to be exposed to the bloody work. We had a small disagreement over that. She threw a frying pan at me—can you believe it John? Now she is going to have to repaper the wall where it's covered with spatter from the pan. She says she is blaming me for everything, and she is going to pray the rosary everyday, says it's the best she can do, stuck married like she is to an Irishman, and yes—send Lori—she's as stubborn as her father. I've told her what my Daddy told me. 'God is good, but don't dance in a small boat,' She put her fingers in her ears and wouldn't listen.

"She'll be praying and scrubbing, polishing body and soul, and fuming all the time now. Lena hates being dependent on anything and being cane bound darkens her mood and deadens her aim. She's like a blackthorn on a moonless night. I tell you it is getting dangerous. But Lori and me escaped with my big book to bone-up on calving. John, I know you're the best, but I've brought you the book to read about it too. I think that's what the sounds have been telling me—bad times are coming. We all need to be prepared. Hoard's Dairyman has an article in it about using lubricants and I've ordered in a supply and some good disinfectants. I should sell everything—should sell the farm too, but for now, I'll be selling Goliath before the next breeding season, and hope that ends the curse. I hope to find another fool who wants the biggest bull and the milkiest cows to show off his herd. There's no way out but through. I've made a bad choice, gone against my heart, and now we will all have to pay. They say its folly to conceal an unhealed wound. So here it is John. You'll help me with this won't you?"

"You know I will Dan. I'll do the reading you want and practice with the jack. Maybe Lori and I will make a game of it to know how to use it and how to trip it. We'll be ready as we can be."

"Yes, that'll be the way then, John. And be careful Lori doesn't see anything about those chapters on breeding in the big book. Lena and I are worried about that—just isn't right for a girl to know particulars, and there are pictures—you know the ones," he said with a meaningful look. You keep the book yourself, and only read what's necessary for the calving task with her."

Dan turned away quickly. "John, you had best put a new plank into Goliath's pen by his manger. He's been working at breaking it and almost has the job done. We can turn him out for the day. Nothing for him to do out there with the cows, but maybe some exercise will take the edge off him. Just be sure no one goes into the cow yard, and I'll be the one getting him in tonight." Dan walked away not looking back. John followed him with his eyes.

Before evening chores, the men set the stage to get Goliath

back into his pen. With Sandy alongside, armed with his pitch-fork, Dan circled the herd to drive from behind. John pounded a bucket, like the dinner bell. When Goliath threatened, low-ering his head at him, Dan waved his fork, and shouted "Get moving Goliath you big galute!" and Sandy barked, showing her teeth viciously. Goliath wheeled away ramming one of the cows, rudely pushing her out of his way as he vented his anger. He cleared his path into the barn, the cows giving way to their king, but in the aisle he encountered John brandishing a stout stick. Goliath regarded John with distain, but greedy for his grain, he stormed into his pen. John slammed the gate behind him and breathed a sigh of relief.

The puller came. Heavy as it was stout, it easily pulled 2000 pounds. With that kind of power in a tool, John wanted Lori to know when and how to use it, so they practiced for an emergency. "Pretend I'm the calf now Lori," he said. "I have to fit through a small space, arms first." He put a chain around his wrist showing her the double half hitch he would fit around the fetlock joint above a hoof. She put a chain on his other wrist and practiced walking him forward. When she understood that, they put the chains onto the puller and she ratcheted him forward. To release him, she had to pull the lever half a notch tighter, reach in and lift the brake. "How fast can you do that Lori?" John asked.

"I'll get faster John," she said.

"If a cow needs help calving, we'll have the puller handy but only use it if we have to," John said. "It's mainly for holding steady and not losing ground. It's best to pull by hand when the cow pushes. A straight pull can hurt both the cow and the calf—and Lori, never panic. I will be the one being sure the calf is coming right and I'll turn the calf a little for its hips to come through. But you must listen to me and do just what I say. Lets practice that."

John launched into a game of "Simon Says." Lori kept up admirably following directions, but got so immersed in touching her left ear that she switched to standing on her right leg, without Simon saying to. By then Sandy was in the game too and John chased them both out of the barn so he could install pegs to hold the calf puller. Then it was a waiting game.

Bell would be the first to calve. It was not uncommon for a cow to follow her instincts and go off alone, rampaging through fences to give birth in the woods. But Bell was different. One afternoon before chores, while the herd rummaged for new spring grass in the night pasture, she came to the barn looking for John to be with her. They were a team. John decided to give her a pen at first, and readied the calving stall. She circled and licked her sides as she laid down and got up. She stamped her feet, kicked at her belly and bellowed her distress. John turned on the radio to some soothing music and took the chains off the calf jack on the wall.

When the herd came in for milking, Bell hadn't made much progress. Lori came to help with chores, bouncing with news from her school day. She said that Dan was working with machinery at the Town gravel pit and wouldn't be home until late, because of a Farmer's Union meeting.

"Lori, it looks like Bell will be calving tonight. Go tell your mother and ask if you can be here to help if I need it. Bell usually is fast, and she has been at it all afternoon, tell her. Get some supper and warm clothes—and be sure that your mother stays in the house. She must take care of that leg and Dan has put me in charge of her following his orders on that—OK?"

Lori looked doubtful, so John added, "And tell her I'll pick her up and carry her back if she comes out here—and tell her you can work the jack just like you can play the piano, 'cus you're all practiced up. Maybe promise an extra hour on the piano," he added. "Skedaddle now, and good luck." John worried a little with Lori gone—glad he wasn't the one doing the telling and wondering if he would see Lori or Lena or no one at all come to help him. But Lori arrived with food for supper, a box of clean rags, and a St. Christopher medal—"so the calf will find its way" Lena said.

After chores, John watched Bell in the pen with growing concern, for he could see the calf coming and realized its size. "See how she lays over on her side when she's down—like she's getting the calf right to be born." John explained to Lori. "You can see those front feet thru all its wrapping. They are front feet Lori, see— they are pointing down so the calf is coming front first." He glanced down at the wide-eyed girl, glad she could help, hoping it turned out well.

"But there is something wrong here—Bell is telling us so— and see the size of those feet!" He turned away from Bell to look at Goliath in the pen across the aisle. He had his nose up over the top board, his massive head tilted slightly so he could see them better, every bit an expectant father, and unchar- acteristically silent—listening and watching. "Let's move Bell into the stall now Lori. I've got to be sure the nose is coming right—remember the pictures—should be setting on those front legs, streamlined as a greyhound. Her bag of waters has broken—that's to make everything slippery and clean. It's a miracle you'll see tonight my girl, and you'll never forget it. Lena and I have helped almost all Hannibal's daughters be born." To himself he added, *Those are the times I've seen her cry, and then, only when it's done and over.* "Your mom has such feeling for the mother, and Dan says he thinks you will be like Lena—says for me to tell you 'keep calm and carry on—flat- foot over still waters.'"

Bell knew the routine and shoved her head into the stanchion. It clanged shut. John explained to Lori what he must do.

"I don't want her laying down just yet, he said. Keep her standing." John pulled off his shirt and his undershirt, rubbing lubricant over his arm until it glistened in the spotlight over the birthing stall. With great effort, like swimming upstream against a powerful force, he entered the cow alongside the front legs, pressing onward into the birth canal, his face turned to look at Lori. As if he was reading Braille, he reported what his fingers told him.

"Well, he's alive, I feel his legs move. Can't find that nose, just the top of his head, yes, I feel his ears. I knew it—the cheeky bugger has his head down, already like his father, and jammed tight. "

John pulled his arm out slowly, now shining amber from the fluid in the bag of waters. He patted Bell. "We can do this my girl, just stay standing. Lori, you keep her up while I get everything we need." He kept talking, telling Lori what they would do.

"We are going to loop the chains onto these front legs, and get the puller ready. You get the pail with lubricant in it. I'll set the puller up. Dunk the chains in the bucket—the war bridle too. We want everything that goes into this cow to be clean and lubricated."

She keeps wanting to lie down and push and I don't want that yet. Do whatever you have to. I'm gonna chain-up his front legs and hook onto the puller, but release cable and push the calf back in. Lots of times the calf will pull his head back into position himself if he has the room to do it. I'll find that out when we pull him forward a little again, and if his head is still down, I'll pull his head into position and put the war bridle on him to keep it straight. Let's hope he cooperates."

Lori was having a talk with Bell. The cow was focused on expelling the calf, so Lori had to get persuasive, saying no—NO and smacking Bell along her neck each time she tried to go down. Bell got nervous and stopped pushing so hard, distracted by Lori, rolling her big cow eyes at her. John shoved the calf back, and worked the legs hoping to coax the calf to pull his head up in position.

"No luck Lori, he's a determined bugger he is—so now comes the test. Get me the war bridle."

Lori fished the cable device out of the lubricant and handed it to John.

Damn, I forgot twine. Go cut me a couple yards of twine and put it into the bucket. Make a loop in its end like I've showed you, and be ready to hand it to me, and don't let Bell lay down. Be quick."

John was biting his lip concentrating on pulling up the head. He had to grab onto an ear, then dive down and get under the nose. When he found the mouth, he put his fingers into it and the calf sucked. He pulled his hand up and the head was in position. Now, he brought his arm out, hoping the calf liked where he was, and reentered with the war bridle, slipping it behind the ears and into the calf's mouth, pulling thru the clip. He kept the cable tight and looped the twine into the end.

"Here Lori—good enough, girl. Now, you hold this snug—don't pull on it but don't let this guy get his nose down. You're leading him, not pulling him out. I'll walk him back to be where he was, and we will let Bell get back to doing her job. I hope she will lie down, but if not, we can catch this calf so it doesn't land on its head and break its neck. Now we'll see if Bell can have this big calf."

Lori was concentrating on keeping the right pressure on the calf's head. When Bell felt the calf back tight inside of her, she began to push mightily and laid down flat on her side. John pulled one leg ahead of the other a little and then pulled when the cow pushed. When the head was clearly coming right, he told Lori to let go and take the twine off. He set the puller up against Bell and hooked the chains in. Ratchet it tight now Lori and we'll use the puller—Lord what a big calf. Come on Bell, you can do it girl. Now we'll work the puller with the cow. Take it up as I tell you—almost there—yes—yes." The head came out and they saw its wide eyes. Take off the bridle, wipe out his nose and I'll keep him coming—it's those shoulders now—damn that bull." Bell made no progress, the calf did not move. "No more, no more, Lori, trip the puller. We'll let him go back a little and pull his legs by hand one then the other. Lori—remember how to trip it—now do it right—Now!"

Lori was almost in tears, but did it fast as she could. John had the slack and used the chains to pull the legs, then leaned back and he and Bell worked together. The calf suddenly lurched forward. "I think he could breathe now Lori, not much time if he's on his own.

"Now Lori, I'm going to turn the calf." John switched hands on the cables crossing the front legs and grasped the calf, turning it. Remember the pictures—he'll fit his hips through if he's at the right angle. Pull up the cable snug and we may have to use this damn puller to get the calf through. Let the cow work—she's the one—she's the one. You get this calf breathing. Bridle's off? Massage his tongue—use a straw in his nose—he's drowning I think."

Bell was flat out on the ground, her head extended, and with a final bellow from her, the calf was free. John grabbed up his hind legs and held them high as he could and a puddle of fluid formed on the ground beneath his nose. " Tickle him Lori and I'll slap some life into him." John struck the calf with his flat hand in the area of the lungs, while Lori pushed a straw up his nose and he sneezed, coughed and sneezed again. She massaged his tongue and he sucked and took his first breath, gurgling more liquids from his mouth. Bell raised her head looking over her shoulder at them, pulled her legs close to her body. John took the chains off and rolled the calf onto a tarp. "Grab on Lori and lets drag our new baby down to the pen while Bell gets up. We will bring her down then and let her mother her big baby."

They knelt in the golden straw, using a gunny sack to wipe down the wet calf. He had a black face with a wide white blaze between eyes full of life, He smelled new. Bell called to him, worried he had been stolen from her, and he answered in his little calf voice as he shook his big wet ears, and blew the last of the fluid out of his nose.

"He looks just like Bell," Lori said. "Isn't he beautiful." She hugged him, rubbing behind his ears where the war bridle had been. John was wet and shining, his muscled arms gleaming as if he had polished them. They shared a moment when time stood still—wordless magic beyond understanding.

"John, you will wait for me won't you?" Lori said. John knew what she was asking and his heart swelled inside him. He looked at her—face splattered with blood, wet with tears with straw in her hair, and he said "You bet Lori," "I'll be waiting to see you all dressed in white lace and satin to marry Prince Charming. But pretty as that will be, I'll be remembering you like you are now."

He turned away breaking the spell. He heard Sandy barking and guessed Dan was home. "Go on up to the house now Lori and tell them how good you've done. I'll put things away and let Bell have her baby back." He heard her joyful chatter as he let Bell loose to track down her calf. By the time Dan entered the barn, Bell was licking him making clean up swept curls all over his hungry face. John was standing in the aisle looking at Goliath.

"Congratulations John. Lori says Bell has given us Goliath's first calf, and he's alive and well."

"Yes, he's a strapping strong bull calf, and yes he's alive but it was tricky Dan. We used the puller you bought. Good thinking on your part there. But the size of him scares me, and you know Bell is a good calving cow. I'm afraid that once again your premonitions are right. There's trouble ahead.

SHINE

I heard it from the butterfly
Whispered by the cherry trees
Who heard it in coyote's cry
Who read it on the morning breeze

SPRING MADE ITS ENTRANCE AS JOHN, DAN AND LORI WORKED to save the new calves being born almost daily. John was sorely needed on the farm at that time and curtailed his trips to Richland, but he filled every spare moment with letters to Eva either reading them or writing them. He even wrote love poems to her and copied one into his journal:

To Eva

Dawn heralds sunrise
In colors pink and gold
And scented apple blossoms
Promise bounty to behold
Like the sun sets snow to melting
Into streams bound to the sea
So my heart fills to breaking
With this splendid mystery

> Unfurling like a petal
> Ahead around the bend
> I sense you calling to me
> My sweet beguiling friend

Their relationship was blooming into a beautiful thing—much like the Sweetheart Rose they both cherished, and with every letter, she reminded him that the management position for her farm was waiting for him. It seemed to John that she was opening the gate— to just a job on one level, while opening her arms to her heart in the deeper sense. He had made progress with the group on his visits to Richland, and felt that, as he had told her, there was hope for him. But even as the emergencies on Dan's farm resolved themselves, new ones emerged.

Just as John was an integral part of Dan's farm family, keeping everyone safe and making the dairy functional, the whole farming community relied on the milk truck driver to deliver news from the grapevine. One spring morning, he brought a personal report and delivered it to John.

"John, do you have a moment, I need to talk to you," said Jimmy MacKee, leaning out of his milk truck window.

"Sure Mac, fire away," said John, and he walked up close to the cab window so he could hear over the chugging truck.

To show that this was important information, Jim turned off the ignition. "Its about Lori. Yesterday after school, my little girl Charlene rode her bike over to play with Lori. Charlene thought they were going to play in the house. My Char doesn't like to get dirty and sure isn't going to go out into the fields where the cattle are, but Lori wanted to get the cows home. She told Charlene to go behind the fence of the night pasture and there she would be safe, and she left Sandy with

Charlene saying that Sandy would protect her. Charlene came home crying, and never wants to come here again to play with Lori. She was so scared she could hardly tell me what happened.

"What happened, Mac?"

"Lori went out into the field where the cows are and one of them charged her. Charlene said she saw the whole thing—Lori just stood there watching that cow come after her, screaming for the dog. Sandy jumped the fence, and ran hell bent for leather out across the field. The cow had Lori on the ground, just ready to gore her, and as she brought her head down, that dog came at her through the air over top of Lori, and got the cow by her nose. Lori rolled over and crawled away, and then ran across the whole field to Charlene while Sandy hung on to that cow who went round and round trying to shake off the dog.

"John, I'm telling you this in case no one else did. Did Lori tell about it? Does Dan know? Charlene seems to think that she didn't say anything. Lena and Dan should sell that cow, or better yet shoot her, and Lori should change her ways or we will all be going to her funeral sooner or later. One thing—I have changed my mind about that flimsy little herd dog. When she came, I wouldn't have given a plug nickel for her, but with a kid like Lori—she is worth her weight in gold. I thought you should know about this, Lori follows you around all the time, maybe have a talk and see what you can do."

"Thanks Mac. As far as I know, Lori didn't say a thing. I'll get her aside and see what she says." All that day, John thought about what he would say to Lori. He was upset that she hadn't kept her promise to him about going alone into the cowherd when Hanna was there. Not only had she disobeyed her parents and John too, but afraid of the punishment she kept the whole thing a secret.

Lori came home from school and very soon was out playing with her sheep buck and Sandy. They were playing "king on the mountain" on a hay rack, when John called her over. The lamb sniffed around John's pockets looking for treats, and finding none, trotted off to nibble some clover where Lena's garden should have been.

"So Lori, I heard a rumor that you were out in the center of the field with the cattle and Hanna almost got you."

Instantly Lori looked down and turned her face away in shame, biting her lip and twisting back and forth, making a groove in the clay with her foot as if she was digging a place to hide in. "Sandy saved me," she mumbled, her face flushed with dishonor.

"You didn't say a word about it. Have you had some other problems with Hanna that you didn't talk about?"

"Well, only that one time in the hay field when she came after me and there was this only one rock,"

"Lori-what field-show me." Lori pointed at the middle hay field. John shook his head "No, there are no rocks in that field, we picked them all off, remember?

"I know, John, except there it was—a big-big rock I could hardly pick up right in front of me, and I got it and threw it and hit Hanna right in the middle of the forehead. Honest!" Lori looked up at him oozing truthfulness. "Yesterday, I wanted to show Charlene I am a daredevil like the Lone Ranger and Superman I hear on the radio. They aren't scared. I'm scared and I need to get over it. Mom says if you have a problem—get over it. I have guardian angels, Sandy and you, and I'm lucky like my Dad—he finds 4 leaf clovers and I find rocks—when I need 'em."

John thought a moment, and then asked, "How do you

think Superman deals with kryptonite, Lori?"

"Kryptonite?"

"Or what does the Lone ranger do when he sees a hundred Comanche warriors on the warpath?"

"A hundred?"

" You don't think they maybe would think about the best way to handle danger? Like maybe go get some help?"

"Get the cavalry, maybe?"

"Now your thinking Lori. They have fear too—and so they do the wise thing and don't get blown up—like your mom does when she lights a fire because she is afraid of being burned, like your dad does when he uses dynamite to blow stumps up. Fear is like Sandy barking—it says "pay attention, there is danger!"

Lori, you must be your own guardian angel for you have a great treasure to watch over. Do you know what that is?"

Lori thought of her marbles but knew that wasn't a good enough answer so she shook her head puzzled.

"Its your life Lori. We all love you. Your mom and dad prayed that they would have a little girl. And I love you. Do you love 'you' enough to watch out for yourself—to care about yourself? It's your job—this life you have. Like Sandy has a job-being a herd dog, and she does it well, you have a job too—being you. Not being Superman or the Lone Ranger—you. Don't you throw away your life being foolish. Your mom cooks and cans and stores away groceries in the pantry, and that's what we have done with you, filling you up with our love. And we expect you will make something of your life—for us and for you and for who ever you love. You are the treasure—shine it—don't throw it away in the mud like its nothing. Shine."

And then John hugged Lori against his chest for just a moment and it was a moment of magic as if Superman, the

Lone Ranger and her guardian angel had swooped her up and
kissed away her fear, and it rained four leaf clovers over the
both of them.

That night John thought about Lori's narrow escape and
the magical way she had eluded death without telling anyone.
He thought about Lena and Dan and himself and the words
he had used, the things he had done to help them all; He
thought about Eva and how much he wanted to be with her.
To express his dilemma, he turned to poetry, making several
attempts on scrap paper, before he copied the best of it down
in his journal, getting out on paper how he felt.

And Can I Stand To Stay?

I climb the ladder into the loft
Each rung worn smooth by my hands.
Polished familiar.
I can feel my way in the dark of night, Bounding up
    exhilarated,
Into the vast storehouse.
The beams show the mark of my draw-knife
As I —years ago—carved the bark away
My steel blades notching and rounding the new golden
    wood
Smelling like rain in the forest glen.
    Beloved stronghold, fit by my own hand, you
    harbor a soaring sanctum
    To hold sustenance for the animals below and
    nourishment for my spirit.

Happens something new out beyond.
Fate pulls back curtains of fog and I see a road shining
    through.
      I hear it calling my name.
      I want to run the golden curve over the horizon.
      I still can run can't I?
Now with nothing chasing me, do I have the heart to
    race toward something?
Like a slave, I have won my freedom toiling here.
Have I burned away my doubts, honed my destiny,
And memorized this space of refuge so I can return in
    my mind?
        But can I bear to leave...?
        And can I stand to stay?
Not yet flying over a space in between,
I find myself loosing my grip on yesterday while
    grasping for tomorrow.
Shadow forms of my companions of everyday, flash
    before me.
Dan hands me a four leaf clover,
Blue eyes a-sparkle with love for his land, his park,
Turning toward dreams that no longer include me,
And I cannot hear his voice singing.
Lena is in her kitchen a-flurry with delicious abundance,
Baking, cooking, serving
For no-one.

Lori astride a half wild pony, is galloping toward barbed
    wire.
She is entangled in ropes.
"Lori-stop—let me help you."
                Oh... how can I bear to leave...?
                But can I stand to stay?
And Sandy is looking for her master, waiting by the
    gate.
The animals have lost their names with no one to call
    them special.
They sadly turn away, blending into the mists of my
    memories.
    "Wait, don't go. Come back,
    I am here" I cry."
Afraid of falling, I claw for my handhold, desperate to
    keep things from changing
As the red clay crumbles away leaving me alone
On an uncharted road called providence.
                How can I bear to leave...?
                But can I stand to stay.

John took a deep breath and closed his journal. He thought
about what Dave had told him about learning to give over
responsibility—that as soldiers, they had not been trained to
surrender. It had been a long, long day. It was as if the worries
of the world had just washed over him leaving him alone with
himself, but he felt like he was in good hands—his own. He
had made up his mind.

SLAM BANG

A FOG HORN DIRGE SOUNDED FROM LAKE SUPERIOR'S TREACH-erous north shore as John began another day. He thought each breath was more water than air under the misty grey blanket. When he reached the barn, Dan was already there, standing by the milk house gazing at the whiteness that was the lake woods, the lake, and on her far side, the lighthouse blaring its warning.

"Socked in for sure, John, but daylight's out there some-where, wantin' to come through, like sure the curse is wantin' to lift, but first—the rocks. Last night I saw the moon and the sun at the same time o'er our swamp—a good sign I think, like it belonged in a dream I had going of better days, if we can just get through to tomorrow."

"Ha, and just who will be having these better days?—Me, I hope." said John, focusing on the better and dodging the rocks that covered over Irish clovers.

"Yes, all of us, its out there just beyond, like the harbor. Funny that I've been remembering a song we used to sing in the trenches when the dismals sunk down heavy as this fog. It was like we all sung together of what was just too terrible—it's like the sound of this fog-horn crying across the lake.

The cannons slew,
Lines they were all cut through.

263

Men on both sides lay—
            dying and dead.
Slam bang.

John heard it now too, unmistakably the words of the fog horn's wail. He shivered. Usually, Dan's songs and ditties cut the gloom that drifted around the tomfoolery of farming in Wisconsin's great north woods, but war and being Irish settled down a darkness in his heart, an underlayment to frivolity, like the undertow of Lake Superior that laid in wait below sparkling water; and the battles, almost daily, to keep life in the living, exacted a dearly sum from his storehouse of cheer laid by for grim times. Indeed, it had been a life and death struggle to birth Goliath's big calves, but Dan had kept his promise to help John and Lori all season. The fog horn blared again, and John remembered the blast of Dan's gun, ending the life of one of his precious Holsteins. Still, with only one broken leg, all the rest survived, and the calf pens over-flowed with romping babies.

Dan walked the length of the barn stopping alongside Goliath glaring at him from his fortified pen. "Remember the man who came to look at this bull, John? He says he's ready to buy." Dan added that the potential buyer was well heeled and thought the farm was a showplace, one he would like to own himself. Goliath began to paw straw over his back, rubbing his massive head along the floor, rumbling his challenge to Dan. "Eh, Goliath," Dan said. He raising his hand up to look like a gun, pointing at the center of the blaze down the bull's nose, and then Dan broke his rule—he looked him in the eye.

"Let's turn him out for the day, John. I'd like you to fan-cy-up his pen so it's fit for a monarch, and tomorrow we will sell his majesty. I'll be back tonight early enough to put him in and help with chores. It's true that I found the bees and missed the honey trying to set records, but I feel the curse will lift like the fog, when we cheer the south end of his Kingship going north—outta here for good." He picked up his pitchfork gesturing out the open rear barn doors as he opened Goliath's pen and hailed his departure with "Take a royal boot in the arse." With a kick and a buck, the bull disappeared like a phantom in the mist. In a jubilant manner, Dan swaggered up the aisle singing to the tune of "Going Thru the Rye," and out the front doors, he danced a jig round to face John, and sang to him a verse from another Burn's song—one he loved to quote because he thought it expressed his way of thinking and living before his ambitions got the best of him.

The war'ly race may riches chase
An' riches still may fly them—O
An' tho' at last they catch them fast
Their hearts can ne'er enjoy them—O

John brought the spreader down with the tractor and cleaned the barn giving special attention to Goliath's pen, thinking all the while about how relieved he would be to have the bull gone. He thought about writing to Eva that night as he scattered the bright straw in Goliath's pen. There was so much he wanted to say, but this past season had kept him very busy, and then there was this other problem that had held him back before this. He had not, until last night made up his mind about leaving this place for Richland. He breathed in the smell of clover hay cured in the summer sun—filling Goliath's manger with it as he thought about Dan, Lena and Lori and all the adventures they had had together. It was an easy life for him, caring about them and the farm, knowing he was needed and still having breathing room—close but still free enough to have a different life—or was he? You haven't told them you were going to leave, a voice in his head scolded him. But there was no time, and never the right moment, he answered as he measured out grain for the bull. Taking his pitchfork with him, he decided to clean the horse barn too, giving him time to think on it. He made up his mind to tell Dan after the bull was gone. It would be the right time.

The fog never lifted. The weak sun finally abandoned trying to shine and slunk off to set somewhere in a happier clime far from the big lake. John's mood darkened as the fog horn sobbed. Perhaps it was that he had leaving to face—or the telling of it—or the fear of something new—or what? By the time Dan returned for chores, John had thought himself out and was overwhelmed with dread. When they opened the rear doors to bring in the cattle, they were already there— bunting each other, crowding, shoving to be first to file in, and claim their stalls, to nestle up warm, and eat themselves full, in the whiteness of the barn. But Goliath was not with them. Dan got his flashlight and cut a swath thru the fog with it, but saw nothing but an empty cow-yard. What to do?

"Leave him," Dan said. "He'll come when he gets hungry— probably sent his girls on ahead to warm up the barn for him. We'll hear him when he comes and we aren't going out in this pea soup looking for him. Lori, turn on Whoopee John, and let's have him cheer the day."

Lori turned the radio up and they worked to the Oompah music of the Six Fat Dutchmen from New Ulm, Minnesota. "Its hard to believe this band can't find gigs now," Dan said.

John nodded and tried to tune out his fear with polka music. Maybe it was all this talk of war with Germany that was bothering him. Like many veterans, he hated the idea of war. He felt angry when he thought of it happening again. His war was the war to end all wars, wasn't it? The atmosphere was charging up for a storm. He could feel the electricity of it.

They were finishing chores when they saw Sandy stalk low and slinky toward the rear doors. Something was out there.

"Lori, go on up to the house now, we will do the last of this. Lena says you have school work to do. Go on now," said Dan, trying to keep the urgency out of his voice. Sandy raced through the barn to accompany Lori back to the house, giving John a warning look as she passed by, looking back over her shoulder anxiously.

Dan turned off the radio. "Did you hear that John?"

John set his milk stool down and came to stand by Dan. They listened. It came again—a low growl like thunder, and then a crash.

"Damn if he's not going to break in! He's attacking the barn itself. Beware cattle at night, John, didn't I tell you?" Dan went to the rear doors and got his pitchfork. He threw John his stick. "I'll open these doors and get him in," he said.

"No Dan, let me, I work around him every day and he tolerates me. I'll sweet talk him in." John had his hand on Dan's shoulder. He felt him trembling, and put a grip on him to keep him back. They heard Goliath hit the barn again—the sound of shattering wood.

"Let go man—its mine to do. Damn you bull—you will do as I say!" Dan shouted.

Goliath had his head against the barn's outer wall, now shouldering along it, and with a mighty thrust he struck the door itself, shaking the whole end of the barn. Whinneboujou's good luck charm fell off its pegs onto the concrete, smashing apart. John picked up the two tomahawks and was about to set them aside to keep them safe, when Dan pulled open the door—to nothing. "Where'd he go?" he said.

Sandy flashed by them into the night. They heard the sound of her fighting something—savage barking, growls, yelps. John felt anger rise in him.

As Dan escaped out the door, John screamed after him "No you don't—your not going without me!" He had the tomahawks tight in one hand and his stick in the other, and he ran straight into the fray just as Goliath hit the dog sending her flying. John splintered his stick over the bull's back, as the bull wheeled toward the dog to finish her off. "You monster! Leave her—get back I say!"

Dan was yelling obscenities at the bull, drawing him away, and the bull charged him. Dan dodged to the side, pushing the fork deep into Goliath's neck, high up between his shoulders; but that just made him mad and now, without a weapon, Dan was defenseless before the bull's towering rage. He stood transfixed, facing Goliath eye to eye, as the bull circled back for the kill. Sandy, like a furry missile, shot from somewhere out of the blackness. She grabbed the bull by the tail, fastening her teeth, hanging on as the bull spun once around trying to get at her, spurting blood, the fork like a giant lance thrown by a picador, rocking back and forth in the heavy muscled neck, and then, head down, Goliath came again.

In slow motion, John saw Dan waiting to take on the bull bare handed. Fueled by years of pent up fury akin to what Crazy Horse displayed in his attack against Custer, John threw away his future, unleashed the demons of his past, brandishing a tomahawk in each hand, and charged the raging bull. With precise savagery he sent his battle ax into Goliath's skull, between his eyes, bringing the bull to his knees, and followed up with the crude tomahawk crafted to till the earth, shattering the bone between his ears, with its sharpened stone. As

Goliath buckled under his own weight, Dan yanked his pitch-fork out and plunged it deep behind Goliath's jaw. They stood over the bull, huffing and sweating, as he crashed down to the ground—two soldiers and a dog. Dan whispered to Goliath as he died—"Slam Bang."

THE MEANING OF POVERTY

LIKE A CLOCK WINDING DOWN, EVENTS TICKED OFF ONE BY one. First, Dan called the man—a well healed businessman looking for show quality cattle, and told him the bull was dead in an unfortunate accident. Though disappointed, he made arrangements to come to see Goliath's offspring. If he couldn't buy the bull, perhaps he could buy the calves. He bought the farm.

John was shocked. He felt like a wild mustang would feel, when someone left the gate open. For a moment, the horse would stand there not believing his eyes, and then rush out the gate to freedom. Dan, practiced in horse trading, weary of the farm with all its trials, and loving his job as Town Chairman and his place with the County Board, had agreed without reservation. Lena saw opportunity ahead and hardship behind. This was her chance to have the life she was suited for.

Only Lori was devastated. The farm, the great barn and the animals within it were all she had ever known. Overnight her world had turned upside down, and John understood her grief. Even though the prospects of a new start, a new relationship and a bright future excited him, John too felt sad, like he was leaving his best and dearest friend. He saw Lori looking out the mow doors above the horse barn, Dave's home when he worked the plow for Dan, and John well imagined how difficult leaving would be for her. What could he give a princess losing her realm?

When the building of the magnificent barn first began,
John undertook to journal down the story of the people
around him, the animals he cared for, and his experience of
the ravages of war, in words so carefully chosen and honest
that they expressed his anguish and fear, his longing and
love—often taking their shape in poetry. He wanted to give it
to Lori, so she might know and remember. So, he wrapped the
journal in a chamois cloth, and hid it in the beam of the barn
loft, certain that it belonged to the kingdom of the barn— this
piece of his heart, this chronicle of his journey. Someday he
thought, it would be found and he hoped it would make its
way to Lori and in that way, she would reclaim her legacy.

Of course! Why hadn't he seen it before? John suddenly understood the story of Iron Hans, the Grimm's fairytale Lori
had told him long ago. In that story, the boy had to go out and
learn the meaning of poverty. Yes, John had explained to Lori
what poverty meant, best he could at the time, and he had
pondered what it meant to him; now, in the instant he thought
of her finding the journal, after having lost everything that
she loved, a new understanding came to him as clearly as if
the Angel Gabriel had announced it himself. In order to grow
up to 'live happily ever after,' the boy in Grimm's story had to
lose everything he had inherited and make a new life without
it; he had to learn poverty, and so did Lori. Already she was
learning to say goodbye, to let go, and in time with the destruction of the barn itself, and by the hand of Divine Providence,
the journal would find her. Such a gift it would be!

John was practiced at knowing what to give. His life was
all about that. He had brought home Ginger for Lori and Lena,
he had helped to purchase Sandy, and on any trip he made, he
bought the most beautiful and rare marbles he could find, so

that he could give just the right one to Lori at special times. The journal-gift was a far-off gift depending wholly upon fate. But for right now, as he planned his imminent departure, he wanted to give her something that he treasured, something he wanted to keep for himself, for he knew that would be a gift she would cherish. The only thing he had like that was the 1st Cavalry badge with Sam's name on the back. He thought of Sam's words—so clear in the vision he'd had in the loft of the barn years before. "I chose you. As I have carried you—now carry me onward, for I have joined my purpose to yours. For I have joined my purpose to yours. Remember me," and he knew this would be his gift.

He bided his time, waiting for just the right moment. It was a summer day in the week he was leaving for Richland. He saw Lori brushing Patches, a heifer she had gentled and trained. Since Dan had sold Tom and Prince, the last draft team on the farm, Lori was pretending Patches was a horse to ride.

"You brush her pretty, Lori. See, she likes it." John and Lori smiled together seeing the heifer acting out, licking her side as Lori brushed her vigorously. I used to have a horse I brushed like that—brushed 'til he shone silver and gold at the same time. He was a grullo. Do you know what that is?"

"No John, tell me. What is a grullo?"

"It is the rarest color of horse, a blue dun buckskin, the color of twilight. His name was Sam and he was my war horse. He was strong, and brave; and he is a big part of me, forever with me, sealed in my memory; so we, Sam and I, think you should have this badge. It was sewn on the arm of a soldier's coat and it was called The Badge of the First Team. Now we want you to have it to remember us by—Sam and me. And when you feel afraid, you remember you have it. You have us!

You can call in the cavalry!"

"Oh John-it's beautiful! Thank you! I will keep it forever and I will always remember you, and Sam."

"I hope you will. Perhaps you will want to give the badge away someday—to just the right person. You will know who, and that way, it will live on—the first team will ride again. Isn't that a good idea?"

"Yes John, I'll remember that every time I look at it." She put the badge to her cheek and embraced John with her eyes— that one look that never failed to take him in.

How to Pass It On

Even though all that could be sold for cash has been ripped away, the barn still stands today, every year a more grey and transparent skeleton, but still standing tall and straight, towering over the squat, common, nondescript little buildings in her shadow. I pray for a miracle—that someone will say—let's save the last great dairy barn in Lakeland County; but time and the undertow of Lake Superior will eventually bring her down under fog, wind and snow, and she will be one with the Manitou of the land and water that birthed her. So I have written something of what happened there—a blend of my memories and John's journal—and like Alice said in Through the Looking-Glass: "It's a poor sort of memory that only works backwards."

My lessons in poverty were many and sharp. All the farm animals died or were sold along with the farm, and I was sent off to school in Superior where no one valued the lessons a girl could learn on a farm. "Its foolish to love living things for they will die and be gone," many told me. My Sandy died after our new neighbor shot the collie for hunting mice in his field. My father asked me to call her out from under the house where she had crawled, so that he could shoot her and put an end to her suffering. Soon after, we acquired a black spaniel dog—all a-wiggle and squirm, yipping joy to be young and belonging, but she ate poison and came wailing down the drive. I ran after her screaming "Help! Something's wrong with Sadie—OH HELP!" But there was no helping her. I opened the door and she dove in to die beneath the washing machine, dissolving among dirty clothes in blood, foam and howling anguish. I learned from my priest that animals couldn't go to heaven. It seemed my poverty bordered on bankruptcy, except that I had set gold into an upper room. For having loved so many creatures, and remembering that I once had a grand kingdom, and a prince who loved me, I had only to think myself beloved to be wealthy.

John went off to Richland and married Eva. They went together to the wedding of his son in Portage. John had been sending his paychecks to the family all those years, so when he showed up, he was welcomed like a great benefactor, and Ida thought how handsome and charming a man she had once been married to. After Eva died, that son wanted John to come live with him, and it was young John Chapman's wife that spoke to me and told me that she knew all about me—that I was their father John's little girl.

I read the last poem of John's journal he called

The Altar

So tired from dragging my memories,
　　Like heavy stones weighing me down,
I came to hide and warm the small thing I call my self
　　In the loft of the barn
From this sacred space,
I observed life- going on without me

Safe, while I tried to bury my secret sack of rocks
   dark stones stained with blood and tears
      in the sweet hay, smelling of my youth.
But like an avalanche, they rolled out unbidden,
     into the strange light of this cathedral,
       to be tumbled into gems,
          that I polished into words.
An offering for the tabernacle
on the altar of the barn.
Nothing lasts they tell me.
    People move on, boards and beams decay.
But the words I've chosen, symbols of my meaning
   are here released, as am I.
Free to create as the winds of change blow through me
And to give it all away again, keeping nothing.
Larger, ever larger as the "I" melts away like a dying ember,
           Consumed in living.

John had crafted the journal's hiding place so cleverly, that it was only when the great beams of the loft were taken down that it was found. His journal, full of notes and poems, told of a decade's odyssey, as he wandered from a "no man's land" of guilt and shame toward a state of mind called "home." He entitled his journal "A Necklace of Words" signed it, and must have intended it to be his legacy to me. Only by the life I led could I acknowledge his influence, and pass it on. *How to pass it on?*

"It's a poor sort of memory that only works backwards."

I thought about that line and what it could mean as I

looked at my garden where my roses grow—old English roses with romantic names. Here in a sun drenched corner, the Sweetheart rose climbs toward the sky in fragrant celebration. The barn's cupola is set among the roses, along with a swallow house I'd constructed from some worthless scraps of wood my son had rescued from the burn pile on the old farm. As I watched, a green blue swallow dipping his wings in a diving salute, circled once and flew off in front of the stained glass windows of my home. I closed John's journal feeling close to him and understanding that I have crafted my life around what we had shared in the dominion of the barn.

As I wrapped the journal in its doeskin chamois, I remembered the feel of the drawstring pouch I kept marbles in as a child. On John's trips to Richland, he bought marbles for me, and gave them out one by one, each marble different from all the others—amber slag, dark blue spiral, cats eye, agate, onyx corkscrew; each one—oh so special, that I named them the best names I could think of— names, like Cloudy, Spooky, Sky... And if only I had them now, a lifetime later, those milky opalescent pearls, and polished bubbles dappled and pierced by color, shot thru on wings of light, crystal spheres as pure as molten love I could hold in my hand. "I wish I had them now."

Then, as if he answered, came to me the words of his poem.

> *They rolled out unbidden*
> *into the strange light of this cathedral to be tumbled*
> > *into gems*
> *that I polished into words*
> *an offering for the tabernacle on the altar of the barn.*

Yes, just like the marbles, I thought as I held, soft and strong, the doeskin package against my cheek. Yes, the scenes in

John's journal, like the marbles, are treasures to take out, like dreams to see and touch—his and mine—polished in the light of remembrance, into stories full blown with his spirit. And I have them now, written down.

"It's a poor sort of memory that only works backwards."

I once had a painting teacher who spoke about capturing light in art. "Everything is the light," he said, his hands gesturing at his canvas, his face aflame with transcendent emotion coming through. I worked to capture that in painting, and also to make windows of stained glass for my home, using rainbow prisms as my palette, making ethereal patterns from fractured diamond light, to play over the ceilings of my life. The glass I use is often layered, making it more difficult to cut. I must grind edges that break badly, and often smear my work with blood from clumsy fingers. Still, my home is filled with stained glass. Was it first love, as a child, for the stained glass windows in the awesome stone cathedrals of Catholicism, where my dreams climbed the rainbow glass rays, up from the kneelers and the cold granite, up and up and out where I knew living things flourished in the light. Or was it first in the barn that I found it? Yes, as did John, in the dust and mist, set a-shimmer by the light coming through the high windows of the loft, an escalade for us to climb out of self. Stained glass, like John, was transformed by fire, and now fills my windows, each color reminding me of old friends—people, animals, trees and the marbles all shining thru each other—a shimmering staircase of memories stained each by the other.

John wrote the story of his circle home—a circle that intersected mine, ran through and about my family and friends; his thoughts came through words that oddly became mine too, until I write our poetry, he beginning again through me—turning a circle within a circle turning, circles running together with no start and no finish— sunshine hoops aflame with life. The barn he crafted, his solace and inspiration, stands strong and young in my mind described, in words—his or mine—I can no longer distinguish between.

Way to pass it on, John!

And so, now I pass it on!

From The Author

A Matter of Honor

I WAS OUTRAGED WHEN I LEARNED THAT THE BIG BARN ON our dairy farm was being demolished and sold off in pieces. Anger carried me back into that long ago life in Wisconsin when the barn was the centerpiece of my existence. When it was clear I could not stop the execution, I began to write an epitaph. Out of my mandate to salvage something of this way of life, to write down John's story and the story of my animals along with the story of the barn, came the makings of a novel. Words spilled out of some hidden place along with tears and laughter. Then along with painful memories came fear. I tried to quit. "I don't want to do this," I told my Writer's Group.

"You have to," was their answer back to me.

It is heart-breaking work to write down to the bones of all that is dear, and set the words that define souls into chapters bound into a cover and call it a book.

"This is too hard for me," I said. And they told me "You can do it."

I found pictures of soldiers headed home out of the fire of the War to End All Wars and made that my cover, for this quest to find home is a story aching to be told. The barn was a place of refuge and inspiration for such as these and for myself. As I wrote about the child in my story, the child I was and still am, I came to understand that my being alive means I carry the flag forward for all those that came before me. **It is a matter of honor to tell their stories,** each one a precious star on our flag. And the pain of looking back dissipates with the telling. Like my Irish father would say,'Tis like the light of day melting the snow covering over.' And there, underneath what you thought hurt too much to bear, is the promise of eternity.

"My barn burned down, and now I see the moon."

THE WAR
TO END ALL WARS